THE
MALTESE MANDARIN

THE
MALTESE MANDARIN

Mark Harland

© Mark Harland 2022

First published by MVH Publishing 2022

A CIP catalogue record for this book is available from the British Library.

ISBN 978-1-7397547-0-9

Book Cover design by Black Swan Book Promotion

Book layout by Clare Brayshaw

Prepared and printed by:

York Publishing Services Ltd
64 Hallfield Road
Layerthorpe
York
YO31 7ZQ

Tel: 01904 431213

Website: www.yps-publishing.co.uk

I dedicate this book to
the people of Malta and their island nation.
You have a historic past.
May you have an equally glorious future.

MARK HARLAND
MMXXI

AUTHOR'S NOTE

I am very proud to call Malta my spiritual home. It gave me my birth and infant nurture so you could say it is my 'real home', not just my spiritual one.

Every time I step off a plane at 'Luqa' I feel I am going home, not arriving in a foreign destination. How wonderful it is that modern aviation can transport me from England to Malta in a little over three hours – without a re-fuelling stop too. In the olden days a stop in the south of France was a necessity lest you might get your feet wet. Today 'Luqa' is a modern 21st century airport served by airlines from more than a dozen countries. Daily, thousands of visitors arrive from all parts of Europe and the whoosh of Airbuses and Boeings has replaced the noisy howl of RAF bombers and fighters when Malta was a bastion of the Empire protecting the trade routes to the Suez Canal and beyond.

To those readers who have not visited the George Cross Island, I urge you to do so. I recently up-dated my little book *MALTA: My Island* to include a short section on travel tips – hopefully of use to first-time and senior visitors especially. I promise you that no nation, indeed no peoples, are more hospitable than the Maltese. The Knights Hospitallers didn't settle on the Island for over two hundred and fifty years for nothing. Don't take my word for it – go there!

This book is a novel and the plot is mine alone. All characters are fictitious but as Maltese family names are few in number it is almost inevitable that some folk might think they recognise themselves and others.

If you spot me under an umbrella in the Upper Barrakka Gardens, Valletta with a cold beer and a notepad, then I'm probably plotting my next novel set in the Island.

Thank you again to Tony Ellul for steering me through the maelstrom that is the Maltese language.

Happy reading – and Sah-ha!

Mark Harland

PROLOGUE

The world entered the third decade of the 21st century in a state of confusion, if not shock. Old orders were disappearing fast and countries that had relied on the status quo for their security and well-being were becoming uncertain about their welfare and futures. How the world had changed in the last two decades since the Millennium celebrations. The fireworks on Sydney Harbour Bridge that had heralded so much hope and optimism had slowly been eroded to a world-wide air of pessimism and a collective culture of despondency, depression and dejection.

Old alliances and friendships, taken for granted for decades, were frayed if not frozen. The 'new Soviets' were meddling where they hadn't meddled before and its leaders were poisoning their foes wherever and whenever they felt like it. A popular British newspaper famous for its play on words dubbed it 'Russian-ing' but it was mighty and populous China that was giving the west the run-around and the most headaches. Since the Beijing Olympics in 2008 the Chinese politburo had run rings around every Western politician including three American Presidents, four British Prime Ministers and now they were threatening Australia with a trade embargo and eternal damnation. Something had to be done.

The NSA – National Security Agency – and their sister organisations consider themselves to be the first line of defence against forces of evil, be they States or Organisations. One of its former Directors, James Bellringer, had dubbed the three main partners – the USA, Britain and Australia – the Triangle of Trust. Sure, there were other members and the 'Five Eyes' might shortly become Six. The 'Five Eyes' of the USA, Britain, Canada, Australia and New Zealand were collectively the world's largest intelligence gathering organisation. But it was the 'Triangle' that the current Director, Ralph Winchester, relied upon the most. But he could only rely one hundred percent on his own people, not here today gone tomorrow politicians with one eye on the polls and the other on their bank accounts.

When not engrossed in briefings with his team at Fort Meade, Maryland he spent simply hours just gazing at the huge world map that dominated one entire wall of his capacious office. As if that wasn't enough to divert him from the routine of endless messages, emails and signals he would also fiddle for hours with a desk-top globe that when he got restless he would spin like a child's toy. The new incumbent in the White House, President Kirk, was a nice guy but hopelessly out of his depth when it came to world affairs and the balance of power. A Congress full of pinko-liberals eating organic carrots didn't help either. On a number of occasions since his recent inauguration he had already had to decide '*Shall we tell the President?*' in the manner of the novel of the same name. Each time, thus far at least, he had told him nothing.

Winchester had made a decision though of his own volition. Press speculation had been rife for months that a sixth 'Eye' was to be recruited. He let those rumours grow without confirmation or denial. When the identity of the country in question came into the public domain the thirst of the media for more information was instantly sated. That 'Eye number Seven' had also been quietly sounded out at the same time was a State secret. For the foreseeable future only a handful of people would know.

1

Bruce McCandless had not particularly enjoyed his two-year stint as Director of GCHQ, the NSA's British partner. Life in boring, provincial Cheltenham had not suited him well. That was putting it mildly. Occasional visits to outstations, some in the public eye and some that didn't officially exist, had kept his morale up. However, it was excellent grounding for his next job. That didn't officially exist either.

The 'farewell dinner' at the posh Queens Hotel on the Promenade had been a necessary song and dance to satisfy the media. He had found the whole charade tedious in the extreme, but it had added two years to his HMG pension pot. He declined the 'gong' of a Knighthood of any Order, preferring the kind of gong that announced that dinner was being served. In the good old days, the names of the Heads of MI5, MI6 and GCHQ were well hidden until the Home Affairs Select Committee had one day decided to interview them, one at a time, on live TV. What the heck! The Americans were horrified, as were the Australians. The whole show assumed that of a *'Carry On'* film farce when the Chairman of the Committee, himself under suspicion of numerous irregularities and malfeasances, announced:

'Sir John Crimson, we'll start with you … the Committee would like to know …' He didn't get any further.

'That's not my real name.'

'What?'

'You didn't expect me to reveal my real name, did you, on live TV?'

Things were never quite the same again. The morning after the dinner, McCandless took the train to London Paddington and then a taxi to Hill Street, Mayfair. The Naval Club was his home when in London. It suited him well, being quite central and not too far from where the nightingales allegedly sang. He'd certainly never heard one himself, but Berkeley Square provided relative peace and quiet in an evening if one needed to ponder or reflect on a tricky situation.

Officially Bruce McCandless had retired. Unofficially he was still working for the NSA, and a few days' leave in London to do what he liked would be a breath of fresh air. He would play the tourist, visit a gallery or two, take in the London Eye and maybe a river trip to Greenwich. Just chill out. He didn't get the chance – at least not yet.

On checking-in at reception a hand-delivered letter awaited him. McCandless chuckled to himself. It could only have one origin – Ralph Winchester. He had called him after the Cheltenham Dinner and had mentioned that the Naval Club was his next destination. The message was simple and had been dictated over the telephone, probably to the girl on reception, Aranca, a Chilean girl from Valparaiso, on exchange for a year from a Club with reciprocal arrangements. She had been carefully vetted. Anglo-Chilean naval and military links were solid.

'Hi Bruce. Meet Alex Pisani for a breakfast meeting at the Ritz tomorrow. All will be explained. You're expected. Have fun. Ralph. message ends …'

After a beer in the bar, McCandless exited the Club, turned left and walked the three hundred yards to Berkeley

Square. He bought a sandwich at Pret A Manger and took a seat under the trees. He read Winchester's message again. The 'message ends' bit was to amuse his naval humour but why say 'have fun?' There was more to this than met the eye. Or even the Eye. To a cynical McCandless the nightingale sounded more like a constipated sparrow.

Like most Brits, McCandless hated breakfast meetings. Totally uncivilised, in his opinion. An American habit that should be thrown back across the Pond like 'trick or treat' and chewing gum. The fifteen minute walk past Green Park tube station to the Ritz in the cooler air of early autumn had at least freshened him up. He could visualise Pisani now. Probably ex-CIA or FBI. Two hundred and twenty pounds, fifty-ish, nicotine-stained pudgy fingers and probably a Bronx drawl that betrayed a humble background before Uncle Sam gave him a break. And what the heck had happened to John Kotch, the normal 'special operations' guy he met in London and other places? He hadn't heard he'd retired. Oh well.

'Yes Sir, can I help you?' The 'Katerina' on her name badge betrayed the receptionist's Eastern European heritage. Weren't they all these days?

'Thank you. My name's McCandless. I have a breakfast meeting with an Alex Pisani. I wasn't sure of the time so I thought eight-thirty was appropriate.'

'Let me check.' She rattled a keyboard, a green waterfall of names appeared and she picked up a phone. It was a short conversation and she soon replaced the handset.

'Sir, a table is reserved in the dining room for you, Table number seven. You won't be kept long.'

Table Seven was by the window overlooking the main thoroughfare of Piccadilly. He scanned the menu and mentally chose the full English breakfast but would wait

3

until Pisani arrived. Doubtless he would order the Eggs Benedict, muffins and pancakes with maple syrup and devour them until the last notch on his belt started to strain. The waiter brought him tea in a silver pot with a proper strainer. No doubt the Yank would order a bottomless mug of coffee. He waited. Then he waited some more.

Then out of the blue a mid-thirties brunette sauntered towards his table, right hand outstretched. In her best Queen's English, which she had obviously practised for his benefit, she floored McCandless.

'How do you do, Mr McCandless. I'm Alexandria Pisani.'

Now he understood why Winchester had said 'have fun.'

McCandless couldn't help but smile at Winchester's little joke. Like his predecessor, Peter Fitzgerald, he had a keen sense of humour. Sometimes you needed it in his job.

2

Alex was drop dead gorgeous. From the moment he spotted her McCandless fell in love. She was a shade under six feet and about a hundred and twenty pounds. She had narrow but muscled shoulders accentuated by a black leather sleeveless bolero on top of a tight white blouse that had lace at the collar and cuffs. Her breasts were high and full – a double D-cup at least he thought. Her narrow waist flared into the long legs clad in pinstripe lycra slacks that disappeared at the bottoms into matching black boots with Cuban heels. Her hair was jet black, slightly curly and fell in tresses onto the top of those shoulders.

Uncharacteristically, McCandless wasn't quite sure what to say. He needn't have worried, she opened the batting although the cricketing analogy, being American, would probably have gone right over her head.

'So, Bruce, may I call you Bruce? I know how reserved you *In-ger-lish* guys can be!' She deliberately elongated the three syllables of his nationality and smiled. The ice was broken. He was putty in her hands but he would try not to let it show. Some hope – as Bob might have said.

'Of course, as long as I can call you Sheila?'

'Huh?' He decided not to educate her into the niceties of Australian social etiquette.

'Lemme guess you were expecting a man, right? I'm John Kotch's replacement.'

'What happened to John? Our last joint assignment in Cyprus and Beirut went like a dream and …'

She cut him short.

'I'll tell you what happened. He developed the same zipper problem common to a lot of bachelors – like you.'

McCandless recoiled, like a cobra when the snake charmer's flute stopped playing. She was obviously well briefed, Winchester had seen to that. What else did she know? She continued.

'Kotch got two members of the secretarial staff, one at Langley and one at Fort Meade in the family way. One had an abortion, one wouldn't. Last I heard he was posted to some awful outstation to cool his ardour. Anyway, let's eat.'

Alex ordered coffee and croissants, McCandless was still digesting the take-out sandwich but still had room for eggs Benedict. The full English could wait for another day.

'Served on an Ingerlish muffin I assume?' The ice wasn't just broken. It was now slush. He was going to have some fun with this girl. Winchester was right.

'So why are you here in London, Alex? It's awfully nice to meet you but as Ralph must have told you, I have officially retired. My NSA days are over. I intend to watch as much cricket as possible and drink nice wines in the sun. It'll be Lords, the Oval and Headingley in the summer followed by Cape Town, the WACA and the WAGGA in the winter …'

'Huh?'

'They're cricket grounds, both here and points east and south. I'll just follow the sun.'

'Ralph has asked me to remind you that you're still on the NSA payroll. An annual pay-check still goes into your account in Jersey. I even know the account number if you ever need it in a hurry.'

McCandless didn't doubt it for a minute. The eggs arrived which brought a timely end to an awkward moment. He instantly remembered a scene from the Bond movie *Casino Royale* when 007 was on a train en-route to Montenegro. In the restaurant car he rendezvoused with the stunning Vesper Lynd representing the British Treasury. Her opening words of 'I'm the money' put him firmly in his place. Without the ten million bucks buy-in for a poker game against international criminals he was impotent. Was Alex Pisani his Vesper Lynd? He didn't like the way this was going. It was about to get even worse.

'Bruce, your connections with NSA will only end completely with your death. The fact is you're needed for a very special mission. You don't have to command a submarine, carry a Walther PPK or live in the shadows under an assumed identity. It's your knowledge and affability that we need right now. It's not an order you understand. This isn't the military. It's a plain, old-fashioned request for help from one friend to another.'

'Well are you going to tell me? Or just keep me in suspenders?' McCandless chuckled at his little quip.

'Bruce, long since gone are the days when Limey agents were bumming each other at Cambridge while our guys were doing the real work in the field. To put it bluntly.' McCandless grinned. She didn't, obviously not knowing who Blunt was.

'Two things you need to know. One – the existing Five Eyes are about to become Six. Two – we know that China is also meddling everywhere she isn't supposed to. It has to stop. From Asia to sub-Saharan Africa the Chinese are exploiting governments in need of aid. Their 'Belt and Road' doctrine coupled with their 'String of Pearls' philosophy is scaring the living shit out of the Pentagon, not to mention the newly elected President. The Five Eyes are struggling, Bruce, and Ralph Winchester has come up with an idea that he thinks only you can put into practice.'

McCandless noticed that Alex was nervously fiddling with what looked like the tip of a crucifix at the end of a gold chain that disappeared into the infinity of her endless cleavage. With a name like Pisani she was obviously an Italian, probably second or third generation. Was she asking for help from the Almighty in the hope he would acquiesce?

Slowly and deliberately with the digital dexterity of a surgeon or a jeweller Alex pulled the 'crucifix' from its pink cavern and into McCandless's line of sight. It was not a crucifix. It had eight equidistant points. Instantly he knew what it was.

It was a Maltese Cross, the ancient symbol of the Knights Templar, the Knights of St. John, the Hospitallers and latterly the adopted national emblem of the Republic of Malta. The rest of the 'breakfast meeting' was a blur. They arranged to meet for dinner that evening. There was a lot to discuss.

3

NSA Headquarters
Fort Meade
Maryland

Director, Ralph Winchester was in a pensive mood. Wasn't he always these days? His retirement from the Army was supposed to signal a permanent move back home to San Pedro California where he could sail all day and watch the giant container ships coming in and out of the Port of Los Angeles. The call from the newly elected President had caught him unawares and he didn't have the heart to decline the invitation to take up the NSA's Directorship. With all the crap going on in the world the President needed all the help he could get. The Covid pandemic, the consequent economic recovery, Russia meddling everywhere and poisoning everyone it didn't like and now this. China. Fucking China again. He threw the thick red file onto his desk and went to pour some more coffee into the polystyrene cup that replaced the chunky mugs emblazoned with the NSA's motif – an American bald eagle clutching a gold key in its talons. Oh no, everything now had to be recyclable and within weeks those cups would become toothpicks. He hated these pissing liberals that preached the gospel of the eco-warrior then drove home in their petrol guzzling sedans to their energy consuming houses. But he didn't want to rock the boat just yet. No Sir. Besides the latest SIGINT on China had given him more than enough to think about in the few short weeks since his appointment.

He decided to put his Deputy Director fully in the picture and picked up the internal phone.

'The coffee's fresh and I need a long talk. When you're ready.'

'Sure, gimme five and I'll be right in.' She didn't tell him her hair and make-up needed refreshing.

Angela Roche had been his choice as Deputy. The President had given him carte blanche. At forty-five Angela was no spring chicken but her twenty years in Army signals and communications had given her the right grounding for this job which would be the pinnacle of her career. At Fort Hood Texas she had been Winchester's personal assistant and confidante and was his first choice as Deputy Director. She wasn't a 'Texas gal' and the chance to return to the Eastern seaboard had been grasped with alacrity. It would give her the opportunity to spend weekends with her elderly parents in her native Maryland. Baltimore to be precise.

Although technically still on the Army payroll at work she wore 'civvies' and blended in easily with the hundreds of staff at Fort Meade. With a short well-managed blonde bob, high cheekbones and a still athletic figure, she could easily pass for thirty-five. When her second husband had blown off with a twenty-something bimbo from Biloxi she had decided to use men rather than marry them. She wasn't bitter, just realistic. She knocked twice on Winchester's office door.

'Come in Angela. Coffee, cream and sugar?' Couldn't he ever remember, she mused to herself? That's men for you.

'Angela the latest intel on China is in that red file. Take it with you and read and digest as soon as possible. For your eyes only of course at present.'

'Sure. You still don't like electronic files do you? Or flash drives? '

'You got it. No matter how many firewalls, anti-hacking devices and whatever else Silicon Valley have developed you can't beat a plain old fashioned file. It's the only one and it's labelled 'Kam Sang Restaurant Menu.'

'Is there any significance in that?'

'Yeah kinda. Way before our time we are led to believe that the original meeting held clandestinely in Hong Kong to commence the overthrow of the then Chinese President Zemin was held in a restaurant of that name. Zemin has long since gone of course but the current 'President Panda' is proving to be an even bigger problem. Panda was the nickname for current President Zhang used by Kirk's predecessor.'

'Don't tell me there's a new plan to blow him out of the sky as well and …'

'No, all the dissidents in Hong Kong are either silenced or lining up for British passports in the hope of starting new lives. Besides, President Zhang rarely travels overseas now as he knows he's a target, especially by his own people. He must be watching his back every day – and night. Word has it that he even declined an invitation to travel on the inaugural high-speed train service from Beijing to Hong Kong.'

'Really? He must be paranoid. Hong Kong is now totally under the control of the CCP. So what's in the file, Ralph? Apart from a recipe for chop-suey?! They both laughed, such was the easy ambience between them.

'Go read it Angela and brush up on your world geography.'

He pointed at the huge world map on the wall which was dominated by two thick red lines one heading directly due west from Beijing the other in a sweeping curve that started in the South China Sea headed south then west in a huge arc that looked as if it had been drawn with a navigator's compass on a naval chart. The line crossed the Indian Ocean then swerved up towards the African eastern seaboard and started to head for the Red Sea and the Suez Canal. Then it faded out but that was due only to the artist's red felt-tip running out of ink, nothing else. It could have gone a lot further.

'Angela, the straight line going overland represents China's 'Belt and Road' mentality and is meant to figuratively recreate the old 'Silk Road' when China traded goods with Eastern Europe – not just silk but spices and all the rest of the goods that at the time only the Middle Kingdom produced. That doesn't especially worry us but the lower red line is rapidly becoming a strategic nightmare. It's known as 'The String of Pearls' and is a continuing build up of naval bases, mostly islands, that China is acquiring either through legitimate Government to Government deals, blackmail or subterfuge. It's seemingly never ending and the word at the Pentagon is that China's ultimate target is Coney Island. That's only a joke of course but the situation is bad.'

'So why isn't the military dealing directly with this?'

'Simple. China has not committed any 'Act of War' in acquiring this necklace. It's warfare in its newest form. China and Russia are becoming masters at it. The current jargon calls it asymmetric warfare. In reality its commercial thuggery backed up by 'goodwill visits' by Peoples Liberation Army Navy (PLAN) vessels. These are intended to be friendly and intimidating at the same time. From their point of view it works perfectly. We have to play them at their own game.'

'OK, how?'

'Take the file home. Let's regroup tomorrow. Happy reading.'

'Yessir!' She snapped a perfunctory salute which was almost meaningless in their new roles.

Three thousand miles to the north-east dusk had just fallen and a couple who had only met that day were about to have their first dinner date.

4

Wheelers of St. James was renowned for its seafood. They had decided to walk, the restaurant being only a short distance from the Ritz. If it rained later they could always get a cab.

They had both changed – she into a black dress that made her look like a high priestess and he into a double breasted navy blue suit that made him look like a retired superannuated Admiral of the Blue. She gazed across the table he had reserved in a quiet corner and her eyes fixed on his jacket buttons which bore a gold anchor motif on each one.

'I thought your Navy days were behind you, sailor?' It was half question half statement. She was well briefed and it slightly unsettled McCandless.

'They were my father's buttons that I had bought for him many years ago. When he died I snipped them off his blazer and had them fixed to this new suit. I even have the little presentation box they were displayed in. Holland and Sherry – London's finest. You won't have heard of them of course.'

'You shouldn't be so presumptive, Bruce. Actually Holland and Sherry have had a sales office in New York all my life.'

'I'm pleasantly surprised. I thought Uncle Sam was still wearing Davy Crockett hats up until …'

She glared at him with cobalt blue eyes that looked like lasers about to cut through steel plate. The waiter brought menus and took their orders for drinks – a spritzer for her and an Indian Pale Ale for him. They studied the fare on offer and checked out the 'specials' board. The choice was staggering and it was a full five minutes before either spoke.

'Gee, this is great Bruce. They even have Mediterranean fish. I think I'll test the waiter though.' She glanced mischievously up and caught his eye.

'Do you have any dendici or lampooki today?'

The waiter looked bamboozled and a little hurt. 'Sorry, Miss, lamb what did you say? We serve only seafood, Miss, and er what did you say then I didn't quite hear?'

Alex softened up and smiled. 'That's OK I guess they might be out of season anyway. I'll take the potted shrimp followed by the pan-fried mullet with a side order of rocket, egg plant and zucchini. Thank you.'

McCandless looked puzzled after this little gastronomic quiz and looking the waiter straight in the eye said 'And I'll take the mussels on the specials followed by the sea bass. No grass, just a few chips. Oh yes and a bottle of your best Muscadet. 2016 if you have it, 2018 if you haven't. 2017 was a terrible year.' McCandless pondered why Americans always wanted to smother good food with green vegetation. He'd never heard of rocket! Maybe she really worked for NASA. He kept that little joke up his sleeve.

The waiter tried hard to suppress a grimace. In his view, and he was a trained Sommelier, there was no such thing as a good Muscadet but the marketing men had done a great job in conning wine drinkers that there was and that Muscadet was the only accompaniment to seafood. Deep down McCandless knew that too. At that point each wanted to ask the other about what they had or hadn't ordered but neither wanted to appear ignorant. Muscadet? Lamb Pooky?

The drinks arrived and in clinking glasses McCandless found it hard to take his eyes from Alex's cleavage. The gold chain was still there and the Maltese Cross. Maybe it was time to dig a little deeper. He decided the direct approach was best.

'So, Alex, before you tell me why we're really here and why you are at least three thousand nautical miles from home, how about telling me your life story. Or shall I probe you with a hundred leading questions? Like they teach you at Spy School?'

She swirled her glass a few revolutions chinking the ice, took a deep breath and said

'OK Bruce, here goes. I was born thirty-five years ago in Hoboken, New Jersey. I'm the youngest illegitimate daughter of Frank Sinatra. I'm the result of his last screw with a casino croupier from Atlantic City. I failed high School, joined the CIA and hooked and screwed my way to the top of the tree, OK?' She paused for effect …

'Or, I was born and bred in Brooklyn, New York City to poor second generation immigrant parents who scrimped and saved to send me and my kid brother to college and then to Princeton. I majored in Math and International Affairs and then went to work for the NSA at Fort Meade in Maryland. Been there ever since. Winchester thinks I'm great but that's only because he wants to screw me. I think he's a red-neck jerk – even if he doesn't come from Texas. Actually he's from southern California I believe. So, Mister McCandless, which is the correct version?'

McCandless tried and failed to suppress his amusement.

'Sinatra was born in Hoboken where his father worked in the docks but I didn't know he went back there to get laid! So I guess it has to be the second option. As for Winchester, well all I can say is the guy has taste.'

She raised her glass towards him.

'Thank you, you've made my day. The first Limey I ever met who knew about Hoboken. Sah-ha!'

The last phrase defeated him. Italian? I take it you are Italian? Second generation Italian American?'

'No, Bruce. My paternal grandfather was Maltese. My mother's side were Sicilian. Pisani is a Maltese name, quite common, but I'm one hundred percent American. Just remember that. Wanna hear more?' He nodded.

'Grandfather worked in the British Navy dockyard in Malta, 1940 through '45. Malta got badly pasted in the war by German and Italian bombers. Postwar Malta was in bad shape – rationing, austerity – you name it. He emigrated to New York in 1946 and got a job in the Navy Yard in Brooklyn. He married my grandmother late in life and my father was the result of that union.'

Her slender fingers started to toy subconsciously with the gold chain and the Maltese Cross glinted in the light of the overhead chandelier. It was almost surreal.

'They're all dead now ….' Her words started to falter.

'This was the chain from Grandpa's gold watch. The Cross was a gift from him to my mother.'

She hauled it up in full view.

'Ten bucks says you don't know what it is?'

Oh yes he did.

She clutched the Cross to her bosom. Her deep blue eyes filled up with what could pass for Curacao liqueur and the tears ran down her cheeks in rivulets of emotion. McCandless took her other hand in his and kissed it softly. He had never in his entire life met a lady like this. She excused herself and went to the ladies room.

A few minutes later and she returned, having repaired her tear-stained make-up.

'Sorry Bruce, I get a bit squiffy when I think of all my family who are no longer with us.' She theatrically crossed herself and briefly glanced at the Heavens.

'They did so much for me and I know they would be so proud to see me working for my country that had become their adopted home. That's the difference you know, Bruce, between us and you Brits. You guys are born Ingerlish and die Ingerlish. Like you have no option. Most Americans are American by choice. They *want* to be American. It's a different ethos.'

McCandless did not disagree. 'So where did the Alexandria come from. That's neither Maltese nor Italian. Is it?'

'You're right. I told you my Grandpa worked in the Malta Dockyard. Well a carrier came in badly damaged by German bombers. Grandpa told me the whole story when I was old enough to understand. It was called the *Illustrious* and many crew had been killed. She limped into Grand Harbour, Valletta for emergency repairs and to offload injured but surviving crew. But the Luftwaffe came back hunting for her. The Ingerlish, sorry the Royal Navy, decided to sail her to the only safe haven and that was the port of Alexandria in Egypt a thousand miles east. Grandpa was one of the workers who stayed on board to continue the repairs. He said that if he ever had a daughter he would call her Alexandria. He didn't but my father did the honours for him. So that's me!'

McCandless was impressed. He knew his naval history. The entrees arrived and he started on his mussels, she on her shrimps. Why the Yanks didn't call them prawns like the rest of the world he would never know. Even Australians called them prawns. 'Chuck another shrimp on the barbie' just wouldn't have the same ring to it, now would it?

'Did your Grandpa spend the rest of the war in Egypt with the Brits?'

'No, after the carrier was repaired he hitched a ride back to Malta on a fast mine-layer called the *Welshman*. It carried much needed supplies and its high speed made it almost impossible for German U-boats to catch. That's also why I have a Welsh middle name Mari and not the usual Maltese Maria.'

'It could have been worse. It might have been Blodwyn.'

'Huh?'

'Never mind. Your Grandpa must have been quite a character!'

The main courses arrived and another waiter with the wine and a corkscrew.

'Just out of interest what the heck was that about Lamb Pooky? A joke of some kind?'

'I was just testing the waiter. A lampooki is a Mediterranean fish, a bit like salmon. The giant shoals migrate past the island and are pursued by Maltese fishing boats. It's a short season and they are a delicacy. Baked lampooki was on the Maltese menu for a few short weeks in the days before freezers were in common use. So Grandpa told me. He always told me he wanted to take me for a visit to what he called 'His Island' but he didn't make it.'

Alexandria already knew more than a little of what was on offer in the Kam Sang Menu on Ralph Winchester's desk. It certainly wasn't chop suey or lampooki. She picked her moment just before the Muscadet ran out.

'OK Bruce. I'll tell you the real reason I'm here with you in London.'

5

Beijing
China

In ancient and not so ancient China, the word 'Mandarin' was a colloquial term given to bureaucrats and scholars who could exert influence in governing circles. They were often wealthy and controlling. Until the Communist Revolution in 1949 you were either a moneyed Mandarin or a poor peasant. There was no in between. In twenty-first century China there is only one centre of power – the Chinese Communist Party. The outer Politburo and the Inner Standing Committee. The latter are the *New Mandarins*. Don't let anybody tell you any different.

The weekly meeting of the Inner Standing Committee had been under way for an hour. Yet more green tea, so beloved of Western vegans trying to emulate stick-thin tai-chi advocates, was handed round the ornate oval table. With cups refreshed the members present once again cast their eyes onto the Agenda. It was normally a routine nod through matters such as internal security, Uighur transit camps and the weekly notice of dissident arrest statistics. Today was somewhat different. The Chairman tapped his pen several times onto the side of his teacup to signal that the Meeting was about to resume.

'The next item, Comrades, is the tricky question of our bi-lateral relations with Britain, the United States and

Australia. We seem to have antagonised all three nations at the same time. I suppose I ought to offer congratulations but we must be very careful not to bite off more than we can chew.'

Right on cue the Defence Minister, fifty-five year old Li Zhan-Shu, reached forward to grab yet another sticky lotus cake. They were a weakness of his but he knew that as soon as the Chairman finished his opening remarks on this particular issue he would be asked to make meaningful comments. Long since gone were the days when every member of the Politburo was in his eighties or even nineties. Age was still venerated in modern China but in the twenty-first century the ruling Party couldn't be seen to consist of Confucius lookalikes walking with sticks and carrying pet linnets in cages wherever they went. Li, nicknamed "Bear" because of his passion for all things sweet and sticky, waited for the nod from The Chairman which he knew was coming soon. The Chairman droned on and on and on then finally finished – probably because he wanted more tea to clear his drying throat. The meeting had by now already lasted four hours.

'As you know we have deliberately stirred up the situation with Australia. Our trade embargo on coal will be hurting them hard. The State of Queensland is virtually built on coal and with the post Covid situation badly affecting its tourist industry it is only a matter of time before it will be forced to seek Federal assistance from Canberra. Our planted climate change activists have worked hard to bring about the decision to scrap coal-fired power stations within a few years. The hugely expensive solar and wind powered replacements will slowly bankrupt them.' He nodded towards the Finance Minister who was starting to nod off. Only money matters excited him.

'That reminds me, Comrade 'Won-Gah', have the necessary disbursements been paid to those who are helping us in the Antipodes?'

The nickname 'Wonga' had been pinched from a British pay-day loan company that specialised in short term high interest loans before it went bust due to criticism of extortionate interest rates and dubious collection practices. The moniker suited him well as his family name was actually Wong and he was the only southerner, a native of Guangdong, on the Inner Standing Committee. They relied on his sharp-edged financial acumen. As Cantonese was his mother tongue he sometimes struggled to keep pace with the 'Mandarin only' orthodoxy of the Politburo. In classless China the Ruling Class spoke Mandarin and that was the end of it.

'The necessary fees have been paid, Mr Chairman.' He hated speaking Mandarin which he likened to gargling with a jar of wasps.

'Comrade Li, could you give us the latest information on the situation in the South China Sea.'

'Mr Chairman, Comrades, as has been widely reported in the Western press, a largely British naval force will, within a few weeks, commence what they call a 'freedom of navigation passage' through the South China Sea. Their shiny new aircraft carrier named after the ruling monarch Queen Elizabeth will, according to unconfirmed reports, leave Singapore and head north and deliberately transit through waters which we have now claimed as belonging to the Motherland and …' He didn't finish the sentence, being interrupted by a noisy intervention from the Interior Minister.

'We can't allow that. We will lose face in the international community. Can't we stop this charade? What about the idea put forward by a junior member of the Politburo that we send a few of our own warships to confront the British and if necessary create a major incident?' The Chairman intervened.

'No! The British have cleverly allowed US Marine Corps planes onto the carrier so any force made against them would then attract the wrath of the Americans. In fact they have gone even further and invited Australia and even the Netherlands to send frigates and destroyers to join them in their flag-waving futilities. Only yesterday 'our people' in Sydney reported two new Australian destroyers preparing to leave what they call 'Fleet Base East' not far from the Opera House. They are so open it's not true. It is the West's biggest weakness and one we will continue to exploit. It won't be long before we manage to achieve what Japan failed to do. One day 'Au-Jau' will become our biggest overseas possession. We already have thousands of patriots living there quite legitimately. Anyway I digress, that is for the future. Comrade Li, please continue.'

'Thank you, Mr Chairman. As you all know, Comrades, our acquisition of most of the islands and atolls in the South China Sea is almost complete. We will be able to monitor every move that the British and allied vessels make. I don't expect any fancy tricks on their part. At least they won't be able to visit their old Colony of Hong Kong!' There was much self-satisfying chuckling around the table.

'That would have looked terrible in the eyes of our own people. I expect their Fleet to head east through the Luzon Strait and then head north for Japan for what they call R & R – rest and recreation. Old habits still die hard in the decadent West and no doubt the whorehouses of Yokosuka will notice increased turnover.' More laughter.

'No, Comrades, I have my eyes on another more distant gem to add to our growing 'String of Pearls' and I want to run it past you now.'

The Chairman stared at Comrade Li expressionless for the next five minutes. What he was suggesting was audacious, even ludicrous. A poker hand too far. But, you know what, it might just be worth looking at.

'Thank you, Comrade Li. There is much to ponder. There will be NO discussion on these matters outside the Inner Committee. Do you all understand? We will take those ideas forward at the next inner Meeting next week. If there are any leaks then it can only have come from the people you see here in this room. We don't have any salt mines but we do have plenty of coal mines with dubious safety records.'

They all laughed. Some more nervously than others. The meeting closed.

6

Blissfully unaware of the current thinking in Beijing, Winchester was back at his desk and hoping that Angela Roche, his colleague and confidante, had managed to read the bulk, if not all of the Kam Sang menu. He didn't have long to find out and just minutes after pouring his first coffee of the day his internal phone rang.

'Ralph. I've read the menu.'

'And?'

'I didn't sleep well. Let me know when you're ready and I'll …'

'Now, please.'

She went straight into his office, knocking only perfunctorily. Unusually his desk which was normally heaped high in files in addition to three computer monitors was almost clear, save for the screens. A copy of a glossy magazine *Superyacht World* looked as if it had been casually tossed aside after being read from cover to cover, the brown ring of a leaking polystyrene coffee cup reminding him to bring some proper mugs from home. Angela noticed the magazine and instantly felt for him. Yachting had been his passion for most of his life outside of his Army career and the prospect of much sailing at San Pedro in retirement had been cruelly delayed by the President's request to head up the NSA – for a couple of years anyway.

'Cream and sugar, Angela? I'm only joking. I have finally remembered. Just a little cream, no sugar.'

She grinned. He was a nice guy.

'So, did you read the menu? Can I take your orders ma'am?' They both laughed.

'To be honest I don't know where to start. Firstly I have to ask, where has this intel come from?'

'Australia. In a nutshell. Our partners in Melbourne collect high quality SIGINT from all manner of sources. Most of them are highly classified of course. But unusually they also seem to have access to personal information. By that I mean human intelligence – not satellites, high speed computers and hackers. It seems they have their own man or woman deep inside the CCP.'

'You're kidding me! You mean James Bond isn't dead yet? Is the CIA involved?'

'Not to my knowledge. After the last bungled attempt to knock the Chinese President's airplane clean out of the sky with a hired international terrorist firing a Stinger missile failed over a decade ago they've been out of favour. Langley have been kept in the dark about a lotta things. Had their part in what was known as 'Operation Opium' ever come to light there would have been all hell to pay. The problem I have Angela is that while the ex-President wanted to build walls this new guy wants to build bridges.'

'Is that a problem? '

'Not normally, no. But the President is not in the slightest bit military minded. You've read the file. It scares the living shit outta me. If the Australians are right then the Chinese 'string of pearls' is gonna end up with Aspreys jewellers in London followed by Tiffany's in New York. And they'll do it without firing a single shot. The Chinese Navy – the PLAN – will have bases from Hainan to Casablanca within a year.'

'So what's their modus operandi? How do they acquire these bases and facilities so easily?'

'Angela, it's with money or fear. Sometimes both. Take say Sri Lanka – what the Brits used to call Ceylon. It's kinda crazy isn't it? It's Sri Lanka but it's still Ceylon Tea. I guess it's a marketing thing. Anyway what the Chinese do is quite simple. They choose a country with port facilities and infrastructure that are run down. Then they sell them a deal to bring it up to date with container facilities and all the modern paraphernalia that goes with it. Computerised cranes, robotic handling and all the rest of the high-tech stuff. The price is always top dollar and the rate of interest exorbitant. The Chinese Finance Minister who apparently has the nickname of 'Comrade Wonga' negotiates all the deals. At the moment we don't know much about him other than the fact he seems to be a token southern Chinese and his real name is Wong which marks him as coming from Guangdong Province. It seems like even the Chinese politburo goes in for tokenism.'

'Like the current liberal President nominating a gun-toting Texan as his Press spokesperson!'

'Yeah, I guess! We are trying to find out more about him. So are the Australians of course. The high interest rates are compounded and quickly become unaffordable to third world countries. That's when they step in and say 'no problem friend, just give us a ninety-nine year lease on the port and we'll call it quits.' Then hey presto they've got a new base.'

'So that's how they do it! It sounds so easy.'

'It is. Anyway, to continue with the 'string of pearls' the biggest and best pearls are those that have a large dry-dock facility. In effect it's the rare black pearl on the string that is the ultimate target of the Chinese.'

'Do we know the location of the 'black pearl' as you call it?'

'We know already that's what they call it. SIGINT picked that up.'

'The Australians think so too. This is the dessert menu. Read it while I pour some more coffee. It's only a one pager. He tossed it to her side of his desk.' It took her only two minutes to read it.

'I've heard of Malta but where is it exactly?'

'Being Army you would not have ever been posted there. The Sixth Fleet has paid courtesy visits there for decades, particularly during the Cold War. It was a major base for the Brits for almost two centuries. Can you believe that? The Maltese asked Lord Nelson to kick Napoleon out of their islands in 1802 – so they did and they stayed there.'

'Didn't they object, you know, to be occupied again?'

'I guess not. Malta had been invaded through history by the Romans, the Carthaginians, the Phoenicians, the Arabs and then the Turks had a go under the command of Suleiman the Magnificent.'

'Shit. Sounds like every power in the world wanted it. Why?'

'Simple. Its strategic position in the centre of the then known world and the fact it had the biggest harbour in the then known world made it a 'must have' location for every military and political power. It's the old adage beloved of realtors, Angela. Location, location, location.'

'So what happened to the Turks? How come they quit?'

'They didn't quit. They were beaten back by the Knights of St. John headed by Grand Master Jean Parisot la Valette. The capital city Valletta was named after him.'

'I didn't know you were a history man, Ralph. This is fascinating.' Winchester reached into a desk drawer and pulled out a small tourist type brochure.

I wasn't until I read this. Here, take it.'

It was titled '*Captain Morgan's Harbour Cruise. Valletta and the three cities.*'

'So how come you have it?'

'Last summer my daughter and her room mate took a vacation to Naples and Sicily – you know Capri, Pompei, Vesuvius and all that volcano stuff including Mount Etna. An optional extra was a day trip to Malta on a giant catamaran. They took it along with a pre-booked harbour cruise from this latter-day Captain Morgan.'

'So what are you trying to tell me? What's the problem?'

'This is the problem, Angela. Listen to this. It's a ninety minute DVD of the cruise.' He popped it into a small portable DVD player, switched it on and then the fast forward button to the play time he had noted. The bilingual female commentator's words left them both cold.

'And on your right, as we approach French Creek, is the biggest dry-dock in the Mediterranean. It is called the Red Dock as it was built as a gift from the People's Republic of China in 1975. It is the length of three football pitches and can accommodate ships three hundred metres long.'

'Ralph, are you thinking what I'm thinking?'

'Yeah. Red China wants it back!'

7

The Naval Club
Mayfair
London

Bruce and Alex were by now totally relaxed in each other's company. It was late morning and they were taking coffee in the quiet reading room just off the main lobby. McCandless now knew why his effective retirement had been delayed. He had been thoroughly briefed by 'Signorina Pisani' as to what the aim of his next, and hopefully last, mission for Queen and Country – and of course the NSA.

'Ralph's plans are only outline at the moment, Bruce. The Red Dock, code name the Black Pearl, must not under any circumstances fall into Chinese hands. You must know something about it. Were you there in the Navy?'

'Yes, many times. Usually just in short stopovers on the way to the Suez Canal and then the Persian Gulf. It was known as the Armilla Patrol. I was on frigates before submarines and, well, you know what subsequently happened after that. I'm assuming Ralph told you? You seem to know a lot about me!'

'Sure, Bruce. I know about Operation Opium. It so nearly came off didn't it? That's why it seems that the current all-powerful Chinese President is so unwilling to travel far from his power base. Anyway our brief is to go to Malta and put certain people in the picture who might be able to help.'

'Yeah, like who?'

'Well the US Ambassador has many contacts as you might expect. Her name is Georgette Fox. I understand she's from Texas.'

'No way! Does she carry a gun? Only joking.'

'We have a brand new Embassy in Malta. With terrorism still a major consideration it's on a new site inland in a place called Attard. Seems like the old one was too insecure. I checked on a map.' She reached into her purse and produced an InsightFleximap of Malta and its sister island Gozo. She pointed to a small township about two miles north of Malta International Airport.

'The Embassy's just here. Look. It's not on the map of course.'

McCandless didn't have to look. On his bedroom wall as a teenager was a 1938 Air Ministry map of Malta given to him by his Uncle Frank who had spent much time there during WW2 and immediately afterwards. It showed that in those days Malta had four airfields, not just one – three Air Force, one Navy.

'So, Bruce, Let's make plans. We could be in Malta some time. I'm officially on indefinite leave but that's a simple cover. I'm going to Malta to 'research into my family roots and history.' What's your cover, should you need one?'

'Well I had always intended to drink a lot more wine in the sun watching cricket. I guess the cricket will have to wait.'

'You seem to know a bit about wine even if the waiter in the restaurant looked mortified at your choice. So how about you researching into Malta's vineyards with a view to writing a small booklet to be published next year. Good idea?'

'Brilliant. Now why didn't I think of that? I've drunk a few of their wines. Nothing to write home about but that was a lot of years ago. Things might have changed.'

'Bruce, to plans and practicalities. When shall we travel? Where do we stay? A hotel or an apartment? What's the weather like? What's the food like?'

'I think you'd better buy a Berlitz Guide. It'll still be hot by the way. Around 30 Centigrade. Your Texan ambassador will be feeling quite at home.'

'Heck, Bruce, doesn't anybody use Fahrenheit any more?'

'Only Stone Age Americans!'

'In that case can we share a cave? Or at least stay in the same hotel?'

Ralph Winchester was right. He was gonna have a lot of fun with this lady.

8

For the third consecutive day Winchester and Angela Roche met in his office. He had heard from Alex Pisani overnight. At least the first couple of pieces of the jigsaw were in place. Within a week he would have two experienced NSA officers on the ground. They were now a hundred percent certain that the Red Dock – the Black Pearl – was the next, perhaps ultimate, acquisition. But how were the Chinese going to do it? Sure, like a lot of tourist destinations, Malta had been hard hit by the Covid pandemic. But Malta wasn't Bangladesh, Burma or Sri Lanka. It was a member of the European Union – or rather what was left of it after the Brits had left and now other members were thinking of following suit. Italy included. The future of the EU itself was starting to look more than a little shaky. Malta might need help. But from old friends like Britain, Australia and the US, not bloody China! He sure wished right now that he knew a lot more about the place.

'Angela, I know you're divorced with no kids and your parents are in fair health not too far away. I want to send you on a mission soon to the Mediterranean. Are you up for it?'

'Great. To Malta I take it?'

'Not exactly but maybe. How are your cooking and waitressing skills and how are your sea legs?'

'What?! Are we talking the Staten Island Ferry here or the Queen Mary? Last time I was in New York I took the boat to the Statue of Liberty and threw up. It was a rough day though to be fair.'

'Well this might be kinda in between. Say about frigate size.'

'What, hell no. There's no way I'm seconding to the Navy even if women do have equal rights these days. Sorry.'

'Angela I can't tell you any more just yet. If my plans come to fruition you'll be a civilian crew member of a civilian ship. When I know more I'll tell you more. Just make sure your US passport is current. Is it?'

'Actually it expired only recently and I keep meaning to renew it and …'

'Leave it with me. I'll have it fast-tracked at the State Department. Your name will remain almost the same and the only alterations will be your place of birth and your occupation. Your family background is Swiss. You were born in Basel and you're now a sous-chef. You need to speak only rudimentary French. Just enough to 'remember' from your early childhood. Got that? I'll arrange for you to go into one of our total immersion courses next week. French only for for five days and nights. OK? Oh yeah and maybe a touch of Mandarin.'

'Oui monsieur!'

She went back to her own office and he poured himself yet more coffee and for the hundredth time picked up the *SuperYacht World* magazine and thumbed it open at the relevant page. Thus far his enquiries had drawn a blank. He might have to come up with an alternative. He had earmarked a million dollars to charter a 'super yacht' for one week only in late fall. It was already in-situ in the Mediterranean and by good fortune its Port of Registration was Valletta. He entered its IMO – International Maritime Organisation No. – into a search engine and within seconds it gave him the precise world location in degrees, minutes and seconds north and east. It was located one nautical mile east of Monte Carlo and hadn't changed position for weeks. Such was the knock-on effect of the Covid pandemic. He'd give it a couple more days then try to come up with another solution. Winchester was a big Humphrey Bogart fan and suddenly he had an idea. First he Googled the name of the vessel he had in mind and then the IMO number, same exercise as before. Where was it? He couldn't believe it. It was berthed in Grand Harbour, Valletta coincidentally also its Port of Registration. His mind started racing.

The basic and initial research he would do himself but sooner rather than later he would have to share his plans, not only with Angela, but with Alex Pisani and Bruce McCandless. Within days he hoped they would be in place on the Maltese archipelago and ready to start.

The Maltese Falcon wasn't just a Bogart movie. It was the name of the most beautiful and sophisticated yacht ever built. Not a motorised super-yacht. A real one. With sails. He went online again to see if it was available for charter. It usually was, at least when its Greek actress owner wasn't throwing parties on it. The website announced that, post-Covid, it would be available for seven day charters at a price of a half a million bucks a week. He emailed off an enquiry via the 'contact us' button and added his preferred dates for the charter, the first full week in October. Then he waited. These days thanks to the internet you never knew where the 'office' was. It could be a business centre in Monaco or even the owner's office in Greece, probably Piraeus. On the other hand if the actress in question was a tax-dodger that 'office' could be anywhere. With the Maltese Falcon already registered in a 'Flag of Convenience' country then the chances are the recipient of the email would be 'offshore' too.

But it was his first choice of vessel to charter that he wanted to clinch first. When he'd said to Angela Roche that the boat would be about 'frigate sized' he wasn't kidding. He reached for the glossy *SuperYacht World* magazine and it fell open at exactly the right page, so many times had it been thus on previous occasions. Ralph just stared at photos of what he considered to be the most beautiful, stunning boat in the whole universe.

That boat was the *'Christina O'* and if his plans came to fruition the notoriety it had achieved in its already long life would be nothing compared to what it would achieve in the next two months. He reached into another drawer and pulled out a DVD entitled 'Trevor McDonald's Secret Mediterranean' and for the next twelve minutes was transported into a world of Presidents, Heads of State and movie stars as they were entertained on board this most majestic of floating palaces.

It had seen the likes of Churchill, Roosevelt, Jackie Onassis and countless celebrities amongst its guests. He watched it again and again and again. Boy, what would he give to be a guest on board. But the person he had in mind was half-way round the other side of the world. Nobody, but nobody, would decline an invitation to cruise on this piece of floating history. Not even the President of the Peoples' Republic of China.

Soon, in fact pretty soon, he would have to tell the President about his idea. Would he buy it?

9

They decided to travel together. Why not? They weren't spies or undercover agents. Sure they both collected pay-checks from the same Agency but shucks, who was to know? After two days shopping in London's West End, Bruce and Alex had equipped themselves with enough semi-tropical attire to fill four suitcases.

The 'I told you the airline baggage allowance of twenty five kilos' was ignored by Alex and her riposte of 'how many pounds is that?' was met with a 'I said you Yanks were still back in the Stone Age. Just double it and add a bit more to get to pounds from kilos.'

So she did and ended up with fifty kilos instead. Oh well no matter, Uncle Sam would pick up the bill. Didn't he always?

The plane was almost full with just a couple of spare seats on the brand new Malta Air 737 Max which had overcome the teething problems with its software.

Bing bong! The Tannoy crackled slightly and sprung to life.

'This is your Captain speaking. My name is Mike Davis and my First Officer is Emanuel Farrugia. Your cabin crew today are Paolo and Maria from rows one to sixteen and from there to the rear you'll be attended to by Katerina and Donna. The weather forecast is good all the way, flight time is an estimated three and a quarter hours. Further announcements will come from my First Officer. Just relax and enjoy the flight.'

The plane took off on schedule on runway 27R, headed due west to the next way-point then banked left beyond the giant reservoirs beneath. Heading south over the English Channel the plane then headed south-east to skirt around the Alps. The views from their side of the plane, the port side, were spectacular. Alex was impressed.

'Boy, it looks like Colorado down there, Bruce. Is that Denver I can see?' He hoped she was joking. She was.

'More likely Berne or Zurich depending on the flight plan and route. The Alps never lose their snow cover, even in summer. Don't believe everything the climate conspiracy nuts tell you.'

Alex was not impressed. She hadn't realised he was a denier. Maybe she should educate him.

He was actually engrossed in a newspaper, the *Times of Malta*, and was only half-listening to her. This was a 'no frills airline' and there were no complimentary papers or periodicals. It must have been left in the rack by a passenger travelling to London from Malta on the outward bound sector as it bore today's date.

'What time do we land in Malta, Bruce? Will it still be light?'

'We're due into Luqa about six-thirty so yes it will still be light but dusk won't be far behind.'

'What is Luqa? Say that again.'

'Luqa. But it's pronounced like Loo Ha as the letter q is silent – in the Maltese way anyway.'

'Jeez, they didn't tell you that in the Berlitz Guide. Any other linguistic challenges to come?'

'Lady, you ain't seen nothing yet. But don't worry about it.'

'Where is Luqa anyway?'

'It's a village near the airport and it was originally RAF Luqa until they turned the main runways into a civilian airport. A highly successful one too.'

'You mean like Andrews AFB?'

'Yes, if you like. Keep reading the Berlitz Guide.' So she did and he went back to the Times of Malta. One of the pages immediately caught his eye and an item on the left column stared out at him. It was an obituary.

PISANI Carmen Maria Assumpta aged 98

In the loving care of Mater Dei hospital.

Requiem mass to held on etc. etc. followed by interment at Cospicua Cemetery

She leaves to mourn her loss a brother Silvo, sons Raymond and Charles, daughters Annabella, Anne-Marie, Teresa and Bernadette, ten grandchildren and two great grandchildren.

Safe in the arms of Jesus.

Lord grant her Eternal Rest.

Enquiries to Tonna & Sons, Rabat.

When Alex 'went to the bathroom' at the front of the plane McCandless tore out the whole page, folded it and stuffed into the side pocket of his lightweight flight bag. Quite why Americans went to the bathroom instead of a toilet he had never managed to figure out. A bathroom at thirty-thousand feet? Yeah right. Only Air Force One and rich Arab Sheiks had one of those in their personalised Jumbos. Somebody else did too but kept schtum about it. Woe betide anyone who spilled the beans or a salt mine, even a coal mine, beckoned.

The shiny white 737 Max with the Maltese cross in crimson red emblazoned on the tail plane, port and starboard, started to make its descent over Sicilian airspace.

The view of Mt. Etna some thirty miles east was a little hazy but just clear enough to see a smoky heat plume coming from the crater like a newly lit cigarette. It auto-suggested to Alex that she would like a menthol cigarette when they landed and cleared the terminal. McCandless decided that this was not perhaps the best time to tell Alex that menthol cigarettes had been banned in the European Union. He hoped for her sake that she'd brought a good supply with her.

Bing bong! 'This is your First Officer Manny Farrugia speaking from the flight deck. We will be landing in approximately ten minutes at Malta International Airport on runway one-three, that is from the north-west. Please remain in your seats until the aircraft has come to a complete standstill on the apron.

'Bruce what did he mean by runway one-three? This place is much bigger than I thought. Thirteen runways huh? I'm impressed.' McCandless decided to leave her 'impressed' for the moment anyway and not to educate her on the arithmetic of runway orientations. That could wait. The plane descended ever lower over Malta's sister island to the north-west and the pilot already had the plane on its correct glide path to terra firma.

'It's a swell view, Bruce. What a beautiful bay down there – never seen sea so blue. Does it have a name?'

'Yeah it must be Salina Bay. We're staying near there, Alex.'

'Check. Is that a girl's name, Salina?'

'No it's Latin for salt. There are salt pans at the head of the bay – at least there used to be. I assume they're still there. Anyway look sharp. That big dome on your left is Mosta Dome. It's massive and it was an easy target for an Italian bomber that dropped a five hundred kilo bomb on it.'

'Shit. How many pounds is that? I'm only joking!'

With a bump and a jerk first the port undercarriage hit the runway followed less than a second later by the starboard and finally the nose-wheels. Merhba ta' Malta! Welcome to Malta.

They didn't yet know it but but they were going to be on the George Cross Island for longer than they thought. A lot longer.

10

The White House
Washington DC

The Director of the NSA was a political appointment, the absolute choice of the President. In choosing Winchester the President had deliberately chosen an 'outsider' far from the Washington establishment. His choice was more than just an outsider. For a start he was ex-Army which was a change from the long line of Admirals and Air Force Generals. And he was a Californian so geographically he was almost an alien. Not since Reagan had a Californian exerted influence in the White House. The meeting in the Oval Office was going well and after the usual pleasantries they got around to the main issue at hand – China.

'So I'm sure you'll agree, Mr President, that we can't go on like this. Did you manage to get a look at the confidential memorandum I had delivered to you before today's meeting? I hope you didn't think I was being presumptive but I thought it would give you the opportunity to consider my suggestion before we actually met.'

'Ralph, I have indeed read your thoughts, even your plan.'

'Mr President, it cannot be a plan until you agree to it and even then we are dependent on others and their acquiescence, not to mention their assistance.'

'You do realise, Ralph, that there is hardly a soul on Capitol Hill, the Pentagon or Langley who would agree with you, don't you? And what about the guys in your NSA? Your thinking is way outta line from the norm. You do know that don't you?' Winchester wasn't sure if that was a question or a statement.

'Let's check these bullet points in your memorandum one at a time. One – that China's posturing on the world stage is as a result of a massive national inferiority complex. Did you dream that one up?'

'No Sir. For centuries China has been mistreated by the rest of the world. The final straw was the invasion by Japan, a much smaller country. With ten times the population China should have wiped the floor with the Japs. They couldn't because they were in a mess. After WW2 the rise of Mao Tse-Tung was almost inevitable. OK the guy was an asshole and a whole lotta people died of starvation but they had over a billion mouths to feed. The Cultural Revolution was an economic basket case. It was only when the moderates like Deng Xiao Ping took over and allowed capitalism and communism to work side by side that the country started to get rich. It was their version of Perestroika. You can get as rich as you like but don't rock the political boat.'

'Which brings us nicely on to the second point in your report. Do you really figure that a re-enactment of the summit between Bush and Gorbachev in Malta is a good idea? Except that the Chinese President is invited instead of the current Russian tyrant?'

'That's exactly what I'm saying, Mr President. It will send a signal to China that they have replaced Russia as a Great Power. They will gain enormous face in the world and I genuinely believe that it will go a long way towards changing their attitudes.'

'OK I buy that. At least I think I do.' The President scanned his eyes further down the memorandum to remind him of the arrangements that had been effected over three decades ago.

'So I meet my opposite number from Beijing on say our new carrier the USS Gerald R. Ford and we wine and dine him until his guts burst and …'

'No Sir. That is exactly what we don't do. By doing that you have already caused him to lose face. You have to understand how the Chinese think. Back in 1989 Bush used what was probably our oldest cruiser, the *Belknap,* to host his side of the proceedings. It was so old and rusty it was almost time to be converted into razor blades. We allowed, even encouraged, the Russians to take their newest cruiser, the *Slava*, on which to do their hosting and the signing of the treaty of friendship. It gave Gorbachev a lot of street cred and it was no skin off our nose.'

'So I turn up in an old *Perry Class* frigate and allow him to arrive in one of their new missile cruisers. Ya know, Ralph, I'm not too sure that would go down too well with Joe Public.'

'Sir, with respect, I don't think you got to the second page of my report.'

There were several minutes of silence while the President re-donned his reading glasses and finished the task.

'Well Ralph, I have to hand it to you. If we can pull it off. Firstly, is the *Christina O* available for the dates you have in mind? If it isn't then your idea is a non-starter.'

'I just heard this morning from their agent in Nice, France that the first week in October is available. The effects of the Covid pandemic have ravaged the cruising industry. At approximately fifty-thousand dollars a day, that's cheap.'

'It'll cost me that in new outfits for the First Lady! She won't want to play second fiddle to the Chinese President's wife. And remember like me she's from Delaware – what did Della wear boy, what did Della wear?'

'Ha-ha yeah I see what you mean. But first the Chinese President has to accept your invitation and I think the best way is for the Prime Minister of Malta to act as a formal go-between. It's all down to semantics.'

'So how do we make sure things go our way? Who is he anyway? And is the airstrip in Malta big enough for Air Force One to land?' Winchester sighed inwardly. That was the problem with most American Presidents. Until they took office they knew almost nothing about the world outside of Texas, Arkansas or whichever State they came from.

'Sir, it might surprise you to know that the main runway in Malta is almost twice the length of that at LAX.'

'Huh?' Then Winchester remembered that California was a million miles from DC so he used another analogy.

'It's longer than JFK, Sir. In fact they only use half of it because it's so long. It was a bomber base for the British during the Cold War, that's why.'

'OK so shall I ask our new Ambassador to Malta to call the Maltese Prime Minister – what's his name again?'

'Edward Borg Vella, Sir. It's in the final note on my Report.' The glasses came back on.

'Well at least it's easy to pronounce.'

'Mr President, the Bush-Gorbachev summit was hailed by the world's press as marking the real end of the Cold War. It was dubbed 'from Malta to Yalta' to emulate the tripartite meeting between Roosevelt, Churchill and Stalin. I cannot think of a more prestigious venue than the *Christina O.* Its pedigree is simply perfect. Here, I've brought you a copy of a magazine called SuperYachtWorld. It has a whole section on the vessel and its rich history. I'm sure you'll find it fascinating.'

'Thank you, I'll catch up on it later.'

In fact he opened the magazine as soon as Winchester left. American Presidents had a penchant for fame and luxury too. They just hid it better.

Later Winchester reflected that at least this President had a sense of humour. On the short flight back to Fort Meade on a Government helicopter he started to make notes. He had told him that he preferred to call the US Ambassador himself. In fact he was going to do nothing of the sort. He didn't tell the President that he already had two serving colleagues on the Island of Malta either. He didn't need to know, not yet and maybe never.

He sent a short email to Alex Pisani.

'Have you arrived yet? It looks like we have a green light. RW.'

There was no 'message ends' but she wouldn't have understood anyway.

11

After clearing immigration Alex and Bruce headed for the main exit and the Taxi kiosk.

'Good evening. Qawra Palace Hotel please.'

'Thank you that will be twenty-five Euros please.'

He paid and the lady attendant handed him a voucher to give to the driver.

'How much is that in real money, Bruce? Like in dollars.'

'Just over thirty US.'

'What? How come? These Eurodollars are worth more than US dollars?'

'Yep. Not so long ago they were almost at parity. That is a reminder that Uncle Sam is not as powerful economically as he once was.'

The driver piled the four cases, two each, into the back of the Mercedes seven seater people carrier and the two visitors sat behind the driver.

'I am Mario. Welcome to Malta. Your first trip to our beautiful island?' Bruce answered for them both.

'Hi, grazzi. No, I was here many times with the Navy. My friend's first visit though. She's Americano.'

'Like the coffee?' They all laughed.

'So where can I take you to my friends? The Phoenicia, the Excelsior I bet. They looked expensive suitcases Miss.'

McCandless shuddered at the mere mention of the word Excelsior. He'd been in command of the submarine *Astute* in the South China Sea when the signal **E-X-C-E-L-S-I-O-R** by Aldis lamp from the US Navy destroyer *John Paul Jones* had triggered the start of illicit action in the South China Sea. Thank goodness it had never got out that the British and American navies had been involved in a plot to bring down the Chinese Government.

'Take us to the Qawra Palace hotel please, Mario. I prefer the north side of the Island myself.'

'Bruce I thought we were staying in the Quarry Hotel some-place?'

'I told you, in Maltese the letter 'q' is silent. It's the OWRA Palace Hotel. Get it?' She smiled.

'I get it Bruce. I have always wanted to stay in a palace.' He didn't enlighten her.

The car set off and it was well dark but the moon was rising in the east like a Chinese lantern. It was almost an omen. Within a couple of kilometres they skirted round a roundabout and Alex saw a sign for a place called Qormi.

'Hey Mario, I guess that's called 'Ormi? Am I right?' squealed Alex excitedly.

'You got it, Miss. I take it is Miss. Signorina if you like. You look sort of Italian. Maltese even.' He could not possibly have known how close to the truth he was.

They by-passed the large township of Sliema and headed out to the Coast Road. Traffic was heavy and people were everywhere. The post-pandemic rush to the sun was in full flow. Slowly but surely Bruce began to get his bearings and at the bottom of a long hill they emerged into a brightly lit horse-shoe shaped bay with a stunning illuminated church on the right.

'Ballutta Bay! I know it. I know where I am now. Next stop Spinola and the famous Dick's Bar.'

'Sorry to tell you,Sir, but Dick's Bar is no more. It's now a Japanese sushi restaurant.'

'What? In Malta. Since when? It's about ten years since I was last here. You could get two beers for a Maltese Lira in Dick's Bar.'

'Then it must be longer than that before you were last here because we have been in the Euro since the 1st of January 2008. Young people think it's a good thing but older folks think the opposite. If you ask my daughter Lexine who is a teenager she will tell you the Euro is great but that's because she holidays in Italy with friends and they don't have to change their money! Lazy. Aren't all teenagers?'

Suddenly the Mediterranean Sea appeared on the right hand side and the almost full moon cast a moonbeam like a searchlight towards them across the still water. It was Alex's first sight of the ocean that bordered three continents and which had nurtured the most ancient civilisations on Earth. Indeed the Ancients had believed that if you had the misfortune to sail out of it then you would fall off the end of the world.

'Nearly there' offered Mario. 'We head into Salina Bay then turn right into Qawra. If you look over there on the other side of the Bay you can see it. That's the Qawra Palace. It's all lit up tonight. Mind you it always is at night.'

Alex was unimpressed. That was definitely not the kind of palace she wanted to stay in.

The car pulled up outside the hotel and parked neatly less than twenty feet from the revolving door that was the main entrance. Mario opened the rear tailgate and lifted the four cases onto the pavement. Reaching into his shirt pocket he pulled out his calling card – 'Marios Cabs' – and passed it to McCandless.

'I do other private work too, not just airport runs for the company. Call me if you need me OK. I'm twenty-four seven.'

'Thanks Mario. Have a couple of Hop Leafs on me.' He passed him a five Euro bill and smiled.

'I take it they still brew Hop Leaf?'

'Of course they do! Some things will never change my friend. Thanks be to God.' He drove off with a cheery wave and a 'Sah-Ha.'

'Alex, you go to the Reception and check us in. Here are the online booking details I printed out before we left London. I'll carry the cases in.'

'What? This place has a smart revolving door but no bell-hops?!'

'What do you think this is – the bloody Ritz? Look sharp. There's a queue at the counter and I'm dying for a Hop Leaf.'

Check in was quick and they took the middle of the three elevators to the sixth floor. Both had majestic sea-view rooms with a good sized balcony facing the Bay and tonight, that moon. It was illuminating a large square stone tower on the other side of the Bay. He wondered if Alex would even notice. They had agreed to meet an hour later in the beautiful Italianate coffee shop that was annexed to the Hotel on the ground floor. He was careful with his instruction. Americans called it the First Floor which could be confusing if she was looking for the Ladies Room – or even the bathroom. He had spent enough time in the Navy visiting Mayport, Florida and San Diego, California to realise that Americans and Brits were divided by a common language. It was a good job they both batted for the same side he had often thought.

They had both changed into more suitable attire for the climate – he into chinos and a polo shirt and she into white jeans with a dark green top, the buttons of which were obviously under not inconsiderable strain. He tried not to notice but the light from the magnificent chandeliers seemed to catch every point of the Malta Cross nestling snugly in her deep cleavage. Not for the first time he marvelled at what a truly beautiful creature she was. A waitress arrived to take their orders. Alex first.

'I'll take a Campari soda and to eat just a slice of New York cheesecake. Thank you.'

'And I'll have a Hop Leaf and a Maltese cheesecake please. Thank you.'

Signorina Pisani was about to discover that when it came to cheesecakes, New York and Malta were a world apart.

'Bruce, up in the room after I'd showered I opened an email from Ralph Winchester. In fact two emails. The first one simply said 'we have a green light' but I didn't get it before we left London. The second one is a fuller explanation. Here read it. It's quite long.'

She passed him the mini iPad which she produced from her purse. The drinks had arrived and she let him read and digest, not that he had eaten yet. She sipped the bitter-sweet nectar that was her default drink and waited. She had to wait longer than she thought because he read it twice.

'God almighty. Not so long ago I was instructed and paid to bring about the downfall and death of one Chinese President and now a few years later I have to broker a peace deal between his successor and our, sorry your, President. Crazy!'

'No, Bruce. We are gonna get the Prime Minister of Malta to do that. How do you pronounce his name by the way?'

'It's simple, just as it sounds – Edward Borg Vella.'

12

They both slept well. Alex had awoken first, slipped into a diaphanous bathrobe and ordered coffee from room service. The small gap she had left in the curtains allowed a shaft of powerful sunlight to pierce her room like a laser. No wonder she had woken up. She opened the 'drapes' to their fullest extent and her jaw dropped. The orange ball of the rising sun on the horizon was like it was carefully balanced on a table of the bluest felt she had ever seen. Somebody had told her that no Sea is as blue as the Mediterranean. She hadn't believed them. But she sure did now. The coffee arrived and she took it onto the balcony blissfully unaware that the steward was leaving in a more excited state than when he had arrived. There was no side to Alex. What you saw was what you got.

With the coffee poured into a dainty espresso-sized cup bearing the 'qp' back-to-back logo of the hotel she lit a Pall Mall menthol, sipped the refreshing caffeine and for the tenth time read Ralph Winchester's email. The dates were tight and the deposit having been made to the Christina O's management company in Nice there was no time to lose. Straight after breakfast she would call the US Embassy and arrange to see the Chargé d'Affaires, Georgette Fox, as soon as possible. Time was of the essence.

They were quite early and the line for the breakfast buffet overlooking the pool was mercifully short. After finding a table for two by the huge picture window they decided to share duties.

'Alex you go get the fruit juices, orange for me please, and I'll get the fry-ups. That OK?'

'What the heck is a fry-up? '

'Well like a full Ingerlish, you know, fried eggs, fried bread, fried bacon, fried sausages …'

'No way José! That is cholesterol on a plate. Is that what they fed you in the British Navy? And what happened to the lime juice – Limey?!' She grinned. She sure had him there.

'OK Alex, if you don't want a fry-up then after you've finished the muesli that resembles parrot food I can recommend you help yourself to a few slices of the hobz and get a few spoonfuls of the local marmalade and some butter.' He pointed to a table that was piled high with all kinds of bread and croissants.

'Huh. What is hobs?'

'It's Maltese bread. It is stunning. That's spelt H-O-B-Z.'

'There's a zee on the end of hob – and you call it hobs?'

'Just try it. You'll see. And don't forget butter and the marmalade. By the way it's called orange jam here.'

'Any more surprises? OK I'll go try it.'

Five minutes later Alex returned to the table with a modest two slices of hobz, two small chilled tubs of Anchor butter and a small side saucer with a few scoops of marmalade. McCandless just watched and waited while he went into battle with his fried everything. Less than two minutes later she had finished eating.

'Well, what's the verdict? Don't tell me you prefer bloody bagels!'

'Bruce, do you think anybody would mind if I lined up and got some more? I have never tasted bread like that in my life. And that orange jam. Wow. You can't buy that in

New York either. Does it come from that place in Spain? Seville or some place?'

'No it's local. Remind me to tell you more later. Come on – it's time for you to call the lady from Texas.'

'I already did before you had even showered I reckon. We're expected at ten o'clock. Where is this place A-Tard? And how do we get there? Is it far away?'

'It's Attard – one word OK? Why do you Yanks always split one word into two? It's about ten kilometres south of here, that's about six miles. If it wasn't still so hot I'd suggest we walk but we'll get a cab on this occasion. I saw a few outside the Hotel in a rank. No problem.'

'Walk?! You were gonna make me walk?'

'You Yanks never walk anywhere. Maybe next time.'

Shortly after nine-thirty they exited the Hotel through the revolving doors and walked into a wall of hot sunshine. It was still fairly quiet with most tourists still sleeping off the excesses of the night before. Had they not been tired after the flight they might have joined in the fun and blended in with the pleb-swarm of visitors from just about every part of Europe including Russians and Eastern Europeans from what was once part of the old Soviet Bloc. It was a timely reminder to both of them that the Bush/Gorbachev Summit of 1989 had truly marked the end of the Cold War. In a few years time would the hoped for summit between the current US and Chinese leaders result in a similar influx of oriental visitors from Beijing, Chengdu and Hong Kong which was now regarded as much a part of China as Hainan? Somehow McCandless doubted it. He should have asked Ralph Winchester what he thought. Perhaps not.

They got in the first taxi in the line and sat in the back. The gruff attitude of the driver was in sharp contrast to the personable Mario the evening before. He didn't even move from his semi-slumped driving position on the right hand side. He reeked of garlic and tobacco at the same time.

'Where to? Sliema? Valletta?' These were the usual destinations for visitors not wanting to endure the crowded buses in the tourist season. Alex took charge which caught McCandless by surprise.

'No. The new American Embassy at Attard please. And try to avoid Mosta. The traffic is always bad at this time of day. Go via Naxxar and Lija. It'll be quicker.' McCandless raised his eyebrows and wondered if she'd been up early studying her Fleximap. The driver turned the ignition key and the car moved out into the traffic flow. This time the sea and the Bay were on their left.

'Driver, what are those big wooden huts over there on the other side of the ponds – are they fish ponds?' The driver grinned and seemed to change personality in an instant.

'If they were then any fish raised there would be very salty. No, they are Malta's famous salt pans used to extract pure salt from the seawater. It's a slow but sure process of evaporation and nature. Been here since Roman times. The sheds are used to store the salt once it has been put into sacks.'

'Thank you, how interesting, Mr er …'

'Debono, Peter Debono. At your service. And I'm sorry I was so grumpy. I worked a late shift yesterday and started early today. We're still catching up after the pandemic. Two kids to feed and another on the way too.' He stifled a yawn but was slightly too late. More garlic. More tobacco.

'How long have you been a cab driver Mr Debono? All your working life?'

'No, not all. Until a few years ago I owned and operated two Malta buses. Then new EU Rules came in and all of us were out of a job. New buses, new rules, new people. With the compensation money I bought this new taxi and registered as a White Cab. I have to work long hours to make less money. Jahasra! But hey, I still eat and in Malta the sun nearly always shines. Haven't you noticed?!'

'You know, Alex, that's something I should have picked up on straight away.'

'What d'ya mean, Bruce?'

'The buses, Malta's famous buses are gone. Mostly orange, brown and reddish coloured. They're gone. I just can't believe it. They were an institution. It's like taking away New York's yellow cabs.'

'It was a sad day for us all my friend. The only place you can see them now is as children's toys sold in plastic blister packs. You know, just for the tourists. All made in China of course. Rubbish, just rubbish. And listen my friends, if you want to buy genuine Malta lace then it's best to buy it in Gozo. Be careful if you buy it in the market in Marsaxxlokk as a lot of it is fake and made in China or Taiwan. Just be careful.' The car reached a crossroads at a village called Bur Marrad and as requested he took the route to Naxxar and the road started to climb.

'Now look left Miss and you get to see a good view of Salina Bay and the salt pans.' Departing the busy little town of Naxxar they headed for San Anton where they saw a sign for the famous botanical gardens and then only a few minutes later they saw the new Embassy. Recently completed it was surrounded by barbed wire and security fences. There was an Army-style guardhouse manned by two uniformed US Marines. Alex showed her ID to the one that came to the window of the taxi.

'We're expected, Ensign.'

'Yes ma'am.'

A button was pressed and the barrier across the road was raised. Peter Debono was staggered.

'I have never been inside the perimeter. Hey, are you guys military?'

'Nope. Just tourists. Can you come back for us at twelve noon please?'

'Of course, see you then.'

Georgette Fox, the American Chargé d'Affaires to the Republic of Malta, was an affable lady. To McCandless's well-travelled eyes she had the pallor not of a red-necked Texan but more of an Eastern Mediterranean citizen. The introductions complete they were ushered into a small day room which was pleasantly furnished with heavily embroidered easy chairs, several chaises longue and a stunning oval coffee table, heavily carved with what looked to McCandless like cedar trees.

'Madam Chargé d' ….'

'Please, Bruce, no formalities here. Call me Georgette. OK?'

'Thank you, Georgette. I'm just admiring the skills of the artisans that carved that table.'

Georgette smiled as she beckoned him closer to the object d'art to take a look. He stared at it.

'Well I thought I was right. It's cedar wood and if I'm not mistaken that is a depiction of the old Beirut harbour with the hills and giant cedars in the background. Am I right?' Georgette was stunned.

'You are the first visitor to this new Embassy who recognises the scene. How clever you are!'

'Well I have been to Beirut but to be honest it was not a pleasant experience. I was on a British warship, HMS Bulwark, assisting British and allied citizens to escape the latest civil war. It was touch and go but we got everybody out. Those giant cedars are of course the Lebanon's national emblem. Just like say the giant redwoods are part of California's psyche. I'm right again aren't I?'

The conversation was halted by a steward coming into the room bearing a tray of two cafetières of coffee and a platter of sweet almond biscuits. At least Ralph Winchester wasn't there to get the cream and sugar wrong. Alex had felt a little out of touch so far so she spoke next.

'Georgette, I'll make a wild guess here. You're from the Lebanon yourself. Am I also right?'

'You are both very perceptive. I was born and raised in Beirut. I was married to a US Marine Corps Officer attached to the US Embassy.' Her eyes filled up. My husband, was killed in that huge explosion that killed so many Marines. By then I was myself a US citizen and I went to live in Texas to be with his family. I continued my language studies and joined the Diplomatic Corps. So here I am. I guess this is the pinnacle of my career. Anyway to business. I have been asked by some people much higher up the food chain to offer you every assistance. How can I help you? What's this about a Summit Meeting? How exciting. On my watch too. Is the President really coming to Malta?'

They talked animatedly for more than an hour. The prospect was amazing. The Maltese Prime Minister was to 'request the company' of the President of the world's most populous nation, China, to attend a Summit meeting with his opposite number from the world's richest nation. And it would all take place on the most prestigious vessel in the world in the territorial waters of one of the world's smallest nations. Georgette Fox was not just a diplomat. She was also a personal member of the United Nations. Could it work? In the words of a Starship Commander, she would 'make it so.'

The taxi arrived on time at twelve noon.

'Where to? Back to the Qawra Palace Hotel?' McCandless was quick off the mark.

'No. Take us to Rabat please, just straight there. Anywhere near the central square. Outside Vince's Bar will be just fine, Peter.'

'How come you know all the bars, Bruce?'

'Once a sailor, always a sailor, Alex. You should know that by now.'

Peter Debono knew that too. Hundreds of Maltese girls had married into naval families so ingratiated into Maltese life had the Royal Navy become in over two centuries. It was something that was hard for outsiders to understand.

13

Beijing
China

A week had passed since the last meeting of the Standing Committee and at this time of year another would not normally have been convened for at least another week. Something extraordinary had happened that had to be acted upon with decisiveness. Within the last few hours an urgent message had arrived in Beijing via the Chinese Ambassador to the Republic of Malta. The President chewed over it a dozen times. His mind was spinning like a top. Initially dismissing it as a scam or a crude joke somebody was playing, he had double checked the authenticity of both the sender and the intermediary. All enquiries proved clear. It was already dark and a cooling wind had arrived announcing that the autumn season in the northerly Hebei Province was not too far off. Leaves were already starting to turn and jackets were donned in the evening. Winters were long and hard in China's capital and trips to the warmer southern Provinces were more common. At least amongst those that could afford it. That was not a problem for the members of the twenty-five strong members of the politburo all of whom had been taken aback by the urgent request from the President and Chairman.

'You are instructed to attend an Emergency Meeting of The Politburo tonight at ten o'clock. Those not able to attend will be expected to join in via Zoom. By order.' This was unprecedented. Something must be up.

By nine forty-five the huge boardroom normally reserved for special occasions started to fill up. The President had taken a leaf from a book he had read which was later turned into a movie. He took the chair, literally at one end of the table so that he could look at any other person present if he wanted to. A huge plasma screen had been hastily erected at the end of the table, facing the Chairman. It would be used for the 'Zoom' attendees. There were pots of green tea at intervals on the table. There were no pre-placed writing pads with pencils. This was going to be another 'no notes allowed' meeting. The President glanced at his Omega Seamaster. If James Bond could have one then, by all the Gods, he could have one. It was now almost ten o'clock and a glance around the table told him that with eighteen seated plus himself and five faces showing on the screen only one member had yet to show. Whoever it was didn't matter. They would start without him. There wasn't any of that 'Quorum nonsense' here in China and even if only a handful of members had turned up it wouldn't matter. Quorums were considered an unnecessary invention of the decadent West. The long hand of the Omega reached the top of the dial. It was ten o'clock precisely China Time. There was only one time zone despite the huge geographical extent from east to west. One and a half billion people kept the same time as Beijing. Full stop.

'Welcome, Comrades. I am grateful you have all made the effort to attend at such short notice.' He used the word 'all' but a glance at the screen told him there were still only four faces on the screen. Whoever it was, he took a dim view, and as soon as the culprit was named he would have strong words later. Suddenly, as if by magic, a fifth face appeared in the top right corner of the screen.

'Ah good. We are all here finally. Again welcome and thank you. Doubtless you are all wondering why this Emergency Meeting has been called. This is why, Comrades.' He waved a single page communication in the air with the printed words facing towards the members and the camera. He pointed to the top of the letterhead and smiled.

'This, Comrades, is the historical emblem of the Republic of Malta, the sign of the Crusaders and is headed Auberge de Castille, Office of the Prime Minister. Permit me to read it out in full to you all.'

The Chairman cleared his throat and took a mouthful of green tea.

To:
'The President of the Peoples' Republic of China
Beijing.

Dear Mr President

It gives me enormous pleasure to extend an invitation to you and your First Lady to visit our beautiful country of Malta, or to be precise, Malta GC.

I have extended a similar invitation to the President of the United States and his First Lady.

In 1989 the meeting held on our beloved island between President Bush and Chairman Gorbachev of the then Soviet Union unofficially marked the end of the Cold War.

In order to demonstrate my even handedness I wish to treat you both with equal respect and generosity.

You might recall the late shipping magnate Aristotle Onassis entertaining Royalty, Nobility and some of the richest people in the world on his magnificent boat the Christina O.

I am delighted to tell you that via intermediaries of impeccable character I have managed to charter this floating piece of history for seven days commencing the first week in October.

As you might expect accommodation on board is luxurious but limited. The two principal Staterooms are the 'Royale' and the 'Presidential.'

Subject to your accepting my invitation I will immediately ensure that the Presidential Suite is reserved for your good-self and your First Lady. I have relegated the American to the 'Royale' suite but you know how jealous they are of the Royal family so this will make amends – in his eyes anyway. Two additional single staterooms will be made available for your interpreters – one each. It is envisaged that you will be aboard the Christina O for three nights following which you might like to stay a little longer to explore the Maltese Islands. You would be most welcome and I can sequester the Corinthia Palace Hotel for you if you wish. It is simply delightful.

In the years ahead and beyond our lifetimes I would like to think that this Summit will mark the end of the acrimony between the two richest and most powerful nations on Earth. It is also my fervent hope that tiny Malta will receive recognition for the role it has played.

For security reasons the invitation will not be made public knowledge until much later.

I look forward to hearing from you.'

Edward Borg Vella

Prime Minister.

When he finished reading the Chairman rolled it up like a Dead Sea Scroll and tied a red ribbon around it. In time he would have it sealed in a glass case and displayed in the Great Hall of the People.

'Well, Comrades. Don't any of you have anything to say?' To a man and woman (there were a token two of them) they simply stared in awe at the Chairman. They were all one million percent jealous. How lucky was he?

'I will of course be accepting the invitation. As you all know the Island of Malta is high on our target list of acquisitions for our String of Pearls doctrine. With good joss the Grand Harbour will become our own Pearl Harbor.' He paused for effect and everyone present smiled politely and nodded.

'The timing is perfect, Comrades. I will be able to remain in Beijing to celebrate our National Day on the First of October and then travel the next day. I will order the Air Force to suitably prepare an Il-76 jet to executive standards. I don't want to arrive in a twenty year old China Airlines B747 which would look shabby alongside the American's new Air Force One. He looked around the table, couldn't spot him and then finally up at the screen. It was the Finance Minister who had 'zoomed in' at the last minute.

'Ah there you are Comrade Won-Gah. You will kindly release the necessary funding for my trip, including the airplane interior conversion. We also need to meet in person tomorrow, Comrade.'

Without realising it the Chairman had just pissed on Wong's matches. He was almost a thousand miles from Beijing entertaining concubine number two in a five-star Shenzhen hotel. It would be the red-eye flight back to Beijing.

'Of course, Comrade Chairman. I have also started to make notes in connection with your visit to Malta. Other financial provisions will have to be made for shall we say …. disbursements.'

That's what he liked about Comrade Won-Gah. When it came to money he was always one step ahead of the shoeshine.

'Pass the oranges, Comrades, the meeting is over.'

In the time honoured Chinese way a crystal bowl of shiny, tiny oranges was passed around the table like a bottle of Port at a Regimental Dinner. They all took one, except for the 'Zoomers' of course. They missed out.

14

The trip to Rabat following the meeting with Georgette Fox was pleasant but, from McCandless's point of view, unfruitful. After a cooling beer and a 'ftira' in the open square outside Vince's Bar, Bruce had decided to come clean with Alex. He unfolded the single page of the Times of Malta that he had ripped from the paper on the plane and read it to her:

PISANI Carmen Maria Assumpta etc.

'Alex, if you look across to the corner of the square you'll see a neat shop frontage with frosted glass windows. See?'

'Sure, why? It's a firm of funeral directors. Tonna and Sons. Is that how you say it? That has to be the easiest Maltese name I've seen yet.'

'Yes but now read to the end of the announcement in the paper.' So she did. She went all quiet but then spoke softly.'

'Oh Bruce, do you think the deceased might be a blood relative? Grandpop never mentioned any siblings but d'ya know what, the lady was about the right age? If he was still alive he would have been one hundred and eight. Boy, you were smart to spot that when we were on the plane. I didn't see you remove that page.'

'I did it when you went to the bathroom at thirty thousand feet ... as if!' She smiled. They were getting used to each other's humour.

'You mean when I went to the loo, Bruce!'

'Finish your beer, honey, and we'll walk across and see if Messrs Tonna can tell us more.' He glibly used the word 'honey' so typical of casual America. And he didn't even realise he'd said it. One day he might deliberately call her 'Melita' and wait for her reaction. They walked across the square and rang the bell at Tonna & Sons.

A pleasant gentleman, slightly balding and in his sixties came to the door and gently opened it.

'Bongu.' He instantly switched to English when he realised he was not dealing with locals.

'Good morning. How can I help you? Please come in.' Gordon Tonna was immaculately attired in the uniform of a funeral director – crisp white shirt, black neck-tie, black waistcoat and the customary striped morning trousers. His polished black shoes were so shiny you could see your face in them, that is if you bent down to take a closer look. They accepted the chance of a seat on a dark leather Chesterfield and introduced themselves. The proprietor sat behind his office desk on which was placed a small vase of purple forget-me-nots, a nice and appropriate touch that lent a touch of empathy and sympathy to an office that dealt with sadness and grief on an almost daily basis. Alex spoke first.

'Mr Tonna, I'm here in Malta on a visit from the US to try and trace any of my ancestors, if I can. My name is Alexandria Pisani and' … she fumbled for the newspaper cutting … 'this recent obituary has led us to you. I know it's a bit of a long shot but I had to start some place.' She passed him the paper which he scanned in under three seconds.

'Alexandria, may I call you by your Christian name, Miss Pisani?'

'Yes, of course, please do.' She liked this guy immediately. So polite.

'Well firstly let me tell you that Madame Pisani's funeral has not yet taken place. It is scheduled for ten days' time. The delay is regretted but as you can see the deceased had a big family. Contacting them all has been a big job for somebody. And Maltese people being so sentimental and family oriented doubtless many of them will want to attend the funeral. Several are living abroad I understand including one in America and one in Australia. We are the Ireland of the Mediterranean so to speak. Thousands of our young people have emigrated over the last sixty years – even more than that! For reasons of confidentiality I cannot pass on any contact details without permission, you understand.'

'Yes, of course. But can you get that permission? I would be very grateful.' She smiled the smile of a honey trap and he cracked. He was already reaching for his desktop day-book clad in dark purple leather and within ten seconds he was dialling a number on his cellphone. He immediately lapsed into Maltese.

'Bongu, Raymond.'

The entire conversation took place in Maltese and ended with the almost automatic 'ciao.'

'I just spoke with the eldest son, Raymond. It's hard to say if he can help you or not but he will if he can. Pisani is a common name in Malta. We are still a little bemused as to why we, based in Rabat, were chosen as the funeral directors when there are other firms more conveniently located in the Three Cities, Conspicua included, where the final interment will take place. Anyway, I digress. I will write down his address and cellphone number. As you might expect he's preoccupied with family stuff, his mother's estate and all the grief and distress that goes with bereavement. I have only met him the once when he came to this office last week. Seems like a nice guy – about my age but with more hair!

Lucky chap, eh? Another couple of years and I'll be able to do a Yul Brynner impersonation.' Like the vast majority of Maltese he had a sense of humour.

'Let me show you out Alex and er, sorry I didn't catch your name Mr ...'

'McCandless but it's Bruce please.' He shook hands with both of them and they walked out back into the heat.

'You know Alex, the name Tonna rings a bell somehow. That is a much less common name than Pisani. Listen let's go back to Vince's Bar. I need another beer.'

'Yeah good idea and I'll have a Campari soda. And what was that sandwich called again?'

'A ftira, pronounced fitera. Try it.'

'Fit era.'

'Now you're making two words out of one! Try again.'

'Fitera, right?'

'You've got it. You seemed to enjoy it. Fancy another?'

'Can we share one? It was huge! What was it exactly anyway? Some kinda fish? Not lamb pooky huh?' They both laughed.

'No, local tuna fish. The locals call it tunny usually, or at least they used to. It's mixed with olive oil, Maltese of course, olives and capers. Served on lightly buttered hobz it is Malta's favourite sandwich and very healthy eating too. You could say it epitomises the Mediterranean diet so beloved of dieticians the world over.'

'What's a caper, by the way? They taste good too.'

'I'll tell you later. Come on this way. The sun's over the yardarm so you can have that Campari. I'll stick to Hop Leaf.'

He slipped his arm around her slender waist without realising it and steered her back to Vince's. This time they found a table and chairs in the shade. It was still hot in late afternoon. Five thousand miles to the east and six hours ahead time-wise it was already midnight. The Chairman of the CCP was hard asleep dreaming about dry-docks and meeting an American First Lady. In Shenzhen Comrade Won-Gah obliged 'No 2' with a 'second coming' not of the Christian variety and ordered a taxi. The red-eye flight on China Southwest Airline to Beijing awaited him. He wouldn't be recognised by either the cabin crew or fellow passengers. With luck he would get three hours sleep followed by another three in his Beijing apartment. He didn't want to give the Chairman the impression he'd spent the previous night in a whorehouse even if he hadn't.

15

Beijing
China

Comrade Won-Gah, the Financial Secretary, was expected. He was ushered into the President's western-style office, an emulation of the Oval Office at the White House with the national red flag with yellow stars in the canton, one large and four smaller ones. The large star represented the Communist Party with the smaller stars representing the People. Smaller meaning subservient to. It had been that way since the flag was first hoisted in Tiananmen Square in Peking on 1st October 1949 and by all the Gods it would stay that way under his Chairmanship. That meant for ever now that he had changed the rules. He didn't want the Motherland's progress to be hampered by Western style elections. That was something that always worried him about the thousands of Chinese students studying overseas in the US, UK and 'Au-Jau' – the great land Down Under. He didn't want any of those students getting infected with the 'democracy virus' – not after being blamed by the West for the Covid virus. That was bad enough. The trade war with Australia was getting worse and the Politburo had agreed to tighten the noose even harder by totally banning all wines from that country. In any case it would give a few years for the indigenous wine industry in China to mature and eventually catch up with those upstarts who had only been a real country for just over two centuries. China had been a nation for over five thousand years and he wasn't going to be pushed around by a bunch of Britons who had decided to spend more time in the sun than in the rain. The spats with Australia's Prime Minister were becoming worse but he was certain that soon, very soon, the Australian Premier would crack and send him a personal gift as a gesture of so-called friendship. Fifty years ago Comrade Whitlam had ordered the RAAF to transport six prize breeding cattle from Queensland to Peking. If only he had known that Szechuan beef had been on the menu for the next six weeks! Don't they ever learn? The future is China's.

'Comrade Won-Gah, good to see you in the flesh so to speak. I take it that it was the flesh that held you up last night? Your neck-tie looked a little askew on the zoom screen I noticed. Ha! I'm right aren't I? Which one was it this time No.2, No.3 or No.4?'

'Wong was caught by surprise but went along with his little charade, relieved that no further questions were asked.'

'No. 2 if you must know, Comrade Chairman. I think she might have to go soon – on costs grounds!'

'Trust you, Comrade Won-Gah, now, to more serious money issues. Take a seat, I'll get us some tea.'

'Thank you, Comrade Chairman, I have made notes since the meeting last night and done some research online. I'll just get my iPad out from my briefcase. Just a second please.' He pressed the release clip from his dark brown highly polished leather case to reach inside. It caught the Chairman's eye.

'Is that made in China, Comrade? A fake copy of a Western brand? It looks superb I must say. Italian perhaps?'

'You're right Comrade Chairman. It is Italian despite the English sounding name of The Bridge. Like Tina Turner, it is quite simply The Best as well as being The Bridge. If you like I'll see if I can get you one on my next trip to Europe.'

'Thank you. I would really appreciate that. Now, to more serious matters. I take it you have sanctioned the release of funds to cover the upgrade to my own personal jet, the customised Il-76?'

'Indeed I have. The five million Yuan should cover it nicely and I understand it will be finished on time. We have matured that marque of aircraft far beyond the original Russian types to such an extent that we are considering renaming it and setting up a production line in Guangdong Province. The Ilyushin patents and trademarks are the only matters standing in our way and …'

'Just ignore them, Comrade, like we always do. What will Russia do? Ban us from importing vodka? Filthy stuff. Now, looking ahead to my visit to Malta, the itinerary will become a little clearer over the next few days. We will need to pay off certain people – what they call in the West greasing palms I understand. What you and I call tea money. You're the money man Comrade Won-Gah – your recommendations if you please?

'Comrade Chairman, matters are already in hand as we speak. The Secretary at our 'Cultural Centre' in the capital city of Valletta is being briefed by the Commercial Attaché and the necessary accounts at the nearby Head Office of the Bank of Valletta have been opened over a year ago. Thus there will be no newly-opened accounts upon which suspicion might be cast. Any disbursements will be paid via the Cultural Attaché.'

'Excellent. Now, Comrade, moving on to the question of Naval Estimates. Has money been allocated in the next Fiscal Year for the new aircraft carrier which remains as yet unnamed?'

'No, not yet Comrade Chairman. Did you have in mind naming it after your good-self?'

'Certainly not. Only the sentimental Americans do that sort of nonsense. Their two latest carriers are named after former Presidents *Gerald R. Ford* and *John F. Kennedy* but would you believe the next in the class is going to be called the *USS Enterprise*?! No doubt it was President Kirk's idea and another Hollywood inspired fantasy to promote the Star Trek movies I assume. They'll be building 'Klingon birds of prey' to fly from its deck next. In fact why don't we invent a new computer video game where our own new fighters called 'birds of prey' attack the *Enterprise* in the South China Sea? It could be a worldwide best seller like Grand Theft Auto!' Won-Gah wasn't sure if the Chairman was joking or not. It was hard to tell sometimes.

'I read recently that the first steel for the *Enterprise* was cut in a lavish ceremony at Newport News, Virginia by two movie stars.'

'Well that backs up what I just said. We'll make sure that we perform a similarly lavish ceremony at Dalian when the first steel is cut for our next carrier. And we must make sure that it's a metre longer than the *Enterprise* for propaganda purposes, Comrade. Now, do we have sufficient funds in the Valletta accounts – enough to bring onside everyone we might need.'

'Oh yes I believe so, Comrade. In fact by the time we've finished I think you'll assume a new name in the history of our great nation.'

'Really? What?'

'*The Maltese Mandarin* of course!'

'I like it Comrade Won-Gah, I like it! A good name for the new carrier maybe?'

'Shall we run the idea past a few people to see what others think, you know, to test the waters so to speak? Excuse the pun. By the way in view of the security situation and the total blackout of news until the summit is imminent, how are we going to maximise exposure in the Western press? Have you given it any thought yet, Comrade Chairman?'

'Well, the Western press don't like me, I can tell you. A few years back after visiting the United Kingdom and enjoying bi-lateral talks with their President 'Cameroon,' I was asked if I had given him any advice. I told him to lock a lot more people up, just like we're doing in our new Province of Hong Kong. A few days later a cartoon of myself and the First Lady departing Heathrow Airport appeared in the newspaper the *Sunday Suppress* with a caption of me saying exactly those words. We must be vigilant at all times, Comrade Won-Gah. Otherwise we will be misquoted by them.'

'I take your point. Well Comrade Chairman, in case we don't meet again before you depart for the Summit, I wish you a pleasant flight. Perhaps you could send me a postcard? My youngest daughter collects foreign stamps.'

'It will be my pleasure Comrade Won-Gah. I will detail an aide to see to it straight after our arrival. In fact on my return I will direct the state-owned China Post Group to issue a new collection of postage stamps to mark the Summit meeting.'

The postcard never arrived.

16

The bus ride back to Qawra from Rabat was an eye-opener for Alex. After the second ftira of the day they walked, hand in hand, the length of Triq San Pawl (St. Paul Street) to the bus terminus almost opposite the gateway to the ancient City of Mdina – the Silent City. Alex just marvelled at the pale yellow houses made from local limestone hewn from local quarries. She had ribbed him.

'Is the q silent in quarries, Bruce?'

'Ha no! You asked me how old these houses are. Well if you said about five hundred years old you'd be about right.'

'You are kidding. No way!'

'Sure, why not? When these were built Manhattan was just a swamp and as for Brooklyn well let's just not go there shall we.'

'Bruce, these buildings are just so beautiful and folks actually live in them. Look at the way little pots and tubs of flowers are grown outside people's front doors. And some are grown up the walls too. What is that one there, that huge pink one? It's gorgeous?'

'It's called an oleander. And that one over there opposite that's a bougainvillea, but they're closely related varieties. See those red and orange flowers over there in that huge terracotta pot? They're called Zinnias and they are highly prized and expensive.'

San Pawl Street meandered like a slow moving river and with the main heat of the day diminishing more people were starting to emerge from their houses to chat and banter on the pavement, or even the middle of the road. Any traffic would have to wait until conversations had finished. The timetable told them that a bus for Bugibba, via Qawra, had departed only a few minutes earlier and the next one would be another twenty minutes.

'See that stone bridge over there on the left? That's the gateway to Mdina, the old medieval capital of Malta before Valletta was even built. Quickly, we'll take a peek before the next bus. Cross over here.'

Just as they started to cross the ancient bridge a peal of bells rang out from the Cathedral to mark the hour – six o'clock. Alex looked skyward to see if the clock was in time with the bells. She was immediately confused. The clock-face seemed to be back to front. Like it should be read from the inside of the clock-tower, not the outside. Bruce interjected before she could say anything.

'Alex, before you ask, many of Malta's churches have two clocks. One is correct, the other is to confuse the Devil. So they say anyway.'

'Aw, how cute is that?'

Cute is not the word that McCandless would have used but after all she was an American and a New Yorker to boot. They wandered down a few streets so narrow that even a high summer sun shone in them for but a couple of hours a day. By now they were all in total shade which reminded McCandless to check his watch made by the Roamer Co. founded in 1888 when Valletta was only three hundred years old. It put time into perspective but isn't that what watches are supposed to do?

'Come on, Alex. Back we go over the bridge. We don't want to miss this next bus.'

'Bruce, this City is just beautiful. Can we come back here on another day please?'

'Sure we can. I love it too.'

He slipped his hand into hers and steered her coxswain-like onto the steps of the bus which had arrived at the stop early. It was absolutely jam-packed with tourists and they were lucky to spot the last two seats which were right at the back on a bench-type seat. McCandless halted by a small electronic display screen near the driver and pressed two plastic cards one after the other onto it until he heard two visible 'pings.' They reminded him of submarine sonar 'pings' which brought back unpleasant memories and he moved sharply to the back of the bus.

'Bruce, didn't you pay the guy? Are buses free like in certain boroughs of DC?' He held up two credit card sized pieces of plastic.

'These are called Tallinjas. They're a prepaid bus pass. I bought them in the hotel gift shop this morning. They're valid for twelve journeys, one each. All you do is zap it onto the sensor pad and it deducts one journey whilst at the same time telling you how many journeys you have left on the card. Eleven left! Here, here's yours. Happy travelling.'

McCandless slid it ever so gently into her cleavage and smiled. She smiled silently back.

The view from the rear seats was good being slightly elevated above the rest of the seats. Rabat and Mdina were over five hundred feet above sea level and the vista before them as the road descended was a revelation to Alex. So many buildings and so many churches in the distance including one that outshone them all.

'Bruce, hey wow! What is that big dome way ahead. That is huge.'

That is Mosta Church or, more accurately, the Sanctuary Basilica of the Assumption of Our Lady. You might have read about it already. That's the church that was hit by a large bomb dropped during the Second World War. It penetrated the roof but it didn't explode. There was a service being conducted at the time and not a single soul was even injured. To the believers it was of course a miracle. And who could contradict that?'

'Ya know Bruce, I was christened a Catholic and raised a Catholic. I guess half of Brooklyn was too what with the Irish and the Italians living cheek by jowl, but sometimes I just wish I had that level of faith. Am I making sense?'

McCandless wasn't listening. He was staring out to sea at least ten miles away. Nautical miles in his case. Glinting in the evening sun were the unmistakable aluminium sails of perhaps the most stunning sailing ship ever built by man. He recognised it immediately. It was the unmistakeable lines of the *Maltese Falcon*. She was coming home.

When they got back to the hotel McCandless opened his own iPad to check his emails. Unlike most women who carried a purse big enough to house a spare wheel and a six-pack of beer, he preferred to travel light. Only one message sat in the in-box that interested him. It was from Ralph Winchester.

'Hi Bruce. Be advised that in addition to the MY Christina O you now have at your disposal the SY Maltese Falcon. It is available for only two days due to previous contractual arrangements. Details as follows etc etc. It is at your total discretion how you incorporate that within your overall vacation. The Maltese Falcon has been chartered in your name but don't worry Uncle Sam has paid for it. Bon voyage. Ralph. Message ends.'

This jigsaw puzzle was getting a little too complicated for McCandless. He needed a 'deep and meaningful' conversation with Alex. He would start over dinner in the hotel dining room.

17

They needn't have bothered 'dressing up' for dinner. Nearly everyone was in shirt sleeve order but shorts were frowned upon. At least a modicum of decorum was achieved. There was only a short line of hotel guests waiting to enter the capacious dining room which had lost its breakfast atmosphere. Gone were the fruit juice dispensers and tables of hobz. Just outside in the lobby McCandless noticed several dozen bottles of wine on display and stepped towards them for a closer look. As he picked one up for a look at the label, a voice bellowed out from behind the small cocktail bar. It was one of the waiters.

'Sir, have you tried it before? It's local. All Delicata wines are local. Here, have a taster.' Taking a small wine glass from under the counter he held it beneath what looked like a small beer tap and pulled a small lever until the glass was about a third full. He passed it to McCandless across the top of the bar.

'What do you think?'

McCandless took the customary sniff of the bouquet followed by a little slurp.

'Not bad. In fact not bad at all. The Cabernet Sauvignon you say? Mmmm. Yes, is it the same as in the bottle?'

'Yes, it is Sir. You can buy it by the glass for a Euro or the bottle is six Euros. I can bring it to your table.'

'Deal! A bottle it is.'

'Give me two minutes. I'm sure you and your lovely wife will enjoy it.' McCandless found it hard not to grin.

'I'll put the six Euros on your room bill, Mr er …'

'McCandless, Room 614. Thank you.'

Most of the residents were eating outside of the hotel at one of the many nearby eateries that seemed to cater for every pocket and taste. From pizzas to pasta to Prosecco, every taste bud was catered for. A decade ago Qawra and its neighbour Bugibba had an indifferent reputation that catered mainly for the 'lower orders.' It was Blackpool with sunshine, garlic and chips. Today the picture was a little different with smart bistros, coffee shops and apartments with prices that reflected the 'up and coming' desirability of an area that epitomised the Island itself.

The mouth watering buffet was a delight to the eye. Alex chose a selection of antipasti and McCandless a veritable smorgasbord of seafood covered in black olives, feta cheese and sun-dried tomatoes. They had barely returned to the table when the wine waiter appeared and hovered like a dragonfly, his left palm balancing the tray and two sparkling glasses and in the other a plain old-fashioned corkscrew that looked as if it had been opening bottles since the Second World War. That's because it had. He deftly removed the cork with the dexterity of a magician and offered it to McCandless in the time-honoured way of all true Sommeliers. He turned next to Alex, poured a modest amount into the shimmering crystal-like glass and offered it to her like she was a Goddess about to taste the elixir of life.

'Madam McCandless, if you please.' She hesitated. Bruce helped her out.

'The lady takes the first sip. This is Malta not Manhattan. Try it.'

'Mmm, nice. As good as Californian I would say. Now back at Walmart I would buy a …'

'Alex, just forget California, Walmart and mama's apple pie. You are zillions of miles away from all that, just as I am away from Queen and Country and roast beef. OK? When in Rome, or even Malta – now what caught your eye for the main course?'

'Do they have lampooki? I still haven't tried it?'

'I don't think so, not tonight. But I did notice pan-fried dendici. Yes?'

After coffee they sat outside on the terrace facing the Bay, the Qawra Tower still illuminated by a now full moon. They talked.

'Bruce, Winchester copied me into his email to you. Why do we need two boats? Surely we only need one for the actual Summit Meeting. Don't we?'

'Sure, but using the *Maltese Falcon* we can also turn the whole show into a social event.'

'We can? Is that a good idea using two boats? I read the files at Fort Meade. The weather was so bad back in '89 that transferring personnel between the *Belknap* and the *Slava* was almost impossible and …'

'Yes, well that was then and this is now. It's late summer not mid-winter. That was just bad luck. They should have known that really bad storms can hit the Island in January and February. That's why the coastline looks so jagged and eroded. The limestone is very soft which is why it is fairly easy to work as a building material. Erosion is hard to predict, let alone calculate. Did you watch Game of Thrones?'

'Yeah sure, who didn't? You?'

'Yes, well the first series anyway. Remember that huge sea-arch in the background behind Daenerys Targaryen, the Dragon Queen, when she got married?'

'Sure, who doesn't? That was an amazing movie-set wasn't it?'

'You're right and wrong. It was amazing but it wasn't a Hollywood movie-set. It was shot at the Azzure Window on the island of Gozo about ten miles north-west of here.'

'You can not be serious!' She did her best to emulate the tennis player John McEnroe at his petulant worst. They were, after all, fellow New Yorkers. They both laughed. They seemed to be doing a lot of that.

'Yes, it's right. I had read somewhere that the final episode was also going to be filmed there but nature intervened.'

'Like bad weather during the shooting?'

'Worse than that. A huge winter storm in 2017 brought the whole structure crashing down into the sea. One day it's there, next day it's not. It was a major tourist attraction, especially since the TV series. It was one of those terrible storms that resulted in Saint Paul being shipwrecked on the Island, effectively bringing Christianity to Malta.'

'When was that?'

'Around AD60 it is believed. At that time Malta was a Roman province.'

'Bruce, can we go to Go-Zo? Tomorrow maybe?'

There you go again. Gozo is one word not two! We sure can but maybe in a few days' time. There's plenty of them. Relax. Tomorrow we'll go to Valletta. And remind me to tell you why your eyes are so blue before we leave Malta.'

'Tell me now please.'

'Not yet. But I will soon. I promise.'

The twin blue lasers nearly cut him in half. It had been a long day but a fulfilling one.

'You know Bruce we've been here in Malta only one whole day but I feel like I've always been here. Does that sound crazy to you?'

'No, not at all. That's the effect the place has on you. It happens to me every time I come here. And don't forget, genetically you are part of the Island. Just remember that.'

Alex didn't need to be told. Already she felt as much a part of the island's DNA as the Mesozoic limestone it was built on. She had never felt like this before in her entire thirty-five years.

18

'Why aren't we taking a cab to Valletta, Bruce? I thought you kept that guy's card.'

'Sure, I did but there's a lot to see on the way that I want to show you, OK?'

Alex nodded. He knew more about the place than she did, that's a given. She thought he seemed a trifle aloof this morning.

'I've been thinking. Before turning in last night I sent a quick email to Ralph. I wanted to clarify the situation with the chartering of the two boats. Seems like the *Christina O* has been directed to come here anyway – something to do with its Port of Registration 'annual review' and its inspection and seaworthiness certification. It arrives on Friday and from midnight that night it's 'ours' for seven days and nights. It's what is called a 'wet charter' that all crewing costs and fuel, victuals etc. are within the quoted price. Paid already.'

'Great so why the pensive mood? Having leveraged the US Chargé d'Affaires to ensure the Maltese Prime Minister's invitation to Beijing was made and accepted, that's our involvement over. Period.'

McCandless so wished Americans desisted from using that one-word sentence. It sounded like an ad for a tampon.

'You're right in that respect, Alex. The arrangements for utilising the ninety-nine metres of floating history will be out of our hands thank goodness. We do not want to get embroiled in that. No, it's Ralph's wish that we similarly use the eighty-eight metre *Maltese Falcon* to put the icing on the Summit cake, so to speak.'

'Any ideas?'

'Yes, a huge one but I don't know if it will work. Ralph is insisting that we get the Chinese President onto the *Maltese Falcon.*'

'Hey, if he's a Humphrey Bogart fan, like me, then just the name might be enough to entice him aboard. But how do we guarantee it?'

'Alex, you might just have something there but how's this for an idea too. I lay awake thinking about it.'

'Go ahead, I'm all ears.'

'Confession time. After you headed up in the lift …. er elevator … last night I cheated on you.'

'You mean you found another Mrs McCandless to confuse the wine waiter?' She grinned.

'Not quite but you're halfway there. I decided I might like another glass or two of that excellent wine so I sneaked back down to the Bar again. The same guy was still on duty. He persuaded me to try another local wine, a half bottle of Falcon Merlot from Gozo and …'

'You mean Go-Zo …. sorry, just winding you up!'

'Then I thought, hey *Maltese Falcon* and Falcon wine. With my brain thus suitably lubricated I then thought, hey, how about having a wine tasting evening on board. Don't forget my cover story, should I need one, is that I'm researching Maltese vineyards for a possible future Guide Book. We can invite a representative from all the major vineyards in Malta and Gozo to come and give a short talk.'

'And bring lots of samples of course for tasting on board. And you dreamt this up last night?'

'Well yes and no. About ten years ago I was on leave in York, that's our York by the way not New York, and an old Navy buddy called Ian Davis invited me to a Yorkshire Guild of Sommeliers wine tasting in Whitby. We had served together on an assault ship called *Fearless* in my very early Navy days and we always kept in touch. I had a few days leave left so I accepted. I expected the tasting and supper to take place in the small hotel we had checked into. But it didn't. The whole evening was on board a sailing ship called the *Grand Turk*. It was actually built in Turkey in the late Nineties and was a replica of an eighteenth century frigate to use in a Horatio Hornblower TV series. It was a great evening. The wine flowed like the Hudson in spring and we all got sozzled and went to Heaven as the expression goes.'

'Yeah. We could ask Prime Minister Borg Vella to act as the host. It will be a magnificent advertisement for the Maltese wine industry. Everybody wins, right?'

'Absolutely! We need to make another call to Georgette. Can you call her this evening maybe?'

'I'll do it when we get to Valletta. It's just a little noisy on the bus. Now, how about pointing out some of the sights to me?'

The bus rolled on with the sea on the left as it followed what is called the Coast Road towards Sliema, perhaps the biggest conurbation on the Island. Every mile or so Bruce pointed to a stone-built watchtower just yards from the water's edge. Qawra Tower. Ghallis Tower. Madliena Tower. St. George's Tower.

'Ya know, Bruce, Jimi Hendrix would have liked this place – all these watchtowers! Ha!'

'Maybe he would. They were all built to watch out for invaders. Let's face it everybody has tried to invade this place because of its strategic importance. But that orange and blue tower a couple of miles ahead, that's new. Well, less than twenty years old. It's the Portomaso Tower and they were halfway through building it last time I was here. A lot of people objected to it on the grounds it looked out of place amongst all the other stone buildings. I quite like it though. There's a bar on the top floor called Bar 22. Let's get a cocktail up there one evening before we leave shall we?'

'Yeah well I agree with the objectors. I think it's vulgar.' McCandless raised an eyebrow. Already she was starting to think like a local.

As they neared Sliema, the traffic got heavier and heavier, such were the effects of a Covid-delayed holiday season. It seemed like half the young population of Sicily and Southern Italy was on vacation on the George Cross Island. McCandless wondered how many of those youngsters even knew that some of their grandparents would have been pilots flying their Marchetti bombers in a vain attempt to pound the Maltese population into submission. Tonight over dinner he would tell the lovely Alex more about Malta's heroism than the tourist guides ever told you. The traffic was almost gridlocked by the time they reached Floriana on the outskirts of Valletta itself. It had taken almost two hours to travel ten miles – as the crow flies anyway. Not that many birds ever flew in Maltese airspace. Not if they knew better anyway.

'Jeez. Ya know Bruce, this place could really do with a subway – like New York. Even London's got one!' By now McCandless was becoming used to the banter and her sense of humour. He was even beginning to enjoy it. They got off the bus outside the famous Triton Fountain.

'Hey, I love that fountain, Bruce. Is that five hundred years old too? Although it looks kinda new to me.'

'I think it's about fifty years old but it looks like it's had a polish and a makeover to me, since I was was last here anyway. The old buses used to park around it. Not now. It's all been paved over to allow pedestrians easy access to it. Hey, let's stand in front of it and take a selfie shall we?'

'Yeah great idea.' Click! She checked to make sure the strong sun had not resulted in a bad take. It hadn't, so she saved it to her main picture gallery on her iPhone.

'Where do we go now, Bruce? I need to call in at the Valletta Branch of the *Middle Sea Bank*. I need to collect some Eurodollars. Do you know where it is?'

'From memory it's about five hundred yards down Kingsway on the right. I mean Republic Street. Old habits die hard.'

'Typical Brit! Queen and Country again huh?'

'You mean King and Country!'

They crossed the bridge that spanned the Great Ditch, a medieval moat built to protect the Capital and the road widened to a broad boulevard that would not have looked out of place in any European capital.

'Listen Alex, there's the bank a couple of hundred yards up front, just as I remembered. You go ahead and then come back and meet me at the Café Royale on the left. See it?'

'Yeah sure. I shouldn't be too long. Get me a long cold drink please. Boy it's hot.'

McCandless secured a table outside the main café but just inside the shaded area. A waitress came to the table to take his order.

'A large Hop Leaf for me please and a Kinnie with lots of ice for my friend please. She won't be long.'

19

In fact Alex was only five minutes but suddenly McCandless wondered why she needed to go into the bank to 'collect' some Euros. He soon found out why. She sat at the wrought iron table and kicked a couple of pigeons out from under her feet. Pesky things were everywhere looking for a dropped morsel of bread or cake. Pigeons were pigeons the world over. She reached for the tall glass and hesitated before sipping from the long drinking straw.

'Bruce, what is this? Smells kinda unusual?'

'It's called Kinnie and it's a local speciality. Go for it.'

'Boy that's different and so tangy and refreshing. Exactly what is it?'

'Remember my telling you about the local oranges and marmalade jam back at the hotel? Well this is made from the same oranges that aren't made into marmalade. It's got lots of aromatic herbs in too.'

'You mean erbs!'

'If you insist. I think it's oregano and rosemary. The latter grows like weeds in this climate. Needless to say the recipe is a closely guarded secret.'

'Like Coca-Cola!'

'I told you – when in Rome. What's that in your left hand?' She passed him a piece of plastic which at first sight he thought was a Tallijna.

'Here, this is yours. I have one too. Purely for emergencies of course – or if you have to pay anybody off.' He stared at it. It was a debit card in his name for the Middle Sea Bank.

'What? So who fixed this?'

'Ralph, who do you think? His tentacles spread a long way. They were ready to collect before we had even arrived. It doesn't ever require a signature, just a PIN number.'

'And are you going to tell me that number or do I have to guess it? Let me guess – 0407 – the Fourth of July?'

'No that's my number, just in case you ever have to use it. Your number is 9988. I just changed it to that to make it easy for you to remember. It's the length of 'our two boats' ninety-nine and eighty-eight metres. OK? That's what you said anyway.'

'So how much is available? Ten million?'

'Ha, this is the Café Royale not Casino Royale. You've been watching too much of James Bond, Bruce. Or maybe I should call you James?'

'Don't you dare, Vesper! Out of interest how much is available?'

'Unlimited. Like the bottomless cup of coffee in most diners.' McCandless didn't know what to say. He was starting to think there was a lot more to all this than met the eye. He went to the Gents' inside and upstairs and thought alone for a couple of minutes before returning to the table outside.

'Are you going to make that call to Georgette Fox suggesting that the Prime Minister hosts the wine tasting and supper on the Maltese Falcon?'

'I just did it while you went to the bathroom. She's up for it and suggested a little idea of her own. She'll call back later to confirm everything after she's spoken with Mr Borg Vella. Does he live in a Palace by the way, you know like Putin in Russia?'

'I've no idea but I know where his office is. Drink up and I'll show you.' He left a five Euro bill on the table tucked under the empty Kinnie can.

'Let's go. This way.' They crossed over the road and walked past an ultra modern building that looked more like a computer generated image than a real edifice.

'Wow! Say, what is this place? It's like another movie-set.'

'That, Alex, is Malta's new Parliament building. It's brand new and it caused a lot of controversy. The architect is world famous. Renzo Piano.'

'I thought he was an Italian musician. Only joking, Bruce. Yeah famous is right. The same guy designed the Shard in London. And that new airport in Japan.'

'You're correct. Anyway we turn left here up these stone steps. Up we go. There's a lot of them but it's not as steep as it looks.'

'Phew! You were right. Seventy-nine I counted. I've never seen steps like those.' She turned around and looked down. It was a long way down but it was a bit like one of those optical illusions.

'They're called Roman steps – wide but shallow. The drop between each one is only four inches and because of that you don't really notice that you're climbing. Clever eh? They were all done during the reconstruction of the whole area which included the removal of the old City Gates and the construction of the new Parliament. Opinion was bitterly divided.'

'So where are we now? Where are we headed?' They kept walking. As if by magic a huge square opened up before them.

'Heck is that a Castle or a Palace up ahead?' She pointed.

'Well actually it's called the Auberge de Castille or more commonly the Office of the Prime Minister.'

'That's his office?! Well it sure beats Block 16 at Fort Meade. Are you sure? He's even got two great cannons outside his front door. And the huge National flag fluttering from the roof – does that mean he's in the office when it's raised? You know like the Queen's Standard flies over Buckingham Palace to signify that she's in residence, so to speak?'

'No, the flag always flies. The two halves, white on the left and red on the right, are a throwback to the Knights of Saint John.'

'And the cross in the left hand corner. What's that?'

'That, Alex, is what makes this Island unique. It is the George Cross awarded to the Island by King George the Sixth in 1942. It is a civilian honour awarded for supreme gallantry. If you like it's the civilian version of the Victoria Cross. To Malta it means everything. That is why you often see the letters G.C. after Malta's name.'

'Wow. How historical. And whose statues are these in the square?'

'They are both of men who for very different reasons changed the whole future of the Island. That one over on the left is of Jean Parisot de Valette. He was the forty-ninth Grand Master of the Order of Saint John and he led the resistance of Malta against the Turkish invaders during the Great Siege in 1565. The new City of Valletta was named after him.'

'New? Four hundred years ago?'

'Yes well apart from the new Parliament building absolutely nothing in Valletta is new. Apart from the other statue over there. Let's take a look.'

'So who was this guy Dom Mintoff. Was he a priest you know like Dom Perignon, the champagne guy?'

'No way, although he held almost God-like status to many Maltese. He was a former Prime Minister which is why his statue is outside the Office of the Prime Minister. He led the campaign for Independence from Britain in 1964 but ironically he tried to persuade the British Foreign Office to totally incorporate Malta into the United Kingdom with two Members of Parliament sitting at Westminster.'

'You mean like say Hawaii when it became State number fifty and sends two Senators to DC?'

'That's a fair analogy.'

'So what happened?'

'The Brits declined, preferring that Malta had total independence. I think it's all worked out for the best. Dozens of civilian airliners arriving every day with thousands of free-spending tourists brings more prosperity to the Island than squadrons of bombers and battalions of troops, even if they did spend most of their pay on wine, women and song.'

'And the Navy?'

'Well spiritually the Navy never really left Malta. You'll see Grand Harbour in a minute. This way.'

'Is it as big as Pearl Harbor, Bruce? I can't wait to see it.' McCandless glanced at his watch. It was five minutes before one o'clock.'

'Come on, step on it. Or we'll miss it!'

'Miss what?'

'You'll see. Come on, we're almost there.'

Walking through ancient iron gates they entered an area known as the Upper Barrakka Gardens. The ornamental ponds, fountains and flowerbeds were a delight to the eye, the cooling effect of the waters being another lesson learnt from the Island's Roman invaders two millennia earlier. The gardens were almost deserted. They very soon found out why. Just beyond the colonnaded arches hundreds of people, mostly visitors, were pressed against wrought iron railings and looking out towards the harbour. There was barely a gap to spare but McCandless once again steered his charge towards the mêlée. A smartly dressed Maltese gentleman in his seventies who was stood right at the front turned round and spoke:

'Are you a visitor? Is this your first time?' Alex was taken aback.'

'Yes. I'm not exactly sure why I …'

'Then change places with me. Quickly. It's almost time.'

Time for what Alex thought? She didn't have long to wait. Peering over the railings brought into her view the most awe inspiring vista she had ever seen in her life. The Grand Harbour. Suddenly some military music sounded over a public address system which reminded her of Sousa. Out of nowhere a khaki-uniformed Army officer marched smartly towards one of the eight huge canons that make up the Saluting Battery. His white pith helmet glinted in the powerful sun and was reminiscent of the Royal Marines or the Welsh Borderers at Rorke's Drift during the Zulu Wars. Snapping smartly to attention alongside gun No. 6 he attached a cord to the firing mechanism with his right hand and with his other withdrew a pocket watch which he studied without moving his head.

At precisely one o'clock he pulled the cord. Half a second later the cordite exploded and two metres of orange flame shot out of the barrel followed by a copious volume of gun smoke. Another half a second later and over a hundred pigeons that had been sunbathing on the ancient battlements took to the air towards the direction of the blue harbour waters and safety. The soldier didn't even flinch. Hopefully he was wearing ear plugs. The large crowd applauded and started to dissipate. The kindly Maltese gentleman bade goodbye to Alex.

'I hope you enjoyed it. I never tire of seeing it. Defending the Grand Harbour is what Malta is all about. Enjoy the rest of your visit and if I can help you here is my card.' With a friendly nod he was gone. It simply read :

Alfie Agius
Jewels and Souvenirs
Merchant Street
Valletta.

'Well, Alex, what did you think to that? Impressive or what?'

For the first time in her life she had been stunned into silence. The smoke and the people had cleared. Just the two of them were left. The view across to Fort Saint Angelo a half a mile away was exquisite. A full two minutes passed as she scanned from left to right to reveal ancient fortifications protecting not just Grand Harbour but four smaller harbours, called Creeks, beyond at right angles to the huge haven itself. She was almost speechless. That third Creek was called Dockyard Creek for good reason. At its mouth facing the Harbour was the biggest dry-dock in the Mediterranean. It was the notorious Red Dock. For the first time since her arrival on the Island she now fully realised the importance of the job in hand. Her job anyway. She was just about to turn away when her eyes suddenly fixed on an amazing sight, the smoke and the noise having initially distracted her. Moored in the Mediterranean style, stern to the quayside, beneath the battlements of Fort St. Angelo was a stunning three masted yacht, its furled sails glinting like silver scrolls in the laser-like sun.

'Bruce, is that what I think it is? Is that the *Maltese Falcon*?'

20

The little drinks and snacks kiosk tucked away in the corner of the gardens gave her time to reflect. McCandless didn't even ask her what she wanted to eat or drink. He just returned to their table she had chosen by the edge of the wall, not just for the view but the shading umbrella that would provide relief from the blistering heat of the Mediterranean sun. He put a tray down on the table and grinned.

'Here comes your first Cisk and your first Maltese cheesecake.'

'The Cisk is a lager right? That's cool but what is this …. this thing? You say it's a cheesecake?'

'Yes, locally known as pastizzia, a delicacy. Made with puff pastry and ricotta cheese, that's goat's cheese to you. Try it. Be careful it's hot!'

'Ouch!' She blew onto it to cool down the chunk she had cut off with the stainless steel knife provided.

'Boy, that is different. I like it. Can you get different flavours, you know, like normal cheesecakes?'

'Of course not. Ricotta is ricotta is ricotta, but you can also have a pea-cake which looks identical until you bite into into it.'

'You're kidding – like black-eyed peas? Now back in Brooklyn we …'

'How many times do I have to tell you? Forget America, you're in Malta with two Islands and five thousand years of history. Not America with fifty states and two hundred and fifty years of dubious unity.'

'You're right, Bruce. I've finished. Delicious! Where are we going now?'

'We'll walk back into the City a slightly different way. I want to show you something.'

Entering the huge square outside the Castille, previously known as the Piazza Regina in colonial days, they turned right into St. Paul's Street and then left into Melita Street. A huge but scruffy door marked the entrance to an unimposing building flying the red and yellow flag of the Peoples Republic of China. The brass plate said it was the Chinese Cultural Office. Yeah right.

'So this is China's Embassy, Bruce.'

'No. This is where they export Chinese culture. So they say anyway. The Embassy isn't even in Valletta it's in Sliema but guess what – they are lobbying hard to build a new one in an area called Pembroke, previously a British Army barracks.'

'Heck. And they're gonna allow that?'

'Well, maybe not, it's all up in the air at the moment. It is suspected that the real reason that the Chinese want a bigger Embassy is to house more staff to fight the asymmetric war they wage so well. In the 'spooks world' it's known as the 'Grey Zone' where anything goes except firing guns. The end result is the same – subliminal control and ultimate subjugation. The Chinese President and his team of 'advisers' will be working as we speak to get the most out of this Summit long term. The Red Dock is only part of the equation. They're trying to infiltrate the communications industry with trendy-named companies like Talkalot and ChitChat but they don't fool us that are in the know, so to speak. They are all State-owned companies controlled by the State i.e. the CCP. The Maltese Government are nobody's fools, believe me. Hopefully we'll be able to have a private chat when we meet Mr Borg Vella at the wine-tasting evening on board the …'

'Oh wow! Does that mean we're going too?'

'Sure. Don't forget I have a Wine Guide to compile and publish and well, let's just say you can be my PA. OK by you, Signorina Pisani?'

'You betcha. I'd better learn more about wine I guess. Especially Maltese wines. So where else are we going now? Can we see some more of Valletta just in case we don't come back again? Please, Bruce?' McCandless already knew that he planned to spend a lot more time in Valletta with this gorgeous lady but she didn't need to know just yet.

'OK can you see where we are now? We've gone almost full circle. Listen why don't you walk down to that bookshop on the right side – see the sign? Agenda Bookshop? Buy a copy of that book I told you about on the plane – the Kapillan of Malta by Nicholas Monsarrat – and while you're there buy another two of those Tallijnas as we'll soon soon use up the allotted trips.'

'He's the guy that wrote The Cruel Sea right?'

'You remembered. If you see a book called 'Letters from Malta' by Mary Rensten don't buy it. I have a copy in my case and I'll give it to you after dinner tonight. It's a lovely book written by a lovely lady. I met her once at a literary festival. In Cheltenham I think when I was stationed there.'

'Sure. Where are you going anyway?'

'I'm going to a hotel down South Street over there.' He pointed.

''Meet me on the corner by that shop called Wembley Stores in say, half an hour? OK.'

'Yes, Sir, Captain.' She mocked a salute like Popeye, smiled and headed off on her own down Republic Street.

It was only five minutes walk north down South Street past the General Workers Union Office and St. Andrews Church, one of only a handful of non-Catholic Churches on the Island. And then he came to his destination – the Osborne Hotel. He had never stayed there overnight, no need to with a comfy bunk awaiting him back on 'HMS Pinafore' back in Grand Harbour. However he had enjoyed many dinners there over the years as an alternative to Baby's Heads, Herrings In and Train Smash. Food on board in the Mess was never too good when the main cooks had been on shore leave and had a skin-full of Hop Leaf, Cisk and God knows what. Food at the Osborne was very civilised, almost genteel. Although five hundred years old the Osborne had undergone several renovations in recent years and it was a prime example of Baroque Maltese architecture. He rang the brass desk-top bell on the Reception desk. Ping! Not quite a sonar but almost. A very smart man in his early seventies appeared and walked immediately towards Bruce, hand outstretched.

'Admiral McCandless, how nice to see you again. You said at Christmas you'd be back again before the year was out.' Admiral was his moniker for Bruce who he knew was now a civilian.

'Hello Charles. Nice to see you too. But sshhhh! I wasn't supposed to be here. Now listen I know it's short notice but I need the best room you have available from this Saturday for three, maybe four nights. A double room. With a view if you have one.' Charles Caruana walked to a small computer screen and hit the keyboard a few times. Old school he might be, but he was no slouch with the modern technology.

'Sorry you're out of luck – no standard or deluxe rooms available. Oh just a second …. I see that our new Penthouse Suite on the top floor is vacant from Thursday. It's top

dollar though and on your pension you need to be careful.'
Charles's humour was his hallmark.

'How much, tell me.'

'To you Admiral, a thousand Euros a night.'

'Deal! Book us in.'

'Us? You mean you're not alone. Don't tell me there's a Mrs McCandless finally after all these years?'

'Not yet Charles. But you just never know. See you on Friday afternoon.'

'Ciao!' And he was gone. He'd spent so much time reminiscing about bygone days and nights he'd almost forgotten the time. Alex was outside Wembley Stores bang on time. She carried a red and white carrier bag with the AGENDA logo on the side.

'So there you are. I'm just looking at all the different wines in this beautifully displayed window. Look! Shall we buy some?'

'No, we'll only have to carry them. Did you get the book? And the Tallijnas?'

'I sure did. And another book called 'Echoes' by a lady called Lou Drofenik. It's split into two parts, Malta and Australia it seems. Why could that be?'

'Probably because whilst half of Ireland emigrated to America so half of Malta emigrated to Australia. But I suggest you read that 'Letters from Malta' first. You can read it in a few days and it'll tell you a lot even if it is a novel. By the way we'll be changing hotels on Friday so that we're more conveniently located for the evening on the Maltese Falcon. That's where I've just been – to the Osborne Hotel. We're booked in Friday for as many nights as we want it seems. They only have the Penthouse Suite available so I booked it.'

'Oh heck, when Winchester sees the tab he'll ...'

'He won't ever see it. Trust me, Alex, just trust me.' So she did.

21

Fort Meade
Maryland

Ralph Winchester was in a cheery mood. It was just after eight in the morning and he was in his office before most of his colleagues. That was fine by him. He could get more done in an hour without phones ringing than the rest of the day put together. All his plans were slowly coming together. He just needed to check that his 'two boats' scenario was still 'on course' and he chuckled at his own little quip.

His desk-top computer whirred up in seconds and he hit the keyboard to Google MarineTraffic.com and entered the IMO (International Maritime Organisation) No. 9384552. In less than two seconds he had the exact position of the vessel in question: 35.53N 14.3E. She was stationary. The Maltese Falcon was back in her spiritual home and Port of Registration. Valletta. One down one to go. Next he entered the IMO for the Christina O 8963818. This time the information took somewhat longer, almost a minute. Eventually it came through. Position 36.63N 13.22E Speed 18 knots. Course 120. She was on her way. Within twenty four hours at the latest she too would be in Grand Harbour for the 'annual Port of Registration inspection' that wasn't really necessary. Winchester was a happy bunny and he spun the globe like a child stopping its revolving with his index finger hoping to stop it in the middle of the Middle Sea. He was getting quite proficient. This time he was only about an inch out and his finger landed somewhere near Corsica! Oh well he was sure Napoleon wouldn't mind. He might have been born in Corsica but his defeat to the hands of Admiral Horatio Nelson in Malta had marked the beginning of the end. With a little 'bad joss' it would similarly mark the beginning of the end for the latest Chinese Emperor. But only a handful of people knew that. For the moment anyway. Publicly, diplomacy was the name of the game.

Twenty-four hours earlier his colleague and confidante, Angela Roche, had flown from New York to Rome on an Alitalia flight to Rome's Fiumicino Airport and a connecting flight to MIA – Malta International Airport. Her new US passport gave her name as Angelique de la Roche. Following the five day total immersion course in French she was good enough to converse colloquially with the other cooks and chefs. The crash course in Mandarin to allow her to address the Chinese Heads of State with more than the somewhat insulting 'Nee How' was to add to the overall appearance of conviviality and welcome. Just in case. Angela would replace the Christina O's second chef whose father had been 'taken ill', fortunately for him while the yacht was still at anchor off Nice on the Côte d'Azur. The equally stunning motorised tender, built by the Italian Aquariva Company, had taken him ashore and then a company car had taken him to Nice Airport for a flight to Paris. When he arrived at the American Hospital of Paris three hours later he found that his father had already been discharged. The suspected cardiac arrest had been a false alarm. It was too late to return to Nice and the Christina O. She had already departed for her next charter. He was mighty sore as he had wanted to visit Valletta and the City named after a fellow Frenchman.

Maybe he would just have to wait for his next annual leave and go as a tourist.

Winchester opened the 'Kam Sang Menu' for the hundredth time and mentally checked off the 'to do' list. Boat 88 was already at her berth alongside Fort Saint Angelo and barring delays Boat 99 would be anchored in Grand Harbour within a day. She was only two hundred nautical miles from her destination and her date with history. Christina O already had an amazing pedigree having been constructed as an anti-submarine escort for the Royal Canadian Navy in 1942 and christened HMCS Stormont. She was built to chase U-boats but today she wouldn't have to chase anything. All she had to do was deliver people, not depth charges.

Alexandria and Bruce were in place in Malta even if both of them didn't know the full story. All they had to do was organise the wine tasting and ensure that all the invited guests arrived.

22

It had been a long, hot day and, after an early supper in the Hotel, Alex and Bruce took a walk along the broad and scenic promenade. The moon was still almost full and beamed its reflection across the Bay towards them. The air was still but at least the temperature had dipped to a manageable twenty-two Centigrade after the thirty plus of the day. The road curved round to the left and as they approached the new Malta National Aquarium the last hints of the orange sunset were leaving its mark. They walked hand in hand and the conversation was easy despite the fact that the tasks in hand were as yet incomplete.

'Ya know Bruce, this whole place is like a floating history book.'

''Rocks don't float.'

'Yeah right but if all this stone could tell a story it would be amazing. From 3,000 BC to now huh?'

'Well actually even before that. There are neolithic structures here that pre-date the Egyptian pyramids by a millennium. Seriously. Some of them make Stonehenge look comparatively modern. One of your former Presidents took a private walk through those stones when he was on a 'State visit to Ingerland' and right in front of the cameras he was asked to say what he thought of it …'

'Yeah, I know don't remind me it was so embarrassing. He said it was 'cool' am I right?'

'Yes, it was something of a cringefest to us Brits but your new guy is coming here in just a few days time. I wonder what he's going to think of Malta?'

'Well the guys at the State Department will have been briefing him of course but how much of the Island he'll actually get to see I'm not sure. He and the First Lady will be spending at least one night at our new Embassy. I'm sure Georgette will have something in mind. Security issues will be paramount of course but with a total news blackout almost until he arrives it shouldn't be too difficult. That new Embassy looked like a Stalag with all those wires, fences and lights. And in the unlikely event of anything going wrong the handful of Marines won't be able to do much. As far as I know there are no US Navy ships to act as back-up should they be needed. Do our ships ever come here on R & R do you know?'

'They used to do in the Cold War. The Sixth Fleet normally had two carriers in the Med. Not now, not with more kit heading for the so-called Indo-Pacific theatre. China is the biggest potential threat which of course is why we're here now.'

'Copy that. Hey do you fancy a drink? Is that a bar back there in the Aquarium? I saw lights on and folks inside.'

'Sure. Campari or Kinnie?'

'Maybe both!'

'Alex, you're starting to talk like a local now, do you realise that?' She just smiled and said nothing.

It was ten o'clock by the time they had finished a Cappuccino in the hotel coffee shop. Bruce just remembered to hand her the copy of 'Letters from Malta' before they turned in for the night.

'A little bedtime reading – it's about trying to trace people and families so, you never know, it might give you a few ideas on tracing your forebears. It's a nice story.'

'Thank you I will.'

'Good night. Sleep tight.'

'You too.' A kiss would have been nice, even just a peck on the cheek she mused. Jesus why are Brits so damned reserved? She might have to take him in hand. And soon too. They only had so many days left in 'Melita, the Island of Honey' and made a note to ask him over breakfast where the name had really come from. He seemed to know everything.

After a refreshing shower she donned her customary diaphanous night-gown and slipped between the cool Egyptian cotton sheets. Time for a read. She picked up the book and started. She was mesmerised and couldn't believe she was on the Island about which she was reading. Tiredness took its toll and she reached the end of Chapter Three and as she was ready to mark the page a small slip of paper fell out of the book onto the bed clothes. Perhaps the previous reader had used it as a bookmark. It looked like a receipt, perhaps from the bookshop where it had been purchased. She looked more closely at it. It was a receipt – from a Bar not a bookshop. It read:

Elvis Lounge
Tourist Street
Qawra

1 pint Hop Leaf	Euros 3.00
1 large Malta wine	Euros 2.00
Total	Euros 5.00

You were served by Alexia

Date: 25.12.20

She re-read it several times. Unless she was very much mistaken Mr McCandless had been here the previous

Christmas despite giving the impression he hadn't been to the Island for a few years. No wonder he knew all about the new buses and Tallijnas. He sure had some explaining to do. And who the hell was Alexia? Had he bought the barmaid a wine? She was falling for this Limey and she didn't need any competition.

23

The President of the People's Republic was in almost holiday mood. Tomorrow was China's National Day, 1st October. There would be a smaller military parade than usual. He wanted to at least give a public impression of a downgrading of the hostility he inwardly felt for the West and America in particular. In a few days he would be pulling the wool over the eyes of the American President. He'd had several conversations with his junior counterpart in Pyongyang, North Korea in recent days. He and 'Rocket Man' had a lot in common, particularly when it came to electoral responsibility. Neither had any! Rocket Man's last piece of advice had stuck in his head.

'And don't Comrade, accept an offer of a ride home in his shiny new SuperJumbo they call Air Force One. After our summit in Hanoi his predecessor offered me a ride back to Pyongyang to save me three days on one of our state-owned clapped out trains. They would have thrown me out at ten thousand metres into the Yellow Sea. Be warned.' He had laughed out loud at that piece of advice. Sometimes he wished that the Americans had parachuted the Brylcreamed little prick into the sea – without a parachute. Then China would no longer have to subsidise their useless neighbour every time the rice crop failed. Why they didn't 'go capitalist' but just keep political control he could never figure out. And woe betide his dirt poor little country if ever one of his rockets landed in the Mother Country by accident. At times he had actually sympathised with American Presidents over their dilemma as to how to handle the little upstart. Oh well, to matters in hand. He called the Defense Secretary who was in personal charge of the refurbishment of the Ilyushin 76 jetliner that was taking him to Malta in forty-eight hours time. Although as Chairman he took overall responsibility for the Defense portfolio he wanted his right-hand man to be onside at all times. In the event of his own demise he had already nominated him as his chosen successor. He didn't want to see his own wife copy Madam Mao and step into his shoes when the time came. She was already far too fond of expensive shopping trips to Japan and Australia. He had reminded her many times not to leave the receipts from Junko Shimada in Tokyo and Myers of Melbourne in her Gucci handbag. If they were lost and found then the Western press would have a field day. That reminded him – he hoped Comrade Won-Gah would do his best to get him a briefcase from The Bridge. Alibaba didn't advertise them.

'Good morning Comrade, I trust this finds you well on the eve of our great National Day?'

'Indeed, Comrade Chairman. I was just about to call you actually.' He lied but he was mindful to keep up his close friendship with the Chairman – just in case. Accidents do happen.

'Is my personal Ilyushin 76 ready? And to my exact specification?'

'As requested, Comrade Chairman. A new communications suite has been added as have the personal recreation facilities – sleeping quarters and a new galley. I have monitored progress on a daily basis receiving photographs by email every few hours. The furnishings are superb with hand crafted rosewood chairs for the matching small dining table. The finest Tientsin carpets have been added and Red Dragon curtaining applied to the windows although you will understand that as it is primarily a military aircraft windows are at a premium and …'

'Comrade, I appreciate that. For future reference we must consider a purpose-built Presidential-style plane like the Americans possess. Even the British have one now. I read that it's a partially converted RAF tanker. Ha! Let's hope that their Prime Minister Doris or whatever he's called isn't a smoker. I must say the plane looked good though. I saw it on YouTube a few days ago. It looked like a flying Union Jack. Is that what the Brits call it? Who the hell was Jack anyway?'

'Comrade Chairman, that reminds me, we have copied an idea from the British Navy. You might recall that one of their destroyers had the audacity to paint a huge red dragon on its bows. It was spotted on their illegal passage through our new Island possessions in the South China Sea a few months ago. Ends up that it was also the name of the ship – HMS Dragon. Accordingly I have instructed that the final touch to the Ilyushin will be a red dragon painted on both sides of the forward fuselage. I hope you approve, Comrade Chairman?'

'Excellent, thank you. A nice touch. Is there anything else we need to discuss?'

'Yes there is. Our PLAAF team have been planning the route you will take to Malta. There is no obvious route. Extra under-wing tanks have been fitted but even then there will need to be at least one refuelling stop, possibly two, depending on wind and jet-streams. The Northern Loop is option one – flying over Mongolia, Russia, Kazakhstan and the eastern part of Ukraine. Option two is the Southern Loop via Sri Lanka and Djibouti. As you know they have already been incorporated into our String of Pearls and with Malta being our next target this route will be very symbolic.'

'Wonderful! See to it.'

'Wishing you and the First Lady a pleasant and fruitful trip comrade. We'll catch up when you get back.'

He couldn't say 'if you get back.' He didn't tell him that one of the four Russian made Soloviev turbofan engines was playing up and constantly overheating. They might have to cannibalise another plane. Another option was to prepare a second Il-76 as a back-up and use it if necessary. Yes, he would do that. Red paint wasn't normally a commodity in short supply in the People's Republic. He picked up the phone and barked orders at a quivering PLAAF senior officer at Xijing airport eight miles away from the capital in Haidian District. They didn't want to announce the President's trip until after he was out of Chinese airspace and so using Beijing's main airport was totally out of the question.

Zhang was too easily recognised and by his own admission it was something he might have to give more thought to in future. In fact quite a lot more thought.

24

She waited until he'd collected his 'fry up' from the hot buffet counter and chose her moment carefully. She looked him straight in the eye and switched on the twin blue lasers.

'Bruce, what the hell were you doing here last Christmas? Don't deny it.' She held up the receipt and stuck it under his nose, printed side towards him. He was taken aback.

'Well, I er, well it's not against the rules is it?'

'You let me think that you hadn't been here since your Navy days. Why have you deceived me? You left this receipt inside the 'Letters from Malta' book you lent me. I'm not happy.' McCandless could just make out the faintest tears forming in those icy blue eyes.

'I thought this was a team effort, just the two of us. Seems not.' The tears grew into a little stream and she reached for the napkin on her lap.

'I've fallen in love with this Island and … I've fallen for this Limey jerk who has been lying to me for the last three days and now it's all falling apart and …' The streams would have turned into rivers except that Malta didn't have any. Not in the summer anyway.

'I'm so sorry, Alexandria, I truly am. If I wasn't a confirmed bachelor I'd have chained you to an altar and looked for a sober priest as soon as I could. You are a gorgeous lady and as soon as I set eyes on you I just knew there was going to be something special between us.'

'You did? So why have you misled me?'

'I haven't, at least not deliberately. Here dry your eyes.' He passed her another paper napkin and poured himself more coffee.

'I'll recap shall I? Let's go back to basics. The Five Eyes, as we call them, have a proven track record of collaboration and success. Agreed?'

'Sure. It works. No doubt about it. The big problem is China. Since Hong Kong was handed back to communist China in 1997 we haven't had proper listening facilities to eavesdrop into the Middle Kingdom. It's a problem. Satellites can't do everything. Some folks think they can but they can't. It takes time and money to shift those Telstars in their orbits and whilst the latter is not really an issue, the former is. Much of the SIGINT we picked up in Hong Kong was channelled through your guys in Okinawa. Now that Okinawa is formally a part of Japan and not a 'US colony' we might as well deal direct with Japan itself. That is why Japan is about to become the Sixth Eye. OK so far?'

'Yeah, but why specifically are WE here. You and me?'

'Winchester's predecessor James Bellringer 'swung it' for me to become the Director of GCHQ when I left the Navy. I didn't really want the job. Cheltenham is about as far from the sea as you can get in England as well. Not exactly a sailor's Shangri-la is it? Going to the Races was the only consolation – you know the Festival, the Gold Cup and all that. When Winchester replaced Bellringer he requested a meeting with me as soon as possible. In fact it was just after your Thanksgiving and he flew over to London for a few days. In fact we both stayed at the Naval Club in Mayfair. There was only one subject of conversation over dinner on the first night. Have a guess.'

'Malta. It's China. Again. We know from our sources via NSA's partners in Melbourne, Australia that Malta is the next Pearl on the String. China will do anything to achieve this. Winchester asked me to come here last December, ostensibly on a Christmas vacation, to suss out the landscape so to speak. He knew from my Navy records that I had been here many times on ships transiting the Med en route to the Suez Canal and the Gulf. So he thought that gave me an edge. He was right. What he doesn't know is my family links go back decades before that. That's our little secret, Alex. OK?'

'Tell me more.' The blue streams had dried up and she sipped her coffee: the appetite, for food anyway, had gone. All she wanted was him. In every way.

'So the point I'm trying to get to is this. If all goes well, post Summit, the Republic of Malta will become the Seventh Eye.'

'You are kidding me. How many people know this?'

'Three. And two of them are sat at this table. More coffee?'

'So exactly how is that going to come about?'

'Malta's Prime Minister, Edward Borg Vella, will be issued an invitation to join the Five Eyes in the not too distant future. The problem is that Malta is officially non-aligned. It isn't even a member of NATO. Even Russian naval vessels have taken advantage of this with minor refits and maintenance work being done in the dockyard.'

'You're joking. And what about PLA Navy ships. Have they come here for R & R yet? One of their frigates was even sent on a goodwill trip to the Baltic last year, I know that.'

'Yes, of course we had that well monitored. It was just a PR exercise to show that no ocean in the globe was 'off limits' to them so to speak. With their new base in Djibouti we can expect to see more of their ships heading north up the Suez Canal and knocking on a few doors in the Med soon. The way they operate it's just inevitable.'

'Is Winchester telling us everything? Are we just pawns to set up the arrangements without being privy to everything? What if something happened to upset the apple-cart.'

'Like what?'

'Like if something nasty happened to the Chinese President?'

'Well a cruise on the world's most exclusive motor yacht the *Christina O* and a wine tasting on the worlds most prestigious sailing yacht isn't like rowing the Atlantic single-handed is it? The security will be tight. Air Force One will be crammed with Secret Service guys armed to the teeth. If anything went wrong the other side we would be held responsible. Nah – it'll be fine. Trust me.'

She gazed into his eyes and held them.

'Now tell me why my eyes are blue.'

'There's a little town in the south-west of the Island called Zurrieq, the other side of the airport. Two thousand years ago it was a Roman garrison town. Romans are famous for their blue eyes, like yours. And you know what occupying soldiers are like with the ladies.'

'Same as sailors I guess, like the one I'm talking to right now.' She grinned.

'Ha! Well legend has it that all the girls with blue eyes born in Zurrieq, inherited them from their ancient Roman forebears. That could be you too. And of course the name Zurrieq is derived from the Italian word for blue – azzurro! Maybe I should call you Azzuria not Alexandria?'

'So this Alexia on the receipt. Who is she?'

'Exactly as it says. She served me. She works there – her parents own it. Wanna meet her?'

'Sure, when?'

'Tonight after dinner. We'll walk round to the Elvis Lounge.'

'Walk?! Americans don't walk. What about a cab?'

'It's not far, trust me. But hey that gives me an idea. Let's get a cab and take a ride to a few places. Give me that card from Peter Debono. Let's see if he's free. We've got all day. Play the tourist OK?'

'Yes Sir, Commander.' She was putty in his hands.

An hour later and Peter pulled his Mercedes up outside the revolving doors of the Hotel. He was in a good mood and had not been called out all night long to collect incoming passengers on delayed flights.

'Bongu, good morning! This is a nice surprise. No suitcases?'

'Bongu, Peter. Nice to see you.' Without making a conscious choice Alex had used a Maltese greeting. With those blue eyes she'd be speaking Latin soon. Bruce arrived at the car a minute behind Alex. She had missed him by her side already.

'Where have you been? I take my eyes off you for one second and you're gone!'

'I just informed Reception that we're checking out tomorrow.'

'Really? So soon?'

'Yes, tomorrow we move to the capital – Il-Belt.'

'Huh? I thought you said we were gonna move to Valletta?' It was Bruce's turn to smile.

'Il-Belt is the nickname for Valletta.'

'OK so that's Hobz, Bongu, Tallinja and now Il-Belt under my belt. Ha! What's next?'

'About another five hundred words to go before you can get by. Now let me get a quick look at this map which I brought along from UK. It's old but it might tell me more than your tourist Fleximap.

'OK Peter, this is where we want to go. In this order please.'

'No problem, let's go!' He let the clutch in and spun the rear wheels. All Maltese taxi drivers fancy themselves as a Formula One driver and Peter Debono was no exception. Traffic was heavy as always and it took almost an hour to reach their first port of call – Marsaxlokk Bay. They pulled up outside the Duncan Hotel and got out.

'Peter, we're going to have coffee here. Can you come back for us in say half an hour? Is that OK?'

'No problem. I'll park up and drop in to my cousin's house just around the corner, up from the church in the square. See you later.' He zoomed off like he was trying to hold pole position at the San Marino Grand Prix.

'It was hot. Baking hot. They took seats outside and grabbed the last table with a shading umbrella. It was commercially sponsored by Cisk lager. The subliminal advertising failed in this case and the young waitress came to take their order.

'Bongu. Two coffees? No problem. Anything to eat?'

'No thank you, but is Mr Bezzina here by any chance please? Walter.'

'Sure he is. Who shall I say wants to see him?'

'Just tell him it's the Admiral. He'll know who it is.'

'Two minutes later and a corpulent gentleman in his late fifties came out of the hotel's door, shielded his eyes from the blazing sun with his right hand and scanned from left to right until he fixed on the couple underneath the Cisk umbrella. His smile was a mile wide, or perhaps a kilometre now that Malta had gone metric. He trotted over to the pale skinned couple who seemed to have been deprived of sunshine and Vitamin D for ever.

'Admiral McCandless. My God. How good to see you again.' Ignoring Bruce's outstretched hand he embraced him and gave him a massive bear hug the likes of which would have done any grizzly proud. The only difference is that the grizzly would not have reeked of garlic.

'Hey Walt, what's all this then.' He prodded his tummy which was considerably bigger than he remembered it. 'Life must be good. How many pounds, er kilos, have you put on? I thought that new young wife of yours would have kept you trim.' Wink wink.

'Well Bruce you know how it is. Yes she keeps me active, if you know what I mean. Four kids in the five years since I last saw you. It is five isn't it? You were on a frigate called the er …. *Braveheart* I think?'

'You know jolly well it was HMS *Brave* not *Braveheart!* Just because I'm English not Scottish like the name of your hotel.'

'Just kidding you. Yes unfortunately Maria is also a very good cook. Too much timpana!' This time it was he who prodded his stomach. Suddenly it dawned on him that Bruce had a companion and a real pretty one at that.

'I'm so sorry Miss er.' His hand extended.

'Pisani. Alexandria Pisani. Hi. Seems like you two guys go back a long way. Listen why don't you two talk while I get refreshed in the Ladies Room.'

'Of course. It's inside on the left just past the fish tank. They're pets by the way not tonight's dinner menu.' Alex picked up her purse and left them alone.

'Bruce, it's so good to see you. Did you ever make Admiral before you quit the Andrew?'

'No sadly not, Walt. You know me – I'm too much of an individual. But I did make Commander.'

'Then what?'

'I took up a civilian job with the British Government in Cheltenham. That came to an end recently now I'm on a special job, a one-off. I can't tell you a lot but hey, do you remember much about that Bush meets Gorbachev summit right here in the Bay over thirty years ago?'

'Of course, how could I forget? It put Marsaxlokk on the map. The weather was terrible and some of those Yankee sailors were stuck here in this hotel for several days. It was so rough that even the US Navy tenders couldn't get back to their ship. Why do you ask?'

'Walt, do you fancy playing host to a few important people next week. Like say an 'al fresco' lunch for four people? You'll be handsomely reimbursed I promise you?'

'Sure, how about timpana, chips and Cisk?'

'Anyway sshh. Alex is coming back I'll tell her later.'

'I heard that, you guys. Don't sshh me! What the heck is timpana anyway?'

25

The Mercedes taxi once again left the starting blocks at Warp Six and shot around the Bay past an open market of cream coloured gazebos to shield the goods on sale and the shoppers from the sun which being noon was almost directly overhead. Hundreds of tourists seemed to be haggling over all manner of souvenirs ranging from jars of honey to replica Malta buses of yesteryear to beautiful lace tablecloths.

'Bruce, can we stop and take a look at that lace – something to take home?' Peter the driver interrupted before Bruce even had the chance to reply.

'No. Don't buy it here. Buy it in Gozo where it comes from. The best Bizzilla comes from Gozo. If you like I'll take you next Monday but not on a weekend – too busy. Mostly with locals taking a break. Where to now, boss?' McCandless opened one end of a long cardboard tube by removing the plastic cap with a 'pop' as he did so. He slowly unrolled it like it was an ancient and historic document.

'Here, Alex, take one end as I unroll it. Careful, it's very fragile.'

'Jeez. Look at the date on this – 1924 and reproduced by the War Office in 1938.' Peter interrupted once again.

'That's even before Mussolini and Hitler started to bomb us into submission. Bastards. We lost a lot of family in 1942. Everybody did. Grand Harbour was the main target of course but a lot of bombs overshot into the Three Cities, especially Cospicua. My wife's family, the Pisanis, were almost wiped out.' There were three seconds of silence before Alex exclaimed:

'Say that again please Peter. Slowly.'

'The Pisanis were almost wiped out. My wife's maiden name is Pisani. Why?'

'Peter, Pisani is my family name. I'm trying to trace any relatives during my visit here.'

'Well the person who can tell you more about the Pisanis than anybody else on the Island sadly has just died.'

'Carmen Pisani? Mother of Raymond Pisani?'

'How do you know that? You've only been here for five minutes.' Alex dug deep into her purse and pulled out the obituary and read it out loud.'

Yes, the funeral is next week, Tuesday I believe. My wife got a call last night from the funeral director in Rabat.'

'Mr Tonna?'

'Heck you seem to know everything. How come?'

'We went to see him just on the off-chance. He was helpful and spoke on the phone to a Mr Raymond Pisani. We're hoping to meet up with him. Mr Tonna was bemused as to why he had been chosen to perform the necessary duties.'

'Well I can maybe throw some light on that. Raymond has a half-brother who lives in Rabat. He is Carmen's first born it seems. He was illegitimate and was cut off from the family. In the old days Malta was very strict about such things and when the local priest played the tune everybody had to dance to it. Not today of course. That's all I know. Sorry. Now where did you say you wanted to go next? Dingli? Nobody wants to go to Dingli.'

'Well I do, here, look at this map. I've put a red ring around where we want to be. OK?'

'A signal station? A Roman signal station? I doubt you'll see more than a few old stones, if anything at all. In any case the road will lead into a cart track just south of Dingli village.'

'It won't, trust me. Just get us there please.'

The road skirted south past the new Kalafrana Freeport container terminal. It wasn't a real Freeport of course because Malta's membership of the European Union prohibited such enterprises. Heading south then west the road curved inland past what looked suspiciously like a disused runway. McCandless leant forward towards the driver's left ear as the windows were open and wind noise quite pronounced.

'So, Peter, what is it now, the old Naval Air Station? It looks busy.'

'Yes it sure is. It's now Hal Far industrial estate with the old runway now a main road running down the middle of it. It works well. Not like the old airfield at Ta' Qali eh. Remember?'

'A bit before my time Peter. Didn't they build the new National Stadium there as well?'

'You're right. Malta beat England there ten nil. Remember?'

'In your dreams. How long will it take to drive to Dingli? Twenty minutes?'

'More than that. But let's take the road past the Blue Grotto and then your friend can see the sea.' 'Yes? Let's do that.'

It was at least forty minutes before they went through the village of Dingli and headed south towards the coast again, the land rising all the time. Their ears 'popped' at about the same time. The road visibly narrowed. Peter Debono looked even more puzzled.

'Are you sure you want to keep on this road? There's just cliffs and cart tracks beyond here.'

'Yes, just keep going until you see a few old buildings and maybe an ariel or two. Up there, look – about a hundred metres ahead. Pull up outside those old gates please.'

Bruce and Alex got out of the Mercedes leaving Peter to enjoy a cigarette and a read of that day's Times of Malta which up until now he hadn't even glanced at. These folks must be crazy. There was absolutely nothing to see, he was sure about that.

'Jeez, Bruce. Why are we here? What is this place anyway?' McCandless dug into his back pocket and pulled out a dog-eared black and white photo and compared it to the scene in front of him.

'Yes this is definitely it. But it looks like only one of those old ariels is still standing now. If we walk just over here then face towards the bigger of those two old buildings we'll be standing where the photographer was who took this shot. Come on.'

'Well, are you gonna tell me where we are exactly? And why we're here. This is just an old dump.'

'Alex, this dump as you put it was once a highly classified listening post operated by the British Admiralty and latterly by the organisation that became merged into the NSA.'

'What?! You are kidding me. When was this?'

'I think from about 1945 until the Brits left the Island.'

'Why here though. It doesn't make sense …'

'Oh yes it does. We are now about eight hundred feet above sea level, the highest point on the whole Island – the optimum place to listen in to foreign and thus potentially enemy radio traffic. By the same token that is why the

125

Romans sited their signal station here too. It's on the old Air Ministry map that I brought with me. Your mob knew what they were doing …'

'What d'ya mean my mob?'

'The Romans! You didn't think I meant the New York Mafia did you?' She dug him in the ribs.

'Ouch. I'll get you later for that.' She smiled, rather hoping that he would, too.

'Keep walking. Just as well you're not wearing heels. It shouldn't be far.'

Two hundred metres later the land suddenly started to fall away from them to reveal a vista of several hundred square kilometres of deep blue sea. Only the tiny outcrop of the island of Filfla ten kilometres distant lay between them and North Africa two hundred miles away. They stood still for a few minutes.

'So you see, Alex, in its day this place was vital to Western intelligence. It even played a crucial role during The Cuban Missile Crisis. Soviet Naval units coming from the Black Sea had to pass Malta to exit the Mediterranean. If Malta does indeed become the Seventh Eye then this place will almost certainly be rebuilt.'

'Jeez. And this is what Winchester wants to happen right?'

'If all goes well, or even badly, depending on how you read it. Some of the old boys who used to work here are still around and living in the Cheltenham area – all in their eighties now of course and one or two in their nineties. As Director of GCHQ I had access to all the files of course. I even had chats with some of them over tea and buns in their own houses. Some of them volunteered to work here almost continuously with short spells in UK. Three years was the normal tour of duty but some of the guys did five or six tours voluntarily.'

'They must have loved it here to do that, don't you think? Ya know, just fell in love with the whole place.'

'Fell in love with the people too. Lots of the guys came out here as single men and married local girls. Many retired out here too. Just collected their pension and led a simple but healthy life in the sun.'

'So the old adage of wine, women and song is true huh? Can you sing?'

'Only when I have a woman and wine.' She smiled.

'Well I can provide one of those.'

'You can eh. I might just put that to the test later. Look, let's drive back to Qawra and just relax for the rest of the day. OK?'

'Aren't you gonna take me to Nashville?'

'What?'

'The Elvis Lounge!'

'Sure, why not. And you can meet your namesake.'

'Huh?'

'Alexia, the barmaid.'

'Yeah, if she's still there.'

'This is Malta, darling, and nothing ever changes. You should have realised that by now.'

Peter stepped on the gas for the journey back to Qawra as he had a pre-booked airport pick-up at six o'clock and it would be nice to see his wife and kids for a meal before going south again to Luqa. The busy traffic did mean he had to slow down through the 'chicane' that is Mosta and Alex gazed skywards to the huge dome that she had seen from the air on the final approach to the airfield just a few days ago. Again, she was beginning to feel as if she had been there for years not days. The road out of town passed over what looked from the car windows like a green valley beneath at right angles to the road.

'What is that Peter? A river or something?'

'Not really but maybe in the winter after some rain. It's called the Wied Tal Isperanza. Wied just means 'valley' in Maltese. In the winter it flows right down to the salt pans which we will see again soon after we have passed through the village of Bur-Marrad. It is famous for a company that hires out commercial vehicles especially ones delivering frozen or chilled food. Oh yes, also a former Prime Minister was born and raised in Bur Marrad.'

'Really, wow. A little place like this? Back in the States our Presidents all seem to come from big cities like New York, Houston, LA and ...' McCandless interjected.

'There you go again, Alex. This is Malta. I hope you're taking note of the Maltese words you're learning every day? And don't forget to add timpana to your list.'

'Yeah and wied! By the way what is timpana? That guy at the Duncan Hotel said his wife's timpana is too good and he puts on weight. So what is it? I can't even begin to guess.'

'It's a kind of baked macaroni with bolognese sauce and covered in pastry. A million calories a mouthful but when it's home-made and washed down with a glass of Maltese red wine – well who cares?'

'Well your friend Walt Disney doesn't does he? Judging by his waistline anyway. What a nice guy though.'

'Hasn't it dawned on you yet Miss Pisani? Everyone in Malta is a nice guy. Unless you're a girl of course.' She didn't say anything. Her silence meant a lot. To McCandless anyway. He suddenly had an idea.

'Peter, don't bother going all the way to the Hotel. Just drop us off at Carolina's Tea Rooms please on the left as we ...'

'I know it. We'll be there in five minutes. The road is clear once we leave Bur-Marrad. See the shop on the left?

That's Azzopardi's hardware shop. It's been there since I was born, in fact probably before my grandfather was born. You can get everything from iron nails to fishing rods.' Two minutes past the salt pans and they were there.

'Thanks Peter, this'll do nicely. Now look I can pay you now for today or tomorrow after you've taken us to the Hotel in Valletta so just say.'

'Tomorrow is fine. Say eleven o'clock. And which hotel in Il-Belt did you say? The Excelsior?'

'McCandless cringed at the mere mention again of the name Excelsior. The nine letters flashed by Aldis lamp from the destroyer USS *John Paul Jones* in the South China Sea had signalled the start of a major and illicit operation against the Chinese Head of State and here he was again, several years later. Except that this time he wasn't sure what the end result was even supposed to be. Maybe it was time to get a normal job. Whatever passed for normal in his crazy life and world.

'Oh gee, Bruce. This place is so quaint. It's a proper Ingerlish tea room. I thought you were kidding me. Honestly.'

'Ha! Carolina is the owner by the way, not one of your Confederate States – just in case you were wondering. Let's take that table by the window and watch the world go by. OK?'

'Yessir Lootenant er Commander.'

'And you can drop all this naval rank stuff. It's bad enough when Walter calls me Admiral.'

'You mean Walt.'

'Pack it in you. Now let's choose – some tea, scones, cream and strawberry jam shall we?'

They left half an hour later and walked, hand in hand, the half mile along the promenade towards the Qawra

Palace Hotel. The view across Salina Bay was exquisite and the sun had lost its ferocity as it started to dip towards the west. A week past the Autumn Equinox the days would start to shorten but for many regular foreign visitors, especially Brits, this was their favourite time to visit the Island. For a Chinese gentleman and his wife it would soon be their first visit and the Maltese sunshine would be a welcome feeling as their native Northern Chinese summer was now a fading memory.

26

Neither Alex nor Bruce felt hungry enough to do justice to the evening buffet on offer. They settled for some local pumpkin soup with hobz and butter and a large glass of La Vallette merlot. Bruce alone knew that they would be tempted later with all kinds of tasty titbits when they went to the Elvis Lounge. It was only just dark but the rapidly waning moon was still leaving a small beam across the Bay.'

'So how far is this Elvis place, Bruce? Far enough to get a cab?'

'No it isn't. We turn left here up Tourist Street uphill for a quarter mile then it's on the right. Let's go! It can get very busy so I hope we can can get a table. If not I'll have to give Joanne an extra kiss and a hug to get us one.'

'What? And who the heck is Joanne? Not another one of your …'

'Alexia's mother. Satisfied?' He detected just a hint of jealousy. That wouldn't do any harm he thought. It might just sharpen her edge so to speak.

The outdoor verandah to the Elvis Lounge was packed with smokers, mostly European holidaymakers but a smattering of locals joined the throng too.

'Evening, Bruce' shouted an English chap in his mid-seventies in a broad Lancashire brogue. 'Welcome back lad. Did yer gerra loook at them new apartments I told yer abart near't National Aquarium? Them's champion. Right gradely. Weren't they love?' He poked his wife in the ribs just as she was taking the final drag from a menthol cigarette and the aroma caught Alex's Roman nose.

'Hey up, Bruce, don't tell me you've gorra wife? Introduce us then.'

Introductions over they moved inside just as the Elvis impersonator, a local Maltese whose moniker was 'Elvis Ellul' came to the fading bars of Blue Suede Shoes. Announcing a twenty minute break to refresh his dry throat back to normality some piped music came over the sound system with speakers in every corner of both public rooms within the Lounge. This prompted an exodus of customers to the front door and whether it was for a fag, some fresh air or a change of venue didn't really matter. The end result was that a couple of tables became vacant and so they made a bee line for the nearest one which had four chairs.

'Bruce shall I ask that nice Ingerlish couple to join us. They seemed so sweet?'

'Sure, why not. I met them several times over Christmas and the New Year. Did you understand them at all?'

'Well it sure wasn't easy. Where did you say they come from?'

'Lancashire.'

'Where's that?'

'Opposite Yorkshire on the left hand side going up. I'll go to the bar. Campari soda or Kinnie?'

'Kinnie please. With a gin in it and lots of ice. Isn't that how the locals drink it?' This lady was getting just a little bit too local for McCandless's liking. Furthermore when meeting Jim and Lynne Bolton minutes earlier she had just grinned when they assumed she was Bruce's wife. To a lifelong bachelor it was most unnerving.

The Boltons joined them at the table just as a member of staff started to come round with platefuls of snacks – mini pizzas and hot roast potatoes. Maltese potatoes of course. McCandless had once enquired as to the name of the variety of potato expecting something similar to the famous Jersey Royals. Instead the young waitress had simply said 'Tina Turner – the best!' Suddenly that very same waitress screamed out:

'Bruuuuce. You are back. Where have you been? She swiftly put the plates on the table and threw her arms around him, kissing him on both cheeks, Continental style.

'Have you seen my mother yet? She's serving in the other lounge. I'll tell her you're here! And who is this gorgeous lady?' She couldn't miss the gold chain and Malta Cross in Alex's cleavage.

'Oh my God. You finally got a Maltese wife! I told you to pick a nice Maltese girl and …'

'Alexia, this is my friend and colleague Alexandria. And no, we're not married.'

'Well it's high time you were. Now come on try these potatoes. Here you are, Alexandria. What do you think?' She bit into the small roastie on the end of the cocktail stick.

'Wow! Boy! They sure don't grow 'em like that in Idaho.'

'Idaho? Is that near Ohio? I know of the Ohio.'

'You do? Because of Olivia Newton-John singing By the banks of the Ohio?'

'No, that was way before my time. My mother would know – and here she is!' Joanne copied her daughter's actions – a bear hug and two kisses.

'Bruce, where have you been since Christmas? No emails, no postcards – nothing. Bad boy!'

McCandless looked a bit sheepish.

'Well I've been a bit busy, you know, with work and all and …'

'Do you still plan to retire here? And did you look at those new apartments overlooking Salina Bay that I told you about? Pisani Construction have almost finished them.' Alex's ears pricked up.

'Did you say Pisani? That's my family name. While I'm here I'm trying to trace any relatives. My grandpa left Malta for the US in 1946.'

'Oh really. Well good luck with that one. It's a very common name. Why don't you try online at maltagenealogy. com? Alexia can try for you in her break. She's good on computers.' Elvis Ellul had finished his break and the opening bars of Jailhouse Rock started to blast over the speakers. Normal conversation became difficult and Lynne Bolton was dying for another fag so she gestured to Alex to join her outside. In less than two minutes they were both in menthol heaven. Jim slurped his Hop Leaf. Not a bad substitute for Boddingtons he thought.

'Sorry if I dropped you in it like, Bruce. Bah, she is a crackin' wench though. And what a lovely pair of … eyes she's got too.' They both laughed.

'Yes she is a fab lady and if she wasn't wedded to Uncle Sam well, I might be tempted you know. Anyway, another beer, old chap? Anyway, mum's the word. Look out the girls are coming back.'

'Bruce, how come Alexia knew about Ohio do you think? Seemed odd to me, that's all.'

'Did you notice she said Ohio. Initially she meant the State of Ohio but then changed to *the* Ohio.'

'Yeah, how come?'

'To Maltese people, even youngsters, the SS Ohio is the most famous ship of all. It is to Malta what the USS Constitution is to America and what HMS Victory is to England. It's the ship that saved Malta in its darkest hour.

'An American ship saved Malta? How come?'

'In 1942 Malta was on its knees. It was running out of food, munitions and above all fuel – kerosene for the Spitfires that provided the air defence. They were bringing oil and kerosene here in drums aboard those mine-layers. Because of their high speed they could avoid German U-boats and even Italian E-boats. You told me your grandpa hitched a ride on the Welshman, right? The Manxman was another one. The problem was they could only transport pitifully small quantities. A big tanker full of fuel oils had to break through from Gibraltar. The first attempt with the SS Kentucky failed. It was sunk. The second attempt by the Ohio succeeded. It was hit badly and its crew abandoned it twice, then re-boarded. Eventually it sailed into Grand Harbour lashed to two destroyers, one on each beam. It was towed into French Creek and with its back broken, it sank, but not before the precious cargo was pumped out. In a nutshell Malta was saved. The Ohio's Captain, one Dudley Mason, also received the George Cross. The GC.'

'Wow. How come we don't hear much about it today? If this was the States there'd be an Ohio Restaurant, an Ohio Bar and even an Ohio Hotel with pictures on the wall, model Ohio ships in glass cases and the whole lot would make an absolute fortune. Every citizen of Cleveland, Columbus and Cincinnati would want to come here on vacation and …'

'Only an American could think like that. But do you know what? You might just have a point there. You might just have a point.'

With a Vera Lynn style 'we'll meet again' goodnight and farewell the two couples left the Elvis Bar shortly after eleven. The Boltons retired to their small apartment down the hill towards the Dolmen Hotel and Bruce and Alex walked slowly back to the Qawra Palace.

'Do you fancy a night-cap from the mini-bar in my room, Alex?'

'No. I fancy one in my room. I slipped a bottle of Victoria Falls Chardonnay into the ice box this morning. It's from Go-Zo!'

You mean Gozo. How many times do I have to tell you …?'

From that night onwards Commander Bruce McCandless RN (Retired) never slept alone on the Island of Malta again. Not ever.

Four thousand miles to the west, at almost the same latitude, Ralph Winchester was coming to the end of his own day. Everything was going to plan. So far so good. The Christina O was less than a day's sailing from Malta and would soon be anchored safely in Grand Harbour, Valletta, under the battlements of Fort Ricasoli in Rinella Creek. 'Angelique' would be aboard as a bona-fide member of the crew. In less than forty-eight hours the President would board the brand new Air Force One for the eight hour non-stop flight to Malta. At roughly the same time the Chinese President would be leaving Beijing but information received from an independent source told him that given the age and condition of the elderly Ilyushin 76 the Chinese arrival time at MIA was, to say the least, not easy to predict.

Winchester re-read the Kam Sang Menu to mentally tick-off the tasks in hand. Then he picked up Alexandria Pisani's staff file, the one that only he and his Deputy ever see.

Marital status: Unmarried. Spinster.

Family: No dependants. No living relatives in the US or worldwide. Orphan-triple checked.

Prospects: Internal Agency future: Limited. Suitable for permanent deployment overseas.

Retention: Expendable.

27

For the second day running Peter Debono pulled his Mercedes up outside the Qawra Palace Hotel. Bruce and Alex were ready with cases packed in the smart lobby just by the glass door leading to the coffee shop.

'All aboard! My friends, it's not a great time of day to drive into Valletta. Traffic will be heavy. What about I drive you past Bugibba and into Saint Paul's Bay. We could stop at Gillieru. Yes?'

McCandless had been there once before on a previous visit, in fact more than once. It was a seafood restaurant that had expanded into a small hotel and was right on the water's edge.

'Yeah that's a good idea, Peter. No point in adding to the traffic on the Coast Road, at least not yet. It will be somewhere new for Alex to see and taste.'

'What was that? I only half-heard you.'

'We were talking about you, not to you.'

'Huh? Where's that place anyway? Gilly what?'

'Gillieru. It's a nice place in a nice location about a road mile away but we could walk.' He winked at Peter who suppressed a grin.

'No way. Let's go.'

They headed north past the Aquarium which looked different in the sunlight. The view across the Bay to two small islands was crystal clear and Bruce decided to play the tourist guide.

'See that slightly bigger island nearer to the mainland?'

'You call Malta mainland, Limey? The States is mainland. Period.' McCandless realised just how much more of an education in language this girl needed.

'You know what I mean. That island with the prominent statue on it commemorates Saint Paul. *The* Saint Paul. OK? The Roman ship on which he was travelling hit the rocks there. He was on his way to Rome to be tried for treason. The church right outside Gillieru was built to give thanks for his survival and is usually referred to simply as the Shipwreck Chapel. You'll see it soon. So legend has it that, but for the storm and the shipwreck, Christianity would not have arrived in Malta. That's why this church is so special. Hey, we're almost there.' The car lurched to the right off the main thoroughfare through the Bay area and downhill. The very attractive Gillieru surrounded by palms was immediately in view.'

'Like it?'

'It's beautiful, Bruce. And is that the church there? Up those steps?' Peter intervened.

'That's it. That's where it all began. But for the shipwreck Malta might be a Moslem State.' He crossed himself. Alex followed suit.

'Peter why don't you park the car and join us on the verandah facing the sea. I'll order some coffee for us all. OK?

'Thank you I'd like that.'

Bruce and Alex walked hand in hand up several steps and into the air conditioned lobby which was a welcome oasis from the thirty-two Celsius outside. A smart Maltese gentleman wearing a white shirt and the Gillieru house tie depicting a lobster was behind the desk checking-in a young couple newly arrived from England judging by the milky-white legs.

'On behalf of the management I wish you a pleasant stay. Here are your room keys with a voucher for a bottle of Maltese wine with your first dinner with us tonight. Enjoy your stay.' Suddenly he saw Bruce and Alex walking towards the outside terrace and bellowed out.

'Admiral Bruce! Hey, long time no see!' He dashed round to the front of the desk and within a few seconds McCandless was subjected to the second garlic bear hug in twenty-four hours.

'You said you were coming back at Easter. What happened?'

'Work and Covid. That's what happened Paul.'

'And of course this beautiful lady is now your wife! No wonder you didn't have time to come here. You were too busy ...'

'Alex this is an old buddy of mine Paul Cremona. Paul may I introduce my girlfriend Signorina Alexandria Pisani and ...'

'How many times did I tell you to choose a nice Maltese girl? They are the best.'

'Actually, Paul, I'm an American from Brooklyn, New York but I have Maltese ancestry and I'm keen to trace ...'

'We'll help you. My brother married into the Pisani Construction Company. By the way did you check out those new retirement apartments I told you about? You know, those across the Bay at Xemxija. They are stunning and they start at only a half a million Euros and ...' McCandless cut him short. Jesus, Alex must be under the impression that he was going to buy half of Malta by now. And his quiet retirement plans seemed to be almost public knowledge.

'Listen, Paul. We'll be here a few more days yet after a special assignment I'm on is completed. How about we come back and do dinner one night next week?'

'Sounds good. The lobster is still our speciality you know that.'

'Mine too!' shouted Alex. 'How did you know? Fresh I hope.'

'But of course. Tell her about the underground pool Bruce. Hey, sorry I gotta go. More arrivals from the airport. It's been non-stop since the pandemic ended. Thanks be to God.' Another crossing.

'So Bruce, that's yet another person who thinks you're about to retire here and buy an apartment from their friend's or family's company. Just how many do you wanna buy? I'm only joking honey. Hey where's this verandah with the sea view and the coffee? Look, here comes Peter.'

They took a table, with an umbrella, with a view right across to Saint Paul's Island. A red and white pleasure boat was in the distance making its way around the promontory north towards Comino and Gozo.

'Bruce, can we take one of those trips before we leave? You know after the 'state visit' so to speak?'

'Sure we can. We can take in Comino, the Blue Lagoon and Gozo on the same day.' Suddenly he had an idea but he kept it to himself. For the time being anyway. But the more he thought about it the more he thought it was a very good idea indeed. Could it work? It just might. Further to the left about a mile distant rose a long hill where all those new apartments were being built. Two tall cranes still swung their loads skywards counter-balanced by huge concrete blocks to further deplete the Maltese countryside of virgin rock in a vain attempt to emulate the desert Emirate of

Dubai. McCandless sincerely hoped this wasn't going to happen and if he was going to move here permanently then a modest stone-built town-house near the water's edge would be his first choice. Life in a steel and concrete tower held no appeal whatsoever. It might suit the wealthy overseas residents who had bought their Maltese passports with money and property but not him.

Coffees over, Peter looked at his watch.

'I don't want to hurry you guys but now is the best time to drive to Il-Belt. I have an airport pick-up to do from Luqa. Some French lady on Alitalia. She needs taking to an Air BnB in Rinella. It came in by email. Says she'll pay in cash one hundred Euros. Easy money.'

The hour's drive to Valletta was a delight to Alex. Each twist and turn of the road seemed to bring forth yet another Watchtower, another seascape and another vista of blue skies and honey coloured stone buildings. She spoke barely a word all the way. This place was a different world in a different time. Just the thought of leaving it when the time came to go home made her eyes water. Where was home anyway? Certainly not in Maryland with her Government job. True, it's where she got paid but it wasn't home. No little house. No white picket fence. No kids. Did he feel the same way about Cheltenham? He already told her he didn't like it. Suddenly a fierce braking of the car jolted her out of her daydream. Peter was mad.

'Bloody karozzins! They stray all over the bloody road. Only just missed that one. I'll get him next time.' Ever the joker.

'Peter, what's a karozzin?'

'A horse drawn taxi, like they have in Mdina.'

'That's another word for my phrasebook. I wanna go back there too.'

'Yeah and Gozo and Comino and …'

'Maybe we'd better stay a bit longer than planned huh?'

'Alex, Baby. There are no plans.'

She smiled sweetly and kissed him softly.

28

Charles Caruana just happened to be the Duty Manager when they checked into the Osborne Hotel. The five hundred year old building had just completed a very tasteful renovation but it still looked and felt as if La Valette himself would walk through the door any second wielding a Templar's sword hewn from the finest Toledo steel. Alex was impressed.

'Jeez. This place feels like a palace yet it's a hotel. The Qawra Palace is a hotel but calls itself a palace. Crazy huh?'

'Well I guess that's marketing for you. I knew you'd like it here. Come on let's go unpack.'

The view from the sixth floor Penthouse Suite was very romantic with an endless vista of stone buildings with flat roofs. Just a smidgeon of blue Mediterranean was visible past a tall church dome that looked like a scaled down version of that in Mosta.

'Is that the famous Saint Johns Co-Cathedral where La Valette himself is buried, you know the guy whose statue you showed me in the big square?'

'No it's Saint Paul's Cathedral. You've seen it before, well a picture of it at least.'

'Are you sure? I don't think so.'

'Ah, then you haven't started reading that book I gave you, Letters from Malta by Mary Rensten. It's on the front cover. There it is – look! You've just unpacked it. There, on the bed.'

'And speaking of beds Commander McCandless you knew there was only one king sized bed in this room when you booked it. Didn't you?'

'Actually we didn't have any choice. The Penthouse is the only room available. Ask Charles, he'll verify that. He said I probably couldn't afford it. Of course he won't ever know that Uncle Sam is paying for it.'

'Well let's hope Uncle Sam never finds out. By the way did the receptionist give you a welcome pack too?'

'No, why? What is that you're holding? Can I see?' She passed him what looked at first like a pre-printed invitation card with the name of the invited left blank. It had been inscribed in fine ink copperplate style Commander and Mrs McCandless. Bruce was mildly amused. This was Charles' attempt at humour. He would chide him later – then buy him a beer. But it was the written and detailed words that created the most interest.

Dear Guest

We bid you a warm welcome to our Islands.
If you are a connoisseur of wines you will be surprised at the range available.
From crisp fruity whites to bold full-bodied Syrahs Malta produces them all.
Please present this token to your wine waiter tonight and a full bottle of the Maltese wine of your choice will be brought to your table.
With the compliments of the Malta Guild of Sommeliers.

Martin Mifsud Hon. Sec.

martin@invinoveritas.com.mt

'Alex, we need to talk to this guy He can do all our spadework for us with regard to the wine tasting reception on the Maltese Falcon. End of problem. Get onto your iPad and send him an email please and tell him we'd like to do his industry a huge favour.'

'Well why don't you just ask Charles downstairs if he knows this Mifsud guy? You just never know.'

'Copy that.' Now he was beginning to speak like an American. He would have to be careful or soon he'd be calling them levels instead of floors.

'Gimmee ten minutes and I'll go back to the lobby and see if Charles can help.' He took the invitation with him in case he had to refer to it.

The lift, which it seems he now had to call an elevator, was seemingly stuck on the ground floor or even the first level, so he decided it might be quicker to walk. Just as well he was on his own as Alex would be waiting till Christmas rather then walk down all those stairs. Finally he emerged into the lobby to see at least a dozen Oriental visitors in what seemed like man and wife couples. They were arguing amongst themselves about which suitcases belonged to who. All the cases seemed to be identical with the same MIA baggage label wrapped around the handles. Similarly they all sported the same airline ID label in the shape of the white 'brushwing' symbol. It was Cathay Pacific's trendy new logo that had replaced the old colonial green and white 'cucumber sandwich' years earlier. The New Order in Hong Kong couldn't possibly have allowed anything as colonial as an English cucumber sandwich to represent what was now effectively an arm of the new and powerful China. A suitcase had been jammed into the doorway of all three lifts to stop them operating whilst the collective throng of Oriental humanity sorted it out. A male member of staff arrived and placed the cases back into the main lobby following complaints by other guests. They cursed him in turn in a language that only they understood.

'Ah, there you are Charles. Have you got a minute?'

'Sure, for you Commander, anything. Don't tell me the future Mrs McCandless doesn't like the drapes?'

'You mean the bloody curtains. Ha! No, Charles it's about this Martin Mifsud chap on this invitation. Do you know him?'

'Yes but I've not known him long. Maybe a year or so. We had a guest from England, Yorkshire I believe, who wanted to visit as many Maltese vineyards as possible in his five day stay here. So to be helpful I called one of the local wine growers called Marsovin. Apparently Mr Mifsud took him all round the Island, even over to Gozo, to taste what was on offer. A Mr Hunter I think his name was. Yes, Howard Hunter. A nice old boy, well into his eighties but boy did he love his wine. To say thank you on his last night here he invited Mr Mifsud and his wife to dinner here in the hotel. Yes now you've jolted my memory it was Mr Hunter who persuaded Martin Mifsud to set up the Malta Guild of Sommeliers. They've never looked back. They organise supper tastings all over Malta at various venues. They launched the Guild here at the Osborne.'

'Charles, do me a huge favour will you please? Can you get hold of Martin Mifsud urgently and invite him here tonight? For dinner as my guest.'

'Well it's not exactly a lot of notice is it! However I do have his personal cellphone number and I know he lives in Floriana only fifteen minutes walk away, so you never know. I'll try. Give me your own cellphone number if you're going out. Who shall I tell him the invitation is from? Can I give him your name?'

'Yeah, tell him it's Bruce Burgundy for a laugh.'

Charles Carvana just shook his head. Sometimes he longed for the olden days when half the British Fleet was in town and all the bars and cafés were full of Jack Tars on the razz.

Walking out into the late afternoon sunshine Bruce and Alex did indeed walk 'south' up the gently inclining South Street to the junction of Republic Street and Wembley Stores on the corner. They paused once again to admire the display of wines on offer which reminded them to take advantage of the voucher from the Malta Guild of Sommeliers that evening. She decided already that she wanted a white wine, he a red. Maybe they would have to settle for a rosé.

'Bruce, what the heck is that up there on that wall? Is it a real airplane or a model?'

'Well to be honest I didn't notice it last time I was here but without even getting close I can tell you what it is. It's a Gloster Gladiator. Looks like a half-size scale model from here. Let's take a closer look.' Alex started to reach for her cellphone to take a shot of it.

'Jeez. It looks like sump'n the Wright Brothers first flew at Kitty Hawk, North Carolina in 1903. I always wanted to see the ...'

'Honey, like I said it's a Gloster Gladiator. It's nothing to do with the City of Gloucester. Gloster is the name of the company that designed and built them. Got it?'

'Well no, not really. So why is it here? And why the heck is this half-demolished building here on the right such an eyesore? It looks like the Acropolis in Greece except it got hit by an earthquake.'

McCandless shook his head. This girl had a lot to learn. Maybe it was incumbent upon him to educate her.

'That, Alex, is Malta's famous Opera House which in its day was one of the finest auditoriums in Europe. In 1942 it took direct hits from Axis bombers. Over the decades there have been many plans to rebuild or redevelop it. Thanks to that architect guy Renzo Piano some changes were made but it still remains a ruin. It's a visible and poignant reminder that Malta suffered terribly in the War but it survived. Most folks like it this way. I admire that.'

'And the airplane? You didn't explain.'

'That's another story altogether, Alex. Malta was so short of defensive fighters that four of those planes that had been stored in crates were rapidly assembled and thrown into the fight although I think only three were actually airworthy. They were Christened Faith, Hope and Charity and gave a good account of themselves and despite being very slow they could 'turn on a dime' and could take a lot of punishment.' He deliberately said 'dime' and not 'sixpence.' One step at a time.

'One of the fuselages is maintained at the War museum here in Valletta. I don't think anyone ever knew which of the three it was. It didn't matter. The George Cross, the GC I told you about, is also displayed there unless they've moved it again.'

'Bruce, will you take me there, please?' She squeezed his hand very tightly.

'Of course I will, of course I will. Let's walk up to the Barrakka Gardens again shall we? This way.'

As they passed the Head Office of the Bank of Valletta they couldn't help but notice some of the Oriental visitors they had seen at the hotel. They were still arguing in a language that McCandless didn't recognise at all. It wasn't Cantonese as he would have picked up the odd phrase here and there from his stints in Hong Kong. Likewise it wasn't Japanese which he would have recognised from his exchange posting at Yokosuka with the US Navy's Seventh Fleet.

They had just entered the Gardens past the lovely ornamental pools and fountains when McCandless's cellphone rang in his pocket.

'Good afternoon. Mr Bruce Burgundy? Charles Caruana asked me to call you.'

'Ah, and you must be Mr Martin Muscadet?' They both laughed. The ice was broken. Not that an ice-breaker was going to be needed in the heat of Malta's summer. They talked for two minutes and arranged to meet for a pre-dinner drink in the Osborne Hotel bar at eight o'clock.

Once again they leant over the railings at the sight of Fort Saint Angelo and the Maltese Falcon still berthed beneath the southern side of the battlements.

'So now you know. This is where the Ohio limped in strapped to two destroyers one on each beam.' he pointed about a mile to the right to French Creek.

'And that is where she settled as the vital fuel was pumped out of her.'

'So this is also where Grandpa's carrier, the Illustrious, limped in too? All shot up with wounded crew aboard?'

'Yes and deceased crew too. But as a top target for the Axis bombers she couldn't be risked lying at anchor too long. The comparative safety of Alexandria beckoned a thousand miles to the east. And here I am talking with a lady of the same name for the reasons you have already told me.'

For a full five minutes, and oblivious of the rest of the human race, Alexandria Mari Pisani stared into the deep blue waters of Grand Harbour and wept buckets. She decided that she never, ever wanted to leave this place. Not ever.

29

They both dressed 'smart cazz' as the current jargon called it these days and just before eight sat in the corner of the bar. Martin Mifsud was smartly attired and showed not the slightest hint of perspiration despite his fifteen minute walk from home. Mutual recognition was swift, there being only a handful of people in the bar. Most residents had already moved into the dining room for dinner.

'You must be Martin. Hello, good evening. Bruce McCandless. I'm guessing that Charles' humour amused you? I do like a glass of Burgundy though I have to admit!'

'Me too. And this beautiful lady I'm thinking must be your …'

'And may I introduce my friend and colleague Miss Alexandria Pisani.' Mifsud shook hands with them both. Bruce took the initiative.

'Let me get us some drinks from the bar. Now I'm guessing you'd like a nice glass of Maltese red wine but you're the expert around here so, please, name your poison.'

'Thank you. You are half right my friend but a Maltese beer, a Cisk, would be nice. As regards the wine I have taken the liberty of bringing a special bottle with me which I have already left with a member of staff in the dining room. He will by now have opened it to allow it to breathe for a while before we eat.' It was Alex's turn to speak.

'Wow. That's what I call planning, Mr Mifsud.'

'It's Martin, please. We don't stand on ceremony too much here despite being occupied by the Brits for two centuries.' He grinned. In fact they all did. McCandless ordered a Hop Leaf for himself and a Campari soda for Alex. The bartender brought the drinks to the highly polished Italianate table and they all raised their glasses. Mifsud assumed the role of 'Toastmaster' and clinked his glass against the other two.

'Your very good health and I wish you a pleasant stay in our Islands.'

'Cheers, it's nice to be here.' Bruce and Alex spoke almost in unison with identical words.

'Are you sure you two aren't married? Only kidding you! Now, how can I help you exactly? A wine tasting I understand. When and where do you want to hold it? Come on – spill the beans.'

Like almost all Maltese, Martin was bi-lingual and loved to slip in colloquial English phrases sometimes into the middle of sentences that were otherwise spoken in Maltese. It was something that Alex had picked up on almost since arriving on the Island. Peter the cab driver had lapsed into such a phrase even when on the cellphone to his wife to complain about the slow traffic. A string of Maltese epithets had ended with 'bloody traffic cops' as if he was a London cabbie en route to Kings Cross.

'Well Martin, it has fallen to Alex and myself to organise a very special wine tasting and some of the information I'm about to impart to you is highly confidential. At least for the moment. Do we have your word?'

'You do. Now please tell me more.' McCandless assumed command like he had done for the last twenty years except that this time he was not on the bridge of a Frigate or at the con of a nuclear submarine.

'Firstly I can tell you that the tasting and supper party will be held on board the sailing vessel the Maltese Falcon currently berthed alongside Fort Saint Angelo and ...' Mifsud gave out a long low whistle.

'What?! How the heck did you swing that one? I've been trying for months to organise a round the Islands cruise for the Guild. Apart from being booked up many months in advance the price they quoted was simply prohibitive. A hundred thousand Euros a day from memory. Your company must have money to burn.'

'Well Martin it's booked and paid for. And yes the company is not short of a bob or two shall I put it that way.' He guessed correctly that Martin would remember when Malta had its own pound and the shillings and pence followed like sheep.

'Ah – like in the good old days eh!' Yet another little English phrase had slipped into the Maltese Lexicon.

'So do we have a date and a time? How many guests and who are they?'

'Martin, let's just say they are important people to our company. There will be about a dozen but how many representatives of Malta's wine industry do you think you can muster? We're planning on next Friday evening, assuming the guests arrive on time. They're flying in from various locations and directions so we have to build in allowances for delays. That's why we have exclusive use of the Maltese Falcon for two or three days if necessary.'

'Wow. So it's costing you a bundle just for the charter alone. I must buy some shares in this company of yours. Is it quoted?'

'Er no it isn't. Let's say it's a private limited company but you'll find out its identity sure enough. Probably on the night.'

Alex already knew from secret emails from Ralph Winchester that the whole evening was going to be streamed live on the internet via a website and Facebook. She would have to be careful. Now they were sharing a room, let alone a bed, it would be tricky to keep any secrets from him. He only had to borrow her iPad for a minute and even more beans would be spilled. She might have to come clean fairly soon. After all they were on the same side. Weren't they?

'Well I know I can persuade at least six wine companies to come along and give a short talk about their wines, including a couple from Gozo. Some of the best wines come from there I can tell you. I take it you have been there?' Alex pulled a face.

'No. It's a sore point, Martin. Mister McCandless here hasn't taken me there. Yet! I can't wait to see Go-Zo.'

'Go-Zo as you call it, Alex, is about half the size of Malta but is only sparsely populated. It is very much greener than Malta especially in the winter after some rainfall. And the wines … oh the wines are just delightful. Some Gozitans claim they are a guaranteed cure for longevity. In fact one of the vineyards is even called Ambrosia. The nectar of the Gods.' McCandless looked at the ship's brass clock above the main bar counter.

'Hey, come on. Let's go and eat. I could eat a horse!' Mifsud knew that horse-meat wasn't on the British menu and wondered how that could have entered the English language. Now if he'd said he could eat a rabbit he would have understood.

The table for three was immediately beneath yet another portrait of Jean Parisot la Valette, this time clad in the full Templar regalia – a red Malta Cross on a brilliant white tunic, a huge Templar sword at the ease position and a small shield defending both his heart and his faith. He was to Malta what

Ataturk was to modern day Turkey. Not that Turks were afforded any elevated status in Catholic Malta. Not after the Great Siege. No way. They looked at the menu which was changed daily. The hotel's chefs were a source of pride and reputation and produced an eclectic mix of Italian, English and Maltese cuisine. Only in Malta could you be offered a choice of Minestrone, Welsh rarebit and Antipasti for entrées, cold cuts with new potatoes, fenek casserole with tagliatelle, baked lampooki with Mediterranean vegetables for main courses followed by fresh figs or spotted dick for desserts. To an outsider the choices would be unfathomable. To a native 'Malteser' it was quite normal. Martin made up his mind swiftly.

'I'm going for the minestrone followed by the fenek. The wine I have brought will accompany it superbly. May I recommend that you try it, Alex. Especially if you haven't had it before in Malta.'

'Sure, I'll go for it. But what is it?'

'Rabbit, cooked in a red wine sauce. Like beef bourguignon except it's rabbit not beef. It's delicious.'

'Er, er OK yeah I'll go for that. You too Bruce?'

'No. I think I'll go for the soup too but followed by the cold cuts. Bearing in mind your Welsh middle name perhaps you should go for the Welsh rarebit. Ha – rarebit followed by rabbit I like it!'

'Bruce, what are cold cuts? Cold cuts of what? It sounds very odd.'

'It means nice slices of cold meat, usually left over from say lunch or the previous night's dinner. It might be beef, pork, lamb ....'

'Sounds gross! Why don't they be honest and just say leftovers?' They all laughed and bang on cue the wine waiter arrived with three glasses with a heavy looking bottle of wine on a silver tray. The cork lay alongside the bottle in the time-honoured way. The waiter poured a tasting volume into one glass and proffered the tray to Alex who immediately looked perplexed. Martin intervened.

'Go ahead, taste it but sample the bouquet first. That's it, swirl the glass around and let the wine climb the glass. See how slowly it runs down the sides? We call that 'having legs' which means a high alcohol content.' Alex did as she was told then held the glass to her Roman nose and inhaled. Then she took her first sip. Then a second.

'Mmmmm. Boy. That is something else. Thank you.' The waiter then proceeded to pour normal measures into all three glasses and put the bottle back on the tray.

'Sir, would you like to keep the bottle and the box when you have finished?'

'Yes please and could you pass me the box please?'

'Certainly Sir.' He retrieved a maroon coloured box from a side table that looked as if it alone was worth more than the cost of a bottle of vin de table in most hotels and restaurants. Embossed with gold leaf on the lid it simply read: St. Jean SYRAH 2016 and underneath was the ubiquitous Cross of Malta, also in gold leaf.

'Impressive isn't it? Now look closely at the label on the bottle.' Martin handed it to Alex. She had never seen a label like it. It wasn't made of paper but of pewter and had been welded to the glass when still molten,

'This is one of our most impressive wines. The vineyard only produces between one and two thousand bottles a year, depending on the yield and harvest of course. They are all numbered and accounted for. Pass me the box please. There should be a little label inside. Oh yes here it is – number 887 of 1680. 2016 was an excellent year and I reserved twenty bottles for myself. The job has to have some perks!'

'Martin, do you still have bottle number 888 by any chance?'

'Yes, my bottles are numbered from 880 to 900 and I'm drinking them in order. Why?'

'Martin, if you want to impress one of the guests on the Maltese Falcon in a unique way would you be so kind as to save bottle number 888 for that evening?'

'I'll be pleased to. Now, where were we?'

Walking home to Floriana with a belly full of rabbit and red wine, Martin wondered why the bottle numbered 888 was significant. Oh well never mind. Tomorrow he would make some phone calls to ensure that all went smoothly on the night. He wondered just who these visitors were. 'Flying in from various locations' gave an indication of wealth, corporate jets and chauffeured limousines. Maybe it was a big company in the food and beverage business he wondered. Remy Martin or Cadbury Schweppes maybe? Either way he wanted to make a good impression for Malta's wine industry. Little could he have realised that within a few days the biggest corporate jet in the world would be landing in Malta for the first time.

30

The socialising and arrangements complete, they retired to bed, but not before Alex had checked her emails. Only one of them was important and she read it to herself several times.

> *99 is on schedule to arrive Grand Harbour Valletta 15:00 hours your time tomorrow. Our asset will be aboard by 18:00 hours and will be available for duty as required. Friday night is good for the tasting on-board 88. I confirm Matilda and wife will be attending as will US Chargé d'Affaires Georgette Fox. White House spokesperson will speak at a special news conference minutes before the Boss departs Andrews on AFO. ETA Malta 08:00 and will transfer to 99 without delay. Arrangements made. Panda will depart Beijing at same time. Share this with McCandless. I hope you're having fun. Now delete. RW*

At least now she could confide in Bruce with a clear conscience. She passed him her iPad and waited. She didn't have to wait long.

'Who the heck are Mr and Mrs Matilda? And why didn't I know? Fox's attendance is fine but …'

'That's the Australian Consul here in Malta and his wife. Winchester's idea. Relations between China and Australia are real bad too, and I guess the idea is to pave the way for better times ahead following the summit. Who is the current Consul anyway, do you know?'

'No idea. Sir Leslie Patterson probably.'

'Sir Who?'

'I'm joking! Sir Leslie Patterson was the fictional Australian Cultural Attaché to the Court of St. James in London. Just a figure of fun.'

'Don't you guys have enough Lords and Sirs already? Jeez. We'd better tell Martin Mifsud about the extra numbers in the morning. Now, remind me why I've fallen for a retired Commander and a semi-retired Civil Servant.' So he did.

Such had been their passion that the curtains remained un-drawn, with the result that the early morning sunrise awoke them both shortly after seven. Alex rose and made them coffee with the facilities provided. As the kettle purred to its climax it reminded her of her own just a few hours earlier. She was so, so happy. Out of habit she clicked on her iPad once again. Another email from Winchester stared her in the face before it registered.

The summit meetings onboard 99 will commence the day after the evening's entertainment. Our asset will be acting as a wine pourer. Angelique will make herself known to you as will Australia's Consul, Shane Warner. He will be presenting an Australian wine as part of the evening, as will Georgette Fox. The State Department will deal with the niceties of the Summit meetings. Not my problem. As you know, the words Winchester and Diplomacy don't normally go together. Nite nite. RW.

She shook Bruce from his slumber, passed him a cup of coffee, then waited until he was fully awake.

'Bruce, read this second email from Winchester.'

'Is this just a belt and braces job? As Martin Mifsud might have said.'

'How do you mean?'

'Well why does he want Angelique on board at all. Who the hell is she anyway? One of your mob? CIA? '

'I don't know Bruce, I just don't know. We'll just have to wait and see. What are we going to do today? Can we do Valletta?'

'Alex honey, nobody *does* Valletta. Valletta will charm and enchant you, but nobody *does* Valletta. Got it? Now, do we have time before breakfast …?'

Still full of cold cuts and rabbit respectively, they had a 'lite bite' breakfast of coffee, figs and hobz with more of the delightful local marmalade and butter. Alex noticed the 'Anchor' label on the small chilled butter packs and assumed there was a naval connection.

'Bruce, are these guys still using Navy victuals twenty years after your Fleet departed?'

'Ha. No. Anchor is a popular brand of butter from New Zealand.'

'They import butter from New Zealand for God's sake? It's ten thousand miles away. How come?'

'It's just tradition. Malta was a stopping point en route to the Suez Canal and all points east. Returning vessels would bring back frozen food including lamb and butter from the Antipodes.'

'Yeah, assuming the canal wasn't blocked by some off-course container ship like that Evergreen something. Winchester still thinks that the so-called accident was sabotage and just a dummy run for a long term incident at a later date.'

'Do you think he was right?'

'Hard to say. Intel and SIGINT picked up nothing, which means probably not. Problem is, it almost certainly sowed the seeds of an idea with some folks – if you understand my meaning. Loss of canal revenues could cripple Egypt's economy fairly quickly. Guess who would come in with money and sympathy?'

'You don't have to tell me. Come on, let's chill. I'll show you Il-Belt. Well some of it anyway.'

Twenty minutes later and they headed once more up South Street and just before the 'Wembley Stores corner' they paused to look into the windows of the Galea Gallery which seemed to specialise in water colours of harbour scenes and ships of today and yesteryear. One stunning picture was of the older USS Constellation against a background of Fort Saint Elmo. Flying the Stars and Stripes from her stern it was a stunning impression of the US Navy's last designed and built sailing 'man of war.' As a ships fanatic McCandless stepped inside to the cooler air. Already it was thirty centigrade and not until the afternoon would South Street be in shade. The painting although completed and signed by the artist was on an easel and still unframed.

Bongu, good morning.' The proprietor, Paul Galea, smiled and replied.

'Good morning. I saw you admiring the Constellation in the window. Like to take a closer look?'

He deftly removed it from the easel and laid it flat on the glass counter. It measured about twenty inches by twelve and unusually for a ship was painted in the 'portrait' style to allow the height of the masts to dominate and delight the eye.

''Kem. How much?'

'Framed or unframed?'

'Unframed but to include postage to the USA please.'

'Sure, for somebody special I'm thinking.'

'You could say that.'

'OK, let's say fifteen hundred for the painting and …'

'I want it couriered overnight please, if possible?'

'It is possible but that will cost a lot. First I need to make a call to TNT. Excuse me.'

Mr Galea reached for his cellphone and pushed a few buttons. This was obviously a speed-dial number and a regular call. Business must be brisk.

'Hello, Bongu.' He spoke the English then the Maltese, uncertain of who exactly would pick up the phone. She wasn't Maltese or English. This young lady was Serbian.

'Marina? Marina Kacarevic? Is that you Marina?'

'Yes, who is that speaking?'

'Hi, it's Paul from the Galea Gallery in Valletta.'

'Hey Paul, don't tell me you've got more stuff to go to China?'

'No America. Just a minute …'

'Sir, where in America? East or west coast the lady wants to know? '

'East Coast. Maryland. Yes thank you Marina, I'll hold.'

'This young lady Marina – she is very efficient. Like a lot of new arrivals from Eastern Europe she worked in the hotel industry until she was laid off because of the pandemic. Very intelligent and if I may say so a credit to her new employers and excuse me … yes, Marina. No it will weigh less than one kilogram and will be rolled and tightly packed inside one of our special aluminium tubes. Yes a US Customs declaration will be attached in the usual way. Value? Just a minute.'

McCandless was as quick as lightning.

'One point four million dollars US.'

'Did you hear that, Marina. Yes one point four million dollars US. You can collect it by 1pm and it will be delivered by 5pm tomorrow Eastern Daylight Time. And the total carriage costs? Two hundred and fifty Euros including insurance. Thank you. It'll be ready. Drop in for coffee next time you're in town. Ciao!'

Alexandria Mari Pisani was absolutely speechless. Mad too.

'What the hell are you doing? I don't want anything to do with an insurance fraud. Count me out.'

'It's not a fraud, well not an insurance fraud anyway. It's a joke I'm playing on Ralph Winchester.'

'OK but who's paying for the joke?'

'He is. Well Uncle Sam anyway. Now all I need you to do Mr Galea is take 1,750 Euros from this account with this piece of plastic here and we're done. As long as the official customs receipt says $1.4m we're good to go. Here's the address. Honey, what is the zip-code for Head Office? Do you have it?'

'How could I forget. 20755, I'll write it down.'

Mr Galea put the blue-tooth electronic bank connector onto the counter and added in the amount to be billed. McCandless punched in 9-9-8-8 and waited. Ping!

'Oh, Mr Galea, I might have some more business for you. If I email you a photo of a new British warship could you do a watercolour for me against a backdrop of Grand Harbour?'

'Of course. But we can Google it now. I will let you have it within three days. What is the name of this ship?'

'HMS Duncan. It's for a friend of mine in Marsaxlokk.'

31

After leaving the Galea Gallery they turned left into Republic Street and just followed their noses. Jewellery shops and boutiques abounded on either side of this beautiful thoroughfare. The architecture was stunning and every building seemed to be the same colour, the colour of honey, such was the effect of five centuries of limestone being bleached by the sun. McCandless was up for a bit of leg-pulling.

'This honey coloured stone is why the Romans called Malta 'Melita' – the Island of Honey. It's nothing to do with bees. Just the colour of the stone. True or false?'

'I'm not sure. You tease me too much.'

'Well it's true, but being of Roman descent yourself you might know that and with your Roman nose and all …'

'Hey just quit that! But I am genetically from Zurrieq probably, yes?'

'Quite possibly but hey we're going in here to this café. It's world famous.' Alex looked up at the stone carved sign above the door:

Caffe Cordina Est. 1837

'Why Bruce, I do declare, this place is almost new! And if it's famous how come I've never heard of it?'

'Because you're from Brooklyn that's why. Come on let's go inside. It looks nice and cool in there.' They found a vacant table and ordered two Cappuccinos and two pastizzias, both cheese. One each. The cheesecakes arrived first fresh from the heated glass dispensing counter.

'You know, Bruce. I could eat one of these every day. Every single day.'

McCandless didn't say anything. He wasn't even listening. His eyes were fixed on a sign hoarding across the road. 'For sale by auction due to bereavement. Five hundred square metres on three floors. Applications to the Agents. Details below.' Then a website which McCandless clocked and memorised. It looked like a restaurant that had seen better days. He daydreamed.

'Are you listening to me!'

'Sorry honey, or should I call you Melita? It suits you.'

'I kinda like it too but Alex is fine. OK?'

The Cappuccinos arrived and looked, smelt and tasted divine. Ten minutes later they paid the bill and left, much to the relief of another couple waiting for a table. It sure was busy. But there again it always was. Every single day except Christmas Day and Easter Sunday. It was obviously the place to see and be seen. It was Valletta's Maxims of Paris and it must be making a fortune.

'OK we turn right here up Triq San Gwan'.

'Is that kinda like 'Trick or Treat?' She managed to keep a straight face for only a few seconds.

'I've told you, In Maltese the Q is silent … They both dissolved into laughter.

'It was my turn to pull your leg this time. Where are we headed anyway?'

'We're going to church. A special church. I'm a Christian like you and although I'm not a Catholic I have to tell you this particular church will blow your mind. Some say that inside it is more impressive than even Saint Peter's Basilica in Rome. Have you been there?'

'Wow. No I haven't. Have you?'

'Yes, many years ago when I was a teenager. I have to say I agree with those that admire this church. Here it is on your left – St. Johns Co-Cathedral. Do not be fooled by the plain exterior. Come on, it's OK to go in.'

'Kem? How much?' McCandless sighed.

'This isn't Brooklyn for God's sake. It's a church not a profit making museum.'

Instantly Alex regretted having made the off the cuff remark. Bruce was right. It was time to show a little respect. High time. She slipped her hand into his and they walked slowly into the cool and darker interior.

'Tread lightly, Alex. Beneath the marble floor are the tombs of over four hundred Knights of the Order, including La Valette.' She was tempted to say 'gee that guy gets everywhere' but she checked herself at the last moment. The lady was learning. She hardly said a word during the next twenty minutes while she absorbed the five hundred year history of the church dedicated to St. John the Baptist. Emerging into the brilliant sunshine and re-donning the Ray-Bans, they were heralded almost immediately by a street musician playing the oboe. Appropriately he gave a pitch-perfect rendition of 'Gabriel's Oboe', a beautiful melody that was adopted as the theme tune for the movie The Mission.

'You know, Bruce. We're on a mission, aren't we? What is freaking me out is that I'm not sure where this mission is going to end. Do you?'

McCandless said nothing. Absolutely nothing.

32

Fifty nautical miles north-west of the Maltese archipelago the Master of the MY Christina O was on the bridge and on the ball. Within three hours, at the most, his beautiful vessel would enter Grand Harbour, Valletta – its Port of Registration.

At fifty-five Stavros Leonides was at the very pinnacle of his career. Almost a year ago he had resigned his Mastership in Dido Cruises and was all set for a retirement in the little village of Oriklini just a few kilometres outside the famous Cypriot city of Larnaca. King Richard the First of England had married his Queen Berengaria at Larnaca during the Crusades. This mission would be his own last crusade. Then he could sail away the golden days of his life in his own yacht 'Heracles', a son of Zeus and the alternative name for Hercules. The twelve month offer and contract for two hundred thousand US dollars, tax-free, was as unexpected as it was welcome. Just a little boost to his pension fund for a year and then the delights of the Eastern Mediterranean and Aegean would await him. The chance meeting he'd had with an American Army General at a regatta in Yalikavak, Turkey had proved to be most fruitful. Invitations to various nautical functions and associated social events flowed at regular intervals. Most of them he'd had to decline but to take command of the Christina O was a once in a lifetime experience. One thing did puzzle him though. He'd been in command of many ships registered under Flags of Convenience including Liberia, Panama and Malta and until now he'd never been summoned for an annual inspection to satisfy regulations. Never mind. Orders were orders and within the hour he would have to decide whether to approach Grand Harbour 'clockwise' from the eastern side of the Island or 'anti-clockwise' via the west coast and the majestic Dingli Cliffs. His mind was made up for him when a secure and encrypted message arrived via the Satellite Communications System known as SCOT which had been bought inexpensively as Royal Navy surplus a few years earlier. He read it several times before it sank in. It was from the owners in Monaco. At least that's where it purported to come from.

> *You are to proceed to a position one nautical mile due south of the Blue Grotto (co-ordinates below) and drop anchor. Be prepared to launch your tender to receive a replacement crew member for your culinary staff. Further instructions will be sent in due course. Head Office.*

Captain Leonides gave the orders to his First Officer Peter Skelton whose dry Yorkshire wit belied his obvious nautical skills and experience.

'Sir, whoever sent that signal knows absolutely nowt about those waters. Bloody wazzocks!'

Leonides had heard many Yorkshire titles before including prats, twats and fuckwits but wazzocks was a new one on him. He was just about to enquire why the originator of the signal was a wazzock when Skelton beat him to it.

'Water there's ovver deep for't anchor chain tha' knows. Three hundred foot, mebbe more. Tek a look at t'chart.

We'll slow down to a knot or two and lower't tender. I'll tek it in tut jetty.'

Captain Leonides wondered if they all spoke like that in Robin Hood's Bay where Skelton hailed from. One day he might just take a look for himself. Skelton had said they were a 'rum lot from't Bay' and coming from him they surely must be. If he was more then slightly bemused by the first signal then the second one coming in thirty minutes later absolutely stunned him.

> *Operation Panda is now good to go. The window of opportunity is short but crystal clear. Only you and I in the whole world know what that means. After collecting your extra crew member you are to proceed to Rinella Creek and anchor. Do not berth. The Dragons and the Eagles will arrive separately for the Summit which will be announced to the world tonight. Good luck. RW.*

So this was it. Now Captain Stavros Leonides knew why he was being paid two hundred grand. In US dollars too, not Euros. The transfer of Angelique de la Roche from dry land to the Christina O was accomplished without difficulty. 'The hey up lass welcome aboard' was lost on the lady from Maryland.

33

'Bruce, shall we go back to the hotel now for some … you know … siesta?' She felt horny.

'No, not yet.' McCandless checked his Roamer and reckoned that assuming all had gone to plan then within two hours or even less the Christina O would be entering Grand Harbour.

'How do you fancy a little boat ride?'

'Sure. Do you mean a little ride or a little boat?'

'Both. The boat is called a dghajsa. Pronounced dicer. Just think of dice or craps. I'm sure you've been to Atlantic City and the casinos. I seem to remember you were descended from a hooker who …'

'Enough! Hah hah. So what is a 'dicer', Bruce?'

'It's Malta's equivalent of a Venetian gondola – a small water taxi if you like. The design is hundreds of years old and they were used extensively to ferry people from ship to shore and vice-versa. Maybe you saw some in Marsaxlokk after we left the Duncan Hotel. You can't miss them, they're painted very bright colours. One guy rows it standing up and uses two crossed-over oars.'

'Yeah, come to think of it I do remember now. So which of us is gonna row?'

'Neither. The rower comes with it. There's a white cab over there look. Let's grab it.'

The driver was pleased to get a fare at this time of day as nearly everyone was taking an afternoon nap.

'Yes, Sir. The Old Customs House did you say? No problem.'

'Thanks, and do think a dghajsa might be available?'

'You are lucky. My cousin operates two of them, mostly just for tourists these days. Shall I call him on his mobile for you? Business has been very slack recently. He will be pleased to be woken up!'

'That'd be great. Grazzi haffna, my friend.'

The road twisted and turned down towards the harbour and passed an entrance to a tunnel called Victoria Gate, the carved lintel above it displaying the name that was yet another reminder that the last Empire to have occupied the Island was the British.

'Here we are – The Old Customs House. And there is my cousin Emanuel Pisani.'

He waved and his cousin waved back. Alex sighed. Yet more Pisanis and she was still no nearer to tracing any forebears than the day she arrived. The website that the friendly staff at the Elvis Lounge had suggested was a major disappointment. The name Pisani had registered a zillion hits in a nanosecond and when Alex had realised that in Malta the name Pisani was as common as Patel in Pakistan or Singh in Srinagar she mentally conceded that she might never solve the mystery. Maybe she would have to come back on vacation on a future occasion and maybe a certain Ingerlish 'Commander' would come with her. She simply could not ever imagine being in Malta without him.

'Sir, would you like me to come back for you? In say an hour?'

'No thanks. But hey do you have a card? I have a special job coming up in a couple of days.'

'Yes, here is my card. Any time to be of service. Oh thanks that's very generous, Fifty Euros! Sometimes I don't take that in a day.'

'You're welcome.' McCandless knew he had overpaid him but he now had three tame taxis drivers if he needed them – all at the same time if necessary – Peter, Mario and now Emanuel.

'Bruce, why the heck did you decline Emanuel's offer to come back later for us. If you think I'm climbing all those steps or steep streets in this heat you are very much mistaken.'

'Relax, Alex. We'll go back in a lift – an elevator to you. Now, climb carefully down into the boat and sit on the centre plank. This isn't the Staten Island ferry but don't worry the Harbour is as flat as a mill pond today.' It was time to take command of his smallest ever commission. HMS Dghajsa weighed less than a ton.

'Full steam ahead helmsman. Head for the Maltese Falcon please, straight ahead.'

Alex was in dreamland as the dghajsa slipped her moorings and headed out across the deep waters of the world's most perfect natural harbour. She tried to imagine she was on the SS Ohio limping into safety with the might of the British Navy protecting her. A gentle dig in the ribs from Bruce brought her back to reality.

'What do you think to that then?'

They were so close to the Maltese Falcon that they had to strain their necks upwards like a cormorant swallowing a fish.

'Bruce, I have never in my life seen a sailing boat as beautiful as this.'

Its plain, simple lines belied the technology that lay within it. The construction itself had been a masterpiece of co-operation between the builders and the designer.

'Was it built in Ingerland, like the Mayflower, Bruce?'

'No it was built in Tuzla, Turkey. Well most of it anyway. The English guy that bought the hull designed the masts, rigging and even the computer software that controls the sails. The masts are made from carbon fibre and they rotate to adjust for wind direction. The sails are made from aluminium – that's aluminum to you – and drop down from the yards when instructed by the computers. It's just mind-boggling. The rig was originally designed to help cargo vessels save fuel. In terms of being 'green' it was twenty or thirty years ahead of its time.'

'You know, Bruce, that's kinda ironic isn't it?'

'Is it? How come?'

'Sure, think about it. The Falcon was built in modern day Turkey and here it is in its home-port Valletta berthed under battlements and fortifications that almost five centuries ago were swarming with heathen Turks trying to invade.'

Not for the first time McCandless reckoned that the new lady in his life was no 'Brooklyn bimbo'. If only he knew what else was going through her mind as she had gone back in time eight decades and imagined she was Captain Dudley Mason GC.

'Port ninety please helmsman. Take us over to Bighi please'.

About two miles distant beyond the breakwaters that marked the entrance to Grand Harbour, McCandless could just make out two white masts and a muffin-top of buff yellow above the stone walls of the Rinella breakwater. He deliberately said nothing, concentrating instead on the sight immediately in front of them.

'Hey, Bruce, look. Another tower but this is different. It's not even facing the ocean. What is it?'

'Actually, Alex, it's a lift shaft built over a century ago to take wounded soldiers up to the Bighi Naval hospital. That's the huge building above us which you can't see properly until you get further back from it.'

'What? Where were they injured? Not in Malta surely.'

'No. In 1915 they were mostly wounded from the Gallipoli Campaign. Mostly British and Australian troops who were evacuated here by sea from the fighting in the Dardanelles. The Turks smashed the hell out of the ANZAC troops and it led to bitter recriminations between Britain and Australia.'

'There you go with that Turkish connection again. Can we go up the elevator and take a look?'

'No, it's no longer functioning. But as I promised earlier I will take you up another modern elevator later.'

McCandless glanced at his Roamer again and then out to sea. The masts had moved nearer and changed course. He just wanted to keep her talking until the ship itself was wholly visible and then he would ask the oarsman to spin round a hundred and eighty degrees and watch her reaction.

'The Navy still used the hospital for many years after WW2 and it was a naval HQ right up until Britain finally pulled out. Before that believe it or not the RN still used Fort St. Angelo as its Mediterranean Fleet Headquarters – hence all the masts, rigging and yardarms you can still see atop the Fort. I think it's used mainly for ceremonial occasions now. In its day I suppose you could say it was the ultimate stone frigate.'

Looking sideways McCandless could see that the Christina O had made the final course adjustments for her entry into Grand Harbour. The fore and main masts now appeared as one, meaning she was on a course heading straight for them. It was time.

'Ready about please, helmsman. Alex, close your eyes please.'

McCandless stuck a hand in the air and spun his index finger in a circle just to make sure. He waited thirty seconds.

'OK Alex, you can open your eyes now. And this, Alex, is the Christina O, the most beautiful 'super yacht' in the whole world. You can take your billion dollar floating palaces owned by Saudi Kings, Russian oligarchs, drugs and arms dealers and tax-dodging businessmen and stuff 'em. This floating piece of history has looks, pedigree and pure class. It's the first time I've seen it in the flesh, only as a radar blip in the past.'

'She is stunning, Bruce, I'll give you that. Just stunning. Oh wow!'

The 'dghajsa-man' suddenly realised, as did all of them, that the Christina O was headed straight for them although she had by now slowed to just three knots. Of course they didn't know that Captain Leonides had orders to anchor at precisely their location. It was time to move out – fast.

'Where to now?'

'Lascaris Wharf please. We're taking the elevator.'

McCandless paid off Emanuel Pisani, generous to a 't' as always. Especially with Uncle Sam's money.

'Where are we going now Bruce? I need a drink. I'm so hot.'

'Me too. We'll go back up topside.'

'Huh? What do you mean topside? We're not on a frigging boat.'

'Cross the road here. Right over there is the elevator I told you about. It will take us straight back up to the Barrakka Gardens, then we can have that cooling drink you mentioned.'

'Jeez, will you just look at that! It looks new. Is it?'

'Well by Maltese standards it's brand new at about a decade old. You could say it's the best of the new alongside the best of the old. A lot of new developments look crass, just awful, but this seems to blend in quite nicely. Anyway, step in. You press the UP button.'

Twenty three seconds later they were almost two hundred feet above Grand Harbour and back to the amazing view across to Fort Saint Angelo and Bighi. The Christina O had dropped both for'ard and stern anchors and lay parallel to the fortifications about a hundred metres from the shore. With the late afternoon sun shining on her white superstructure and buff coloured funnel she looked a picture of pure floating elegance. Perhaps only one other vessel in the world, the Royal Yacht Britannia, could match her for looks and prestige but she had long since been relegated to museum status by 'here today gone tomorrow' politicians who learnt little and cared less about their country's pride or maritime history.

'Beer or Kinnie, Bruce? I'll go to the kiosk. Let's send RW an email shall we? You know to tell him that '99' has arrived safely.'

'A Hop Leaf for me please. And I'm sure he already knows but yes just confirm it for him.'

Back at the hotel a half an hour later Alex opened her iPad. There was an unexpected message in her in-box.

At RW's request I am now our asset aboard 99.
I will make myself known to you at the wine tasting on
88 Friday evening.

Angelique

34

The White House
Washington DC
17:00 hours Eastern Daylight Time

The hastily announced and convened press conference had caught most of DC's Press Corps by total surprise. Wearied by a former incumbent who accused each and every one of them of bias and 'fake news' and worn down by pandemic related PR exercises, most of the Corps actually failed to turn up. In the words of the Pretty Woman – 'big mistake'!

Newly elected President Kirk had chosen his Spokeswoman very carefully. Looking back at the choices made by his predecessors he'd decided that the best ones had been female. They had to sound as if they really believed what the President wanted them to say. Women made better actors he figured but on this occasion it really didn't matter. This was no act. This was realpolitik in the truest sense of the word. Sheryl Baguley had been stolen from GlobeNewsCorp when her contract had been terminated following a heated 'on air' argument with a Congressman who'd been accused of receiving bribes to influence State contracts from a Chinese-owned electronics company. The case hadn't yet gone to court and Baguley had been harangued for presuming guilt and not innocence before the trial. Cometh the hour, cometh the woman. She was exactly the person Kirk needed for this role. She was also a 'dead ringer' for Liz Hurley and despite her slight Southern drawl she could speak the 'Queen's Ingerlish' when called upon to do so.

Looking and sounding more like Elizabeth Taylor in 'Cat on a Hot Tin Roof' she strode to the lectern and laid the two pages of notes in front of her. She didn't need the auto-cue. That was for dumbos and Presidents with a speech impediment. This press conference was going out live on 'all stations coast to coast' and timed to coincide with evening news bulletins for maximum impact – on the East Coast anyway. California could carry on surfing. Who cares about cowboys and Californians anyway? The Director of the NSA sure did but he knew a lot more than the President. A whole lot more.

'Ladies and Gentlemen, Good afternoon.

What I am about to impart to you will be looked back in the years ahead as a historic moment in the annals of international diplomacy. Most of us were still at High School when the Bush-Gorbachev Summit held in Malta in 1989 marked the end of the Cold War. The world was never the same again and the Summit led directly to a new life for millions who had for over four decades been enslaved within the Soviet Empire.

Today it is the Chinese Dragon not the Russian Bear that is causing so many problems to the West. The Dragon has taken it upon itself to enslave the Uighur peoples and incarcerate them in camps that are reminiscent of Stalin at his worst. Vast swathes of American and allied industries have been destroyed by China as it dumps millions of tons of cheap steel into our marketplace. Is there any wonder that Detroit is almost deserted and Pittsburgh reduced to rust? Tit-for-tat tariffs are not the answer. America and China must learn to co-exist on the global trading platforms of the twenty-first century.

Our two Navies have come perilously close to accidentally starting a War in the South China Sea. The only two people on Earth who can ensure this doesn't happen are the Presidents of our two great nations. Back in 1989 it was the then Prime Minister of Malta, Dr. Eddie Fenech Adami, who graciously acted as host and go-between. Emulating his fellow citizen and former Premier, the current Maltese Prime Minister, Edward Borg Vella, has invited President Kirk and President Zhang to attend a new Summit. I am delighted to tell you that both have accepted and ...'

The Press Corps simply erupted into a tumult of noise and hand waving. A barrage of questions were fired at Sheryl Baguley.

'Why did the President agree?!'

'Are you kidding?'

'Is this some kinda joke?'

'We should be nuking 'em not talking to them!'

'What the heck do we have a Navy for?'

'Has the State Department sanctioned this?'

'Will the press be invited?'

'When is it going to take place?'

The last question seemed to bring calm and order to the proceedings. Sheryl raised her right hand as if she were taking an oath which brought almost total silence to the briefing room.

'Thank you. Now if ya'll allow me, I'll continue.'

She always lapsed into Texan when she was irritated.

'If you check the history books you will see that the previous Summit took place on two warships, one American one Soviet. This time round an effort is being made to de-militarise the whole thing and create a neutral and civil ambience from the start. Accordingly I can tell you that the super-yacht Christina O has been chartered for this purpose.'

Wows and low whistles echoed around for what seemed an eternity but which in reality was probably about ten seconds.

'And before ya'll start texting your newspapers and TV stations and Twittering like constipated blackbirds – you might like to listen to the rest of the briefing.'

She was obviously irritated again.

'The Christina O was chosen for two main reasons. One – it is already in the central Mediterranean and luckily was available. Two – it has a pedigree of hosting the mighty and the powerful. Former guests include John Fitzgerald Kennedy, his widow the subsequent Jackie Onassis and of course Sir Winston Churchill. And wasn't it Sir Winston himself who once famously said that Jaw-Jaw is better than War-War?

So I'll answer that last question first. I can tell you that the first round of Summit talks will commence in just over forty-eight hours time. As I speak the President and First Lady are boarding Air Force One at Andrews AFB and by the time this briefing is over will almost certainly be airborne. For security reasons no further details will be released until the President is aboard the Christina O. Our understanding is that President Zhang will be departing Beijing any time now bearing in mind that China Time is twelve hours ahead of EDT he'll probably be timing his flight over the South China Sea in the early morning sunlight ...'

'Yeah to get a good view of those islands they've stolen' bawled out a junior reporter from an East Coast tabloid. He'd hit the nail right on the head but nine thousand miles east things were not going entirely as planned.

Sheryl answered all the questions asked by the journos except one. She knew that no press would be invited. Then she wrapped up the briefing. She thought she'd done a good job but being a modest kinda gal she wouldn't crow about it. If only she was going too. She'd read about Margaret Tutwiler and how she'd made herself indispensable to former President George HW Bush to such an extent that she'd accompanied the American delegation to Malta in 1989. Maybe the talks would fail initially and there would have to be a Round Two. Then she could emulate Elizabeth Taylor as well as Liz Hurley. The former had been on the Christina O with Richard Burton. She wouldn't have minded a slice of him, either.

35

Beijing
China

Xijiao military airfield is less than ten miles from downtown Beijing. It had been the scene of intense activity in the last few days. The race to customise the Ilyushin-76 to the standards required by President Zhang for the long-haul flight to Malta and the Summit had been a tight one. All the extra internal furnishings had been applied, drop tanks fitted to increase range and the gleaming exterior paintwork polished to perfection. The huge red dragons on the front of the fuselage, port and starboard, reflected brilliantly in the modern LED lighting of the special hangar that was now reserved for Red Dragon One. Shortly after dawn the plane was towed out by tractor to the apron. Because it was designed primarily for cargo and military use it didn't have a nice passenger door that could be manoeuvred precisely into line with a red carpet. Other than the huge tailgate that could be raised to allow the embarkation of troops and equipment, the small number of crew would embark via a small ladder that was manually operated under the plane's belly. That would not look very dignified for a President of the People's Republic and his First Lady so there were no official photographs of the boarding. Instead CCP official photographers took shots of the plane to catch the dragons prancing in the orange early morning sun as it rose above the Yellow Sea and cast its warming glow over the Motherland. All was well. So far.

The plane took off on runway 18 due south and being designed with a high wing for assisted take-offs on short fields it didn't need all the runway despite being loaded to its maximum with fuel. It then headed on a bearing 200 and headed for Hainan Island, over a thousand miles to the south-west, for its first scheduled refuelling stop. It was important to keep those tanks topped up. They had a long way to go.

Red Dragon One levelled out at twenty five thousand feet and the pilot set the autopilot. Back in the cabin the President and Madam Zhang relaxed in the two rows of Business Class seats that had been sequestered from a China Airlines B747 before it was permanently grounded. The global pandemic had hit all the world's airlines and big four-engined passenger planes were being phased out or mothballed in the hope of better days ahead. All but two anyway. Zhang had heard from his own intelligence people that the B747s that were Air Force One and its backup, an identical replica, were being replaced by two new B747-8s before the production line came to an end. He went green with envy when he imagined the new plane flying his opposite number into Malta International Airport in a few hours time. Almost as green as the tea which a steward brought to him from the improvised galley that had been hastily fitted into the forward part of the plane behind the crew area.

Zhang gazed out of one of only four windows, two port and two starboard, but not being designed for civilian use they afforded poor visibility of the countryside below. Mentally he ticked off the tasks he had dealt with the night before. Comrade Won-Gah had seen to all the fiscal details he was sure. He would repay his diligence and loyalty handsomely in the not too distant future. He glanced across to his wife who had somehow obtained a copy of Il-Bizzilla, Air Malta's in-flight magazine. She was talking animatedly to their interpreter, another female. She seemed particularly engrossed in the retail property section. Wasn't she satisfied with one of the new western-style condos he'd reserved for them that were being erected on the Paracel Islands in the South China Sea? Typical woman, he thought. Never bloody satisfied. Perhaps it was indeed time to get a concubine or three like Comrade Won-Gah. Yes, he would ask him for advice when they next met. Whenever that was. He decided on a couple of hours sleep. He'd been up half the night making various calls and effecting certain emails. The PA system's 'bing bong' awoke him from his dreams of living in the sun.

'This is the Captain speaking. We are about to make our final approach into Hainan. Please fasten all seat belts.' There was no 'cabin crew, doors to manual' as there weren't any doors. Zhang looked at his Rolex Oyster Perpetual which he had just bought a few days earlier. He didn't want to look like a schmuck at the Summit meetings. Could that be right? They had been in the air for four hours. This sector was supposed to have taken only three hours or less. He hadn't changed the time on his watch and in any case China only had one time zone. He questioned the Captain just before disembarking for the half-hour refuelling stop.

'My apologies, Comrade Chairman. The number two engine was seemingly losing oil pressure so purely as a precaution we turned it off. As you know they were Soviet designed and ...'

'Yes, yes, yes. Will it be fixed on the ground here or shall I book into a local hotel while you fix it?'

'I guarantee we'll be leaving in just thirty minutes, Comrade Chairman.' He didn't say whether they would be flying with three or four engines though.

Sure enough ninety minutes later they were at ten thousand feet heading almost due south to overfly the first of the Islands that had been incorporated into the String of Pearls. Zhang wondered why they were flying so low. So low in fact that he could make out fishing vessels and PLAN patrol boats. His curiosity was short-lived and came to an abrupt end when the First Officer came to his side.

'Comrade Chairman, the Captain has invited you to join him in the cockpit to get a better view of the new base our Patriotic Forces have constructed. This model of the Il-76 also has a glazed nose like an old-fashioned Soviet bomber. Perhaps you'd like to …'

'Yes thank you, First Officer.'

Ten minutes later the President of almost a billion and a half people was lying prostrate in the glazed nose of the thirty year old plane. Looking down at the horseshoe shaped coral atoll upon which sat a shimmering new runway he felt somewhat uncomfortable. It wasn't as if the PLA men and women three miles below him could see him and wave. And the cost. The cost! Only he and Comrade Won-Gah alone amongst the Politburo knew the full cost of these Pearls. The post-pandemic downturn in trade had hit China harder than most people had realised. He crawled back into the cockpit and thanked the Captain for the opportunity to get a bird's eye view. His conversation was interrupted by a warning buzzer and a large red light, one of four, flashing at one second intervals.

'It's that No.2 engine again. Turn it off!' The First Officer thumped another button and the flashing red light went off completely.

Zhang returned to his seat feeling a little queasy. He had twisted his lower back whilst emulating a WW2 bomb aimer and now Red Dragon One was down to three engines. The Captain came back into the cabin and spoke directly to the President. Incredibly the two women were still yacking.

'Comrade Chairman, there is no cause for alarm I do assure you. However as a precaution we are now changing plans and we will not overfly any more of our new territories. We will soon turn west over the Malay Peninsula and head straight for our next intended stop, Nagumbo in Sri Lanka. By doing this we should still make our original ETA and as we burn up fuel the plane's load will decrease and we'll actually pick up speed. These old planes are tough old birds. Now if we had re-engined them with our own Yangtze engines that we pirated from the Rolls Royce Trents that we reverse engineered we could fly on only two engines and …'

'Yes, yes, yes. Do what you think is best. Wake me up before we arrive at the next Pearl.'

'Certainly, Comrade Chairman. Sleep well.'

He didn't tell him that the back-up Red Dragon Two had already left Hainan Island on a direct course for Nagumbo. Just as a precaution of course.

Back in Beijing the New China News Agency, the voice-piece of the CCP, had just announced that President Zhang was headed for a Summit with his opposite number in the White House, President Kirk.

'Our esteemed President and Chairman is currently on his way to Malta for an urgent Summit Meeting. It is believed that Trade is the number one item on the agenda. Plainly the Imperialist Americans are feeling the pinch as the once almighty dollar takes second place to the RMB Yuan as the world's reserve currency of choice.'

It was of course total bollox.

Feeling a little nauseous from the back pain President Zhang reached into the little rack on the back of the seat in front of him, one of the smaller crew seats used by PLAAF personnel, just in case he needed the sick-bag but what else he retrieved made him go as green as the pak-choi he'd eaten for his last supper. It was a map of the eastern Indian Ocean with various red circles that had been drawn of varying size and latitude. In the name of all the Gods, what was this? Across the top in crude Chinese characters effected with a cheap red felt-tip pen were two letters and three numbers followed by three words.

MH-370 Possible crash zones.

And then it dawned on him. This Il-76 had been one of several such aircraft detailed to assist in the international search operation for the missing Malaysian Airlines B777 that had mysteriously disappeared on a routine flight from Kuala Lumpur to Beijing a few years earlier. The wreck had never been found and over a hundred citizens of the People's Republic had lost their lives. And here they were heading out across the very same stretch of water with only three operating engines and two thousand miles to go. In his eyes it was the worst possible feng-shui. Sick bag number one filled up but Red Dragon One droned on towards the next Pearl on the String.

36

Midway across the Atlantic, Air Force One was approaching the Azores, a potential diversion field in case of problems. There weren't any. Well only one and it might cause a slight rethink to the flight plan. A feisty Atlantic jet-stream had created an eighty knot tail-wind and was looking to knock almost an hour off the projected flight time. The scheduled ETA of six o'clock in the morning might be more like five o'clock. The Captain had to decide whether to throttle back the four huge General Electric turbofans or arrive an hour early. In fact was Malta International Airport (MIA) even open to traffic that early? He didn't know but he'd better find out pretty soon. He didn't want to annoy over a hundred thousand Maltese citizens living on the flight path when he flew in on runway one-three, the provisionally designated flight plan.

Back in the main cabin the President and First Lady had enjoyed a dinner of Maine lobster and a prime rib-eye steak. After reading the briefing notes from the State Department he had retired for the night, satisfied that the forthcoming Summit would be every bit as successful and historic as that held at Marsaxlokk over three decades ago. He'd watched the live feed when Sheryl Baguley had conducted the White House briefing with such aplomb. Maybe he should have brought her along too but accommodation on the Christina O was limited and his official interpreter on board, a nationalised Chinese American called Nancy Kwok, was effectively his sole member of staff. He had no notion whatsoever that 'Angelique' was already in place. Quite simply he didn't need to know.

If only things were going as smoothly on Red Dragon One. Conversely it had hit a headwind which reduced their ground-speed by fifty knots. On the ground at Nagumbo they rendezvoused with Red Dragon Two, which with four fully working engines had flown a shorter route. Not for them a sight-seeing detour to the South China Sea. The carefully laid plans were starting to fall apart. President Zhang rejected outright the idea of switching to Red Dragon Two which although was externally identical to its twin was bereft of the added comforts. The two PLAAF Captains discussed the matter at length while both planes were refuelled.

'The next stop at Djibouti is out of the question Comrade. Let's file flight plans for Tripoli in Libya which is only twenty minutes flying time from Malta. I did Libya over a decade ago to evacuate our compatriots during the civil war there. Malta was the in case of need diversion field.'

'No, let us stop at Djibouti to off-load a member of crew who has been taken ill. We'll get the News Agency to put out a false report. Then we'll fly to Tripoli, then Malta.'

'Agreed, Comrade. Perfect.'

There were ample photo opportunities for President and Mrs Zhang on the ground in Djibouti, posing in front of the forward fuselage with the bright Red Dragon as a backdrop. In a week's time or less it would look great on the front page of the China Daily and the Shanghai Star, not to mention Hong Kong's South China Morning Post which was now fully under the control of 'patriotic staff' and not sycophantic pro-western scribblers. They almost slipped up but at the last minute just remembered to take a photo of a 'sick crew member' being gently stretchered from the huge tailgate of the Ilyushin. And just to add to the air of benevolence, prominence was given to several, now empty, crates of Covid Vaccine that had been delivered to somewhere else in Africa almost a year ago. The PLAAF crew member who doubled up as a photographer would be well rewarded for his diligence at a later date.

After two hours on the ground the two Red Dragons took off for Tripoli at an interval of five minutes with 'Two' as a back-up just in case it was needed. It wasn't, well not just yet anyway. The four hour flight to Libya was relatively uneventful and arrangements were made for the President's entourage including the crew to stay overnight at the Chinese Embassy. They would arrive in Malta at the right time, just a day late.

Meanwhile Air Force One was ahead of the game and flying almost exactly due east as it entered the Mediterranean Sea. The Captain had indeed throttled back slightly and at about five o'clock he asked for the President to be awakened by an aide.

'Mr President, Sir, we will be landing in Malta in just over an hour's time at approximately six a.m. local time. We'll be arranging coffee and a 'lite' breakfast shortly, Sir.'

'Thank you, Steward. Is it light yet? I hear it's a great view coming into Malta.'

'No Sir, it's still dark but the Captain says that as we're flying into the sunrise we should see daylight well before landing. Perhaps you would like to join the Captain and First Officer on the flight deck as we land,'

'Hey that'd be great. It's my first trip to Malta.'

He could have added that it was only his second ever trip out of the States and the first one was a perfunctory flight to

Ottawa to say Hi to Eye Number Three, Canada. He settled back with coffee and doughnuts for the next half-hour and made small talk with Nancy Kwok. He showered, shaved and changed clothes into a lightweight suit more suitable for Malta's late summer warmth and waited for the nod to go upstairs to the flight deck. He didn't have long to wait after that. The steward returned and ushered him up 'topside' as Bruce McCandless might have said if he was there. To the east the faintest flecks of orange and pink were starting to illuminate the horizon. With just a hundred miles to go the big Boeing started to descend slowly but surely towards Melita and her date with destiny. Malta's Air Traffic Control was well briefed as to the importance of the next flight due in and who was aboard. Denise Grech was only twenty-five and newly qualified. She was thrilled to find she was on duty at the same time as the arrival of Air Force One. What a story to tell her grandchildren one day. She, a village girl from Marsaskala, was going to tell the American President's plane that it was OK for it to land. About fifty miles out the headphones clicked and came to life in the First Officer's ears.

'Good morning Air Force One. This is Malta ATC.'

'Copy that. Good morning Malta.'

'We had your ETA as o-six hundred. You're early my friend.'

'Yeah, friendly tailwinds, ma'am.' He'd picked up on the female voice – and the politeness.

'Your early arrival is a little bit of a problem. We have a midnight to six curfew at MIA, barring emergencies of course. Can I suggest a compromise? Just give me a few seconds please.'

The First Officer passed the President, who was now sitting in the jump seat directly behind him, a spare headset and plumbed the jack into the socket.

'This is Malta again. I'm delaying your landing by just a few minutes and I'm changing your runway from one-three to three-one. Do you copy that.'

'Copy that. Roger.'

'Good, you are clear to land on three-one any time. You are the only bird in the sky for two hundred nautical miles.' Denise knew that all American aviators preferred nautical miles to kilometres.

'Malta, can I have your name please. The President would like to say Hi.'

'It's Denise Grech – that's GOLF ROMEO ECHO CHARLIE HOTEL – and I'd be delighted to welcome President Kirk to our Islands.' The President took the initiative while the pilots noted the runway change and associated course corrections.

'Good morning Miss er Greek and thank you. I can just see you guys in the growing light now. Looks like I can see two islands ahead – hey no, three. Which is which?'

Denise knew from the radar screen exactly where Air Force One was.

'Mr President the first island you see is called Gozo. The small one behind it is called Comino and the big one is my home – Malta!'

'I've never heard of Go-Zo. Whose is it?'

'It's our sister Island, Mr President. If you have time you should visit also.'

'Yeah, I'd like that. Go-Zo did you say?'

Ten minutes later and Air Force One positioned onto the glide path three miles out. The view from the capacious cockpit was perfect. To the right was the container terminal at Kalafrana with its computer controlled cranes dipping in precision to load and unload the giant metal boxes so typical of maritime trade in the twenty-first century. The vista ahead was a quilt patchwork of tiny fields that looked like one of those tapestries made from discarded clothing. In the early sunlight and divided by honey-coloured stone walls, they were like nothing either the crew or President had ever seen before. It was, to them, absolutely enchanting and a million miles away from the prairies of their homeland. The auto-voice counted down the height above the ground. 'Eighty, sixty, forty, twenty.' They landed smoothly on runway three-one and decelerated from one hundred and fifty knots to ten in less than six thousand feet of smooth asphalt. The Captain turned to his First Officer.

'Jeez. How long is this sucker? And we only used half of it.'

'Air Force One, Merhba ta' Malta, welcome to Malta. Proceed left onto runway two-four and follow the security truck to Hard Standing Four. Over.'

'Copy that. Thank you.'

Operation Panda was proceeding to plan. All they needed now was the Panda. But Pandas don't travel well, particularly in the heat.

37

There was no hurry to disembark Air Force One or 'de-plane' as the ghastly American jargon called it. Nobody de-boats so why should anyone de-plane? As soon as the Boeing came to a standstill it was surrounded by Pulizija ta' Malta vehicles bearing their green and cream livery. It was now public knowledge that the President was attending the Summit but any potential terrorists would have to have been out of the trap like a greyhound to achieve anything. It wasn't going to happen, but the Maltese authorities were mindful of the CIA's conclusion that the PanAm Jumbo blown out of the sky at Lockerbie in Scotland in 1988 had almost certainly been caused by a bomb planted in a container in Malta for transfer to the doomed plane. No chances were being taken. The President always travelled in his customised bullet-proof Cadillac dubbed 'the Beast' but on this occasion there was insufficient time for arrangements to be made. The Commissioner of Police was Victor Tabona and he made it his personal responsibility to ensure the President's safety for the duration of his stay.

Barely a handful of people knew that the US President had actually arrived, save for some airport employees including Air Traffic Control and a few ground handlers. Oh yes and a farmer's daughter called Suzanne Azzopardi who lived just on the northern edge of the small town of

Mqabba. Up at dawn to attend to the family's small herd of goats she hadn't seen Air Force One land but as soon as it turned left and taxied towards its hard standing she saw the early morning sun glinting off the blue and white fuselage. She had seen big planes before but never one this big. Within seconds she realised what it was – the President's plane! A year earlier she had watched a DVD called 'Jumbo – the plane that changed the world.' In a flash she ran inside and grabbed an iPhone that she shared with her three sisters. Luckily the plane was still taxiing towards her but Suzanne knew it had to turn right soon towards the hangars and the service and maintenance hangars that were now such an important part of Malta's economy. Switching the cellphone to 'camera' she framed the giant plane in the viewfinder and zoomed in with her thumb and forefinger and waited for the turn that she knew must come. Click, click,click. She took three shots, the final one showing the whole plane from nose to tail and showing the famous Stars and Stripes in all its glory on the tailfin. Within seconds she was on the phone to call the newsroom of the Times of Malta newspaper. Who knows, they might even pay a couple of hundred Euros for the scoop?! Within twenty minutes the photo took pride of place on the online version of The Times and within two hours the front banner of the proper paper itself in a hundred plus shops and newsagents across the Maltese Islands. There might soon even be a Souvenir edition, or even a special supplement. It wasn't just the two hundred Euros that thrilled Suzanne. It was seeing her name in a paper that was now splashed across the world with the underlying accreditation: Photo by Suzanne Azzopardi. Maybe now she could think about turning her hobbies of photography and writing short stories into a journalistic career. After all there wasn't much of a future in goats despite the continuing demand for ricotta and Maltese cheesecakes. Was this the break she was looking for?

The guy with the two bats who looked as if he was playing table-tennis in thin air lowered and crossed the tools of his profession. His job was over. The Captain applied the brakes and the four huge turbofans spooled down to zero. Nobody aboard had the slightest inkling that Air Force One was parked on the same spot that four decades earlier had been reserved for Vulcan bombers as part of Britain's nuclear deterrent. There was a moral in there somewhere.

A mobile flight of stairs was pushed out manually from a nearby hangar towards the port side forward door of the Boeing. There was a moment of panic when it was realised that it wouldn't reach! No problem. Servicing Lufthansa Jumbos had become commonplace at the new commercial aviation centre and a suitable brand new ladder was soon wheeled out. The door was opened to reveal the American eagle logo and crest of the President on the inside of the door. Victor Tabona wanted to be the first Maltese citizen to welcome the President to his homeland. After all he was personally responsible for his safety whilst he was on the Island and now the whole world knew where he was thanks to a goat-herding young lady. He didn't want the President's visit to be plagued by paparazzi and overly curious citizens and tourists. They were more of a threat than terrorists but convincing the Secret Service agents on-board might be a different matter.

Having seen the President on TV earlier in the year trip three times ascending steps to Air Force One he measured his strides carefully. He didn't want the American security personnel to think they were dealing with an Inspector Clouseau of Pink Panther fame. No Sir, Malta had come of age and he wanted to demonstrate the Island's suitability not just for this Summit but for future international conferences for the next century. Why not? The very name Hospitallers denoted hospitality did it not? Victor hadn't been Commissioner during the Commonwealth Heads of Government meeting (CHGM) a few years earlier but as his Deputy he had watched, listened and learnt. He was absolutely determined that nothing would go wrong. Victor was greeted by a steward at the top of the steps and ushered inside. Within seconds he was frisked by security staff who apologised but said they had a job to do. He understood only too well. Their responsibility was awesome too. Within two minutes he was drinking coffee with the de-facto head of the Free World.

'So you see, Mr President, that the suddenness of the arrangements means that the usual protocols cannot be observed. My first responsibility is to get you and the First Lady aboard the Christina O with a minimum of disruption and as little fuss as possible. Here, let me show you on the map.'

Victor produced a detailed map of the southern part of the Island and laid it out across the small table that he, the President and the two senior security staff were sat at. He took a red marker pen out from his inside pocket and drew a ring around their location. Then he drew another ring about three inches to the north-east on the map. The second red ring was surrounded by blue water.

'So we're here – and we need to get you there.' The red pen hovered like dragonfly over the northern expanse of Grand Harbour.

The obviously senior of the two Secret Servicemen intervened.

'Jesus. Are you telling me that old tub isn't even tied up alongside? What if …?'

'Sir, with respect, the Christina O is in fine shape and is a darn sight older than your SS United States which I understand is no longer fit to go to sea. Now if you don't mind Mr ... Gangster was it?'

'Geister. Hank Geister. Lootenant.'

'Mr Geister, this is my plan. I have acquired a black unmarked people carrier, in fact two of them. Complete with smoked glass tinted windows that can only be seen out of and not into. One is for the President and First Lady's luggage. The other is for my staff.' Geister was appalled.

'Where is the President gonna go? On a bus?' Victor Tabona decided to humour this wise guy.

'We had actually considered that as an option.' He lied and had trouble containing a smile.

'However we have decided that you, Mr President, will be taken to the Christina O on a boat and ...'

'Gee, that sounds great! I've got a boat of my own at Wilmington in Delaware and you know what, since being sworn in I just miss being on the ocean without a care in the world. Where and when do we get on this boat. What is it a 'Sunseeker 45' like mine or a ...'

'No, it's a Marine Police launch. And it has heads, a refrigerator stocked with cold beer and a crew of three who all speak English. The press and the public will assume you are in one of the two blacked-out vans taking you through the Three Cities to Rinella just here.' He pointed to the map again. Geister looked like he was going to puke. He spoke again.

'How is the security detail getting to Christina O?'

'It isn't. You're all staying at the US Embassy here in Attard.'

This time Victor pointed two inches due north on the map. But don't worry, you won't have to walk. I'm laying on a mini-bus. It'll be here soon. The flight crew will be hosted in Officers Quarters by the AFM – the Armed Forces of Malta – for the duration of the trip. I understand that a couple of scenic pleasure flights have been arranged for them. Not for the President of course. He will remain on terra firma or even aqua firma. and the Pulizija Ta' Malti will guard him as their own I promise you.'

He pointed to the badge on his jacket which bore a Templar's shield mounted on a Malta Cross protected by a heavy belt. Underpinned in Latin were the words 'Domine Dirige Nos – Lord Guide Us.'

Geister frowned heavily. The President just smiled. Four miles away a much in love couple were just about to have breakfast.

38

Bruce went for the bacon, eggs and fried bread whilst Alex went for the fruit, hobz and marmalade. Boy was she gonna miss the Maltese bread when she got back Stateside. Already she was dreading it. How long did they have left in Malta? Four days? Five days? In a way she was glad she didn't know. All she did know was that it was going to be the saddest day of her life.

The first editions of the Times of Malta were already in the dining room and splashed across the front page was the big blue and white Boeing – Air Force One – on the runway. It looked like it hadn't even stopped yet, and a pair of frightened quails taking flight from the scrub vegetation on the near side of the perimeter fence got caught by the camera's lens.

'Well at least he's gotten here in one piece and on schedule. I wonder how he's getting to the Christina O?' Bruce couldn't resist the quip.

''Well he sure as hell won't be walking. None of your mob ever do. I hope somebody has bought him and the First Lady some Tallinjas!'

'Smart ass. That's our President you're talking about.'

'You mean your President. I have a Queen remember?'

'Ha! Anyway now we know that President Zhang has been delayed twenty four hours what shall we do today?

The wine tasting on the Maltese Falcon is now scheduled for tomorrow night, not tonight. So the Summit talks proper won't start until Sunday now …'

'Correction, Monday. Nobody will want to offend by having the talks start on the Sabbath. You're forgetting this is a deeply Catholic country.'

'Yeah I hadn't thought of that. I hope Martin Mifsud has been advised of the delay?'

'Sure. I think you'd better check.'

'I called the Embassy. Georgette has it all in hand. We're just bit-players in all this now I think.'

Neither of them were absolutely sure about that and the silence was deafening until the eggs and hobz were finished. Bruce broke the silence.

'So, Alex. Wherever you want to go today just say. I'll take you.'

'Three guesses.'

'Gozo?'

'You got it!'

'Well listen. Valletta is not the most convenient place from which to get to Gozo. It really isn't. And it can be time consuming by bus but on the other hand that is the best way from a scenic point of view. So let's compromise OK?'

'I'm sure not walking, Bruce. Ha!'

'OK how about this for a plan? After breakfast we walk out of the City Gates, or at least where the City Gates used to be, and get a bus to Cirkewwa. I think it's number 222 but we'll check.'

'Jeez. The President's only just arrived and already they've named a place after him?'

'What?'

'Kirk Ewwa! Only joking. Sure, how long will that take?'

'At least an hour. And today is a good day to do it because tomorrow and Sunday will very busy. At weekends every man and his dog want to go to Gozo.'

'You said compromise?'

'Yes let's call Mario the other cab driver and see if he can pick us up when we come back to Cirkewwa off the ferry. Yeah?'

'Good thinking Batman. How long is the crossing? An hour?'

'Nothing like. Maybe twenty minutes. It's almost a straight line but the route curves around the south-west of Comino, the smaller island that separates Malta and Gozo. You get a great view of the Santa Marija Tower which looks red in certain lights, especially at sunset. You also get a peek towards the Blue Lagoon which is just magical to swim in.'

'Yeah, I saw it in some brochures I picked up. Shame we don't have the time to go there. Real shame.'

'Come on. Call Mario to pick us up say six-ish at Cirkewwa. Chop chop.'

A few miles to the south-west President and Mrs Kirk had 'de-planed ' from Air Force One and got in the back seats of a modest but comfortable black Mercedes 500 saloon. The driver was a newly qualified Police Constable with ambitions to specialise in personal protection. And here he was driving the President of the United States of America. Talk about starting at the top and working your way down. Victor Tabona occupied the vacant front seat. A standard police car acted as back-up and followed at a discreet distance of about a hundred metres.

Meanwhile the two black vans containing the President and First Lady's luggage and a handful of Tabona's staff set off from the military side of the airport and headed north towards the Three Cities via the Marsa racecourse, Paola and

Cospicua. There was a cop car at the front and another at the rear, both with flashing but silent blue lights. One of the cops had tied a small Stars and Stripes to the mirrors of one of the vans to give the impression that it might contain the President. Just for a laugh he tied them to the van containing the luggage. Stuck in slow moving traffic en route they were pointed at by many pedestrians waving cameras and cellphones taking souvenir photos of the mini-motorcade. If only they knew. A half an hour later and they arrived at a jetty in Rinella. Traffic cops had sealed off the main road to the quayside to add to the illusion but the luggage, and Nancy Kwok, still had to be transferred to the Christina O. A small twenty metre Marine Police launch was waiting and the crew manhandled ten large suitcases aboard – two each for the President and Ms Kwok and six for the First Lady. She wanted to look every inch as glamorous as Jackie Kennedy and Elizabeth Taylor. She would be spending at least four nights on board and didn't want to be outshone by Madam Zhang. Would she be attired in outrageously expensive clothes from Gaultier, Versace or maybe Christian Dior? Or maybe in a classic Chinese 'cheong sam' with slits up the sides almost as far as her underwear? She just hoped that the four hours she'd spent at Saks Fifth Avenue would be worth it. Not to mention the four thousand bucks.

Meanwhile the President's real car had arrived at the Blue Grotto at the head of the Wied Ta' Zurrieq and after leaving the Mercedes walked a short distance to a jetty thronged with tourists of several nationalities waiting in turn for their chance to board small four-seater motorboats which would take them into the famous Blue Grotto. Of course they were recognised instantly and were mobbed and cheered by all of them, most of whom wanted a 'selfie' with the most powerful man in the world. That's just human nature. 'Lootenent

Gangster' would have had several litters of kittens if he'd been there. There wasn't a problem and after a couple of dozen handshakes and autographing several baseball caps the President and his Lady were escorted down a narrow but secure gangplank onto the quarterdeck of the patrol boat. Within two minutes they were sipping cool cans of Cisk beneath a white tarpaulin that had been erected to provide shade. The mooring ropes were cast off fore and aft and the boat backed out in reverse into the deep blue sea. Normal maritime etiquette would have been to give three short blasts on the hooter but who cared? Nobody. Next stop Grand Harbour, Valletta but Victor Tabona wanted to show him a few of the sights before delivering his precious human cargo to the Christina O.

At about the same time the 222 bus to Kirkewwa was passing through Naxxar, then Mosta on its slow route north to St. Paul's Bay.

'Bruce do we go past that Gillieru place? Can we stop for a drink? It's hot!'

'No. We're taking the new by-pass. It was built a few years back. Probably with European money. The EU is very good at giving away other people's money. That's one of the reasons we got out. Listen, if you like I'll ask the driver if he can stop for one minute at the café at the head of the bay. It's been rebuilt since I first started coming here but they sell cold drinks.' He walked down to the driver with his request. He returned all smiles in seconds.

'No problem. He said he was needing a cigarette.'

'Nice guy.'

'I told you, everybody's nice in Malta. We're almost there. A Cisk or a Hop Leaf?'

'Neither. Get me a Kinnie. In fact make it two, I'm thirsty.'

McCandless just grinned. The lady was almost a local. And he hadn't even asked her yet.

Patrol boat No. 70 was rounding the south-east tip of the Island then started to turn left past the Port of Kalafrana with the cranes they had seen on final descent for landing a few hours earlier. The President was now on his second cold Cisk and removed his jacket and neck tie. He was all ears and eyes as Victor Tabona acted as tourist guide and bartender. The First Lady was already too hot and requested that she went into the much cooler cabin which was partly air-conditioned. Victor was in full flow and pointed to his left towards a huge sweeping bay past the container terminal.

'And that Mr President, is the famous Marsaxlokk Bay where the Bush-Gorbachev Summit took place over thirty years ago.'

'Ya don't say. Gee.' He'd read the files and although the talks had been hugely successful despite the physicality of it.

'The weather played a terrible role and almost scuppered the entire programme. But you know it's all clear for the next few days and you'll have a great time. Just an idea if I may, Mr President. You didn't have time to see the Blue Grotto but as it looks as if Sunday is going to be a free day so how about suggesting to President Zhang that the four of you take in a trip to the Blue Lagoon on Camino. I can arrange the necessary transportation. Great photo opportunities too. The bathing is just magical.'

'Yeah I saw it at a distance from the air. The lady on Air Traffic Control pointed out Comino to me. She was real helpful. I'd kinda like to meet her. Let's go for it. Cheers.'

'Sah-ha! And Victor opened another two cans of Cisk. Like his compatriot Alexandria Pisani he was already getting to like this place and he'd only been here a few hours.

The 222 bus ground its way slowly but surely up Xemxjia Hill. Since Bruce's last visit a thousand high rise apartments had been built on the hillside and by the number of small boats moored in the Bay a goodly proportion of residents were aquatically minded. Many more and you'd be able to walk across the whole Bay without getting your feet wet.

'How far is it Bruce. Are we nearly there?' She sounded like a kid in the back of a family car on a long journey.

'Nope. We have to go up some steep hills to the village of Mellieha then down some steep hairpin bends to the beach and then up again …'

'Jeez. I didn't realise Malta has so many hills.'

'The hilly terrain is all in the north of the Island but this is the only way to the ferry terminal. You'll love it when we get there. The views on the way are breathtaking.'

He was right. Alex had never seen such vistas of sun, sand and sea in her entire thirty-five year life. She just sipped on her can of Kinnie without saying a single word until the bus pulled up at the terminal. There were tourists everywhere and a ferry had just berthed on its return from Gozo, the front bow door gaping open and upwards like a giant whale as a stream of cars drove off onto dry land. Bruce bought 'round trip' tickets for them both and they rode the escalator up to the boarding gantry. A polished and prominent blue plaque read 'This terminal was partially funded by the European Union.'

'Bruce do think they have ever thought about building a tunnel to Go-Zo? Be kinda quicker wouldn't it? Or even a subway. Ya know, like the subway to Hoboken …Ha!'

'There you go again. Actually, there is serious talk of constructing a tunnel but the main problem is not the geology – it's the cost.'

'Well maybe those Euro guys will pay for it. And we both know who'll offer to build it and pay for it otherwise don't we?'

'Yes. Bloody China!'

Patrol boat No. 70 was making steady progress up the coast at a distance of about a mile from it to lend better views of the Island. The boat just maintained a steady ten knots and with almost no wind and swell the sea was dead calm. Victor pointed out the sights as they skirted up the coast. Delimara Point, St. Peter's Pool and the entrance to the long creek that was Marsascala. They both glanced skywards several times to watch planes heading south and then turning right on 'finals' to Luqa. This did not go unnoticed by the President.

'Boy, sure is a busy little airport you guys have here ...'

'Mr President, there's nothing little about it with respect. It is one of the Island's biggest assets that we inherited from the British, apart from the old dock facilities. We have two main runways both of which are used depending on the wind of course. You landed on the long one just to be safe. We don't get many Jumbos here.'

'You seem well informed on aviation, Victor.'

'Well you see we have a major problem with refugees fleeing from North Africa so we purchased several small but useful maritime patrol planes from your American Beech Company. Once in a while I'll take a trip as an observer just to keep up to speed with the overall situation. The EU has been of little or no assistance but with the help of friends and our own initiative we get by.'

'Jeez. I'd heard about this. If we can help more just ask our Chargé d'Affaires. In fact I'll see her at the reception party on the Maltese Falcon soon so I'll mention it to her. Georgette Fox is one feisty lady. Have you met yet?'

'No, Sir, I have not yet had the pleasure.'

'Great, well, look how about you come along too? Do you like wine?'

'Mr President, every Maltese person likes wine! Especially if it is Maltese wine. We are a proud and patriotic – just like you Americans. By the way I mentioned that my staff were arranging a treat for your flight crew. I thought they might like to go on a couple of those patrol flights I just talked about. They'll get a bird's eye view of the whole Maltese Archipelago.'

'They'll love to I'm sure. Just make sure the guys don't get too much of your beer – and your women!'

Two more cans of Cisk later the boat hugged the honeyed limestone and the entrance to Grand Harbour itself was in sight. With the stone mountain of Fort Ricasoli towering above them to their left No. 70 did a swift Port 90 and headed past the long harbour mole. Two minutes later and the course correction was repeated.

'On your right is Fort St. Elmo and ahead of us directly, Mr President, is your floating home for the next few days – the one and only Christina O. Isn't she just beautiful?'

The President nearly dropped the almost empty beer can. The can might not have dropped but his lower jaw sure did. About a dozen miles to the north-west another couple were getting off a boat, not onto one.

'Welcome to Gozo' shouted six taxi-drivers all at the same time.'

'Round the Island trip?'

'Somewhere nice for lunch?'

'Victoria?'

'Marsalforn?'

'The Inland Sea?'

'The Citadel?'

'Honey let's haggle with the drivers and get an all-day deal and take in the whole place shall we? How about this guy over here – the only one who's not shouting and touting?'

'Sure I'll ask him how much …' McCandless was too slow off the mark. Alex had spotted that the reason this driver was quiet was because he had just lit up a Pall Mall menthol cigarette and as quick as a flash Alex had seen the green and white pack disappear into his shirt breast pocket like he was trying to hide something. That's because he was. The deal was done at a hundred Euros for the whole day and they would stop for a nice lunch break. His name was Eddie. The car was a five seater white Fiat and was air-conditioned. It was almost noon and the sun at its highest and hottest – almost thirty-three degrees Celsius. The road climbed west out of the pretty little port of Mgarr towards Victoria, Gozo's administrative capital. They had barely gone half a mile before out of the blue Alex leant forward.

'Pull the car in Eddie you little asshole!'

'You feel sick? I can open the windows.'

'Just pull in please.'

So he did, with the two inside wheels on the semi-arid scrub and the offside wheels still in the road. The inside wheels crushed some wild aniseed which grows like wildfire in the Maltese countryside. Instantly the smell of Pernod filled the air which was accentuated by the heat.

'Eddie where did you get these?'

She slid her right hand into his shirt pocket and retrieved the pack of menthols.

'Who's been a naughty boy then? Aren't these now illegal under EU Rules?' Eddie looked a bit sheepish but decided to come clean. These guys were obviously tourists not plain-clothes police.

'My cousin, Paulo, he gets them from Sicily for me every month when he takes his boat there. Just for personal use you understand. I'm not a dealer.'

'I believe you Eddie. Thousands wouldn't. Now look we'll call it two hundred Euros if you throw in a sleeve of those Pall Malls. Deal?'

'Deal. You want one now?'

'Has the Pope got a balcony?'

President Kirk and his First Lady were thrilled beyond all expectations. He wasn't piped aboard like he was when he had recently visited the new destroyer the USS Zumwalt in Mayport, Florida. He was trying to remember why it had struck a chord with him when Victor Tabona had mentioned Fort St. Elmo. Of course – the ship was named after Admiral Elmo Zumwalt, one of America's most celebrated naval heroes. He wondered if the late Admiral had ever visited Fort St. Elmo during his lifetime's service to the world's biggest navy. Although there may have been no direct link the connection ticked another little box in the President's mind.

After being formally greeted by Captain Leonides he introduced his First Officer Peter Skelton to the President and Mrs Kirk. Skelton was tempted to use a Yorkshire greeting of 'Now then, hey up' but managed to keep to the formal 'How do you do, Mr President.' He would hopefully get the chance for an informal chat or two over the next few days as he had an idea that he wanted to run past him.

Two stewards ushered the Kirks to the Royale Suite two decks below the boat deck where their luggage already awaited them. Instantly they were transported to a floating Heaven. The brass portholes afforded a million dollar view of the Valletta battlements that made any movie-set look like a papier-maché mock-up. They were both enchanted beyond words.

The grand tour of Gozo delighted Alex with every next bend rounded. Every road seemed to lead to another church, honey-coloured village or stunning seascape. They stopped at a small seafood restaurant by the water's edge in Marsalforn in the north of the island. Eddie drove off to see his cousin Paulo for a coffee. Perhaps he was running low on menthols, having just traded away a whole carton.

For the first time Alex ate locally caught lampooki – baked with olives, tomatoes and almonds. The latter came from Sicily and together with California they were the world's two biggest suppliers. If the harvest failed in one it was up to the other to meet the demand – at a price of course. Maybe almonds should be added to the menthols in Paolo's manifest.

By the time Alex had finished lunch she had fallen in love again. This time with lampooki. It was a growing list. By late afternoon they had 'done Go-Zo' with the exception of the Inland Sea and the site where the Game of Thrones had been filmed. Alex would have loved a selfie of where Daenerys Targaryen had gotten married. As the ferry passed the Santa Marija Tower on the return leg to Malta she and Bruce stood on the port side deck and turned to speak to each other in almost synchronised unison.

'Shall we go back there again one day?'

39

Back in Grand Harbour all was well on the Christina O. The President and Mrs Kirk unpacked and for the first time the First Lady acknowledged that even she might have over-packed. With the Chinese President and Mrs Zhang being delayed at least a day she would not feel obliged to 'dress up' formally tonight for the first of the on-board dinners. In her own way she was quite relieved. Maybe she could just unwind with Nancy Kwok, the President's official interpreter.

'Honey I've put in a call to Georgette Fox our new Chargé d'Affaires here in Malta. She's invited to the wine tasting evening tomorrow on the Maltese Falcon but with arrangements being delayed I thought she could come on board for supper tonight too. OK with you?'

'Sure, Hun. I've heard she's a very feisty and interesting lady. But who will you be talking to with three women talking non-stop, you might not even get a look-in for once!'

'That's what I figured too so I'll while away the time with the Captain and that Robin Hood guy, Peter something.'

'Lemme guess you're going ashore to …'

'Nope. Staying on board. Victor Tabona's strict orders. Don't forget our own security guys are not here. They're at the new Embassy and … shit, it only just occurred to me that the briefcase with all the nuclear launch codes is also with Geister. But heck, the Chinese aren't going to start anything, are they? Not with their President here having a Pow-Wow or a Ying-Tong or whatever they call it in Pandaland.'

'That reminds me Honey – no indiscretions in front of the cameras. No jokes about slitty eyes. Don't forget how the Queen of England's late husband, the Duke of Edinburgh, embarrassed everybody when he got caught on camera.'

'Yeah, what a great guy though eh? Did you know that he and the Queen lived here for two years when he was in the Royal Navy? Yeah! He was Captain of a destroyer called the Magpie or the Quail or sump'n like that.'

'Yeah I read that too. And did you know that the Maltese Directorate of Restorations was spending a lot of time and money turning their old house into a museum?'

'I didn't know that, but Victor, the police guy, did tell me that on the day of his funeral at Windsor Castle, the ancient saluting battery someplace near here gave him a nine gun salute at twelve noon. One salute for every decade of his life. That's what I call class. No chance I'll get anything like that for sure.'

'You can say that again. But you never know you might get a carrier named after you – about twenty years after you're dead.'

'That's just given me an idea. Thanks, honey.'

The sun was going down and was definitely over the yardarm. Mario the cab driver turned up on time at the ferry terminal. Alex gave the orders.

'Take us home to Valletta please Mario.' And she didn't even realise what she'd said.

'Sure thing, but do you fancy a cooling drink on the way back? There's a nice little bar called the Apple's Eye at a place called Golden Bay. It's not too much of a detour and you can watch the orange ball of sunshine sink into the sea directly ahead of you.'

'Go for it Mario. Two Cisks and one Campari soda coming up.'

They followed the road through Mellieha and down Xemxija hill past the cafe they had stopped for refreshments earlier in the day. Then instead of picking up the by-pass road they turned right and followed the sign to Golden Bay and Manikata. The orange sun was setting directly in front of them and in fifteen minutes time would disappear towards Tunisia. On the outside terrace and facing due west they toasted a 'perfect day.'

The ancient battlements of Valletta turned from honey to gold to sable and an aura of calm descended on Grand Harbour. Lights twinkled on moored vessels and at intervals along the fortifications that had witnessed history like no other. Soon the world would be watching but until the Chinese arrived, formalities would be kept to a minimum. Georgette Fox arrived shortly after sundown and two crew members had been detailed to take the Christina O's tender to pick her up from a jetty in Senglea just around the promontory. Curiously she was carrying a portable cooler of the kind you might take on a family picnic. Once on board the Christina O she asked for a steward to attend.

'OK see these? Eight bottles of wine – four white and four red. Please place the white wines in a refrigerator and keep the reds at room temperature. Take care please. They are very special.'

'Yes ma'am. I'll see to it.'

Five minutes later and a Lebanese, a Chinese and an American lady were sitting outside on the deck overlooking the pool which reflected a mosaic floor in the pattern of a dancing bull. It could be electrically raised to form a dance floor when required. There would be no dancing tonight – just inane chatter about fashion, furnishings and facials.

Weren't girls just the same the world over? The chef Marco Pierre Marceau from Geneva came up on deck to introduce himself and his new assistant, Angelique de la Roche.

'Good evening ladies. Can we please take your orders for dinner tonight? We are at your service and we pride ourselves on being able to provide almost anything you like.'

'Oh really, wow!' exclaimed the First Lady. 'Anything?'

'Well almost anything but we 'av run out of pangolins so pangolin pancakes are out. But as ze Chinese people are not 'ere yet anyway ...'

Everybody laughed, even Nancy Kwok who had been accustomed to a Western diet for twenty years since becoming a naturalised US Citizen. She decided to match Pierre's humour.

'Will we be having Peking duck when the Chinese arrive? Or is it called Beijing duck now.'

'Ha! To me canard is canard wherever it comes from. Would you like that this evening? Perhaps as an entrée? It is no problem.' They all agreed and smiled.

'And for a main course can I suggest a filet mignon with asparagus tips and Maltese pommes de terre? They are just amazing and I sent for a supply as soon as we moored a few hours ago. And for dessert I am 'appy to offer you fruita fresca a la Mediterranean – Chardonnay grapes from France, peaches from Sicily and some locally-sourced figs which were also obtained since arriving.'

The ladies clapped politely in anticipation of the feast to come.

'And for wine may I suggest a ...' Georgette Fox interrupted him.

'I've brought the wine from my own collection. Can you please serve us a bottle of the white, chilled as cold as you can get it and the red at room temperature.'

'Of course mesdames. Angelique will call you to the dining room in approximately one hour. In the meantime a steward will attend to your every need. Bon appétit!' Two decks down in Arry's Bar, the atmosphere was a little different.

President Kirk had read-up about the famous 'Arry's Bar on board, named of course after its founder the Greek shipping magnate Aristotle Onassis. The covers on the bar stools were made from whales' foreskins and the de-facto leader of the Free World just couldn't wait to emulate JFK and order his own favourite tipple from the bartender. How ironic he thought that the Kennedy clan had introduced Prohibition and here he was on JFK's old barstool! A good job also that these stool covers had been made before the ban on whaling. It wasn't long before Victor Tabona joined them as he wanted to run a few security related ideas past the President. With tomorrow being an unexpected free day, not to mention the Sunday, he wanted to make sure that the President was both entertained and protected.

The sight of the American President, a Maltese policeman, a Greek captain and a Yorkshireman First Officer drinking and singing in a ship's bar would have obtained a zillion hits on any social media platform. Thank goodness nobody took any photos but even if they had the accusations of 'it's fake news or it's photo-shopped' would have echoed round the world in seconds. But this was real and Peter Skelton's idea that the President should forego having a carrier named after him and instead name it Bonhomme Richard hit home hard. The current Bonhomme Richard had recently been almost destroyed by a fire when alongside in San Diego and in all probability would never sail again. Skelton further suggested that when completed, its shakedown cruise should be to the Yorkshire Coast where its namesake had gained notoriety in the Battle of Flamborough Head in 1779. The wreck had never been found following the battle but perhaps a ceremony of some kind could take place in the area where it was believed to have sunk. The President took mental notes and was determined to speak to the Secretary of the Navy on his return to DC. What a great idea and a chance to visit Yorkshire too. If he won a second term.

After several rounds of drinks and amid much mirth it was suggested by the bartender that each of the four men sang a song representing where each of them came from. With glasses recharged to provide Dutch courage the President went first and gave a creditable rendition of 'What did Della Wear?' immortalised by Perry Como. What price a video of that on YouTube thought the bartender?

Captain Leonides just about got away with singing his version of 'Who pays the Ferryman?' composed by Yannis Markopoulos but as he sang the words in Greek the others didn't know if he got the lyrics correct or not. What if he had? So what! The moral of the song was that if you put a gold coin in the mouth of a deceased person prior to cremation then the coin could be used to pay the ferryman to take him to Hades. More drinks were poured. Then it was Victor Tabona's turn. He chose 'Viva Malta' a popular tune sung by Freddie Portelli which he sang in Maltese of course. A polite round of applause followed. More drinks. And then it was Skelton's turn. They should have known that decorum was about to be abandoned when he removed his trousers and stood up on his barstool. Reaching for his iPhone Skelton found a version of 'On Ilkley Moor Baht'at' and sang along with gusto to all eight verses of it. He then sat down before he fell down. What on earth would the whale have thought about somebody standing on his foreskin and singing all that? Captain Leonides was used to it. He often called Skelton down to the Bar if the guests were short of a little entertainment. More drinks. It was midnight by the time the all-male merriment had ended. The President slunk off to the Royale Suite and was relieved to see that the First Lady was nicely asleep. Boy, had he had a good time or what?! Tomorrow was another day. Or was it today already?

40

Fortunately for the New China News Agency there were no more delays to the flight plans of the Ilyushin-76s bearing the President and Chairman of the People's Republic. At 6pm China time the main headline was:

> 'The President and First Lady have arrived in the historic Island of Malta for bi-lateral talks with America's President Kirk. International trade and the scaling down of tension in our Southern Seas are the main items to be discussed. Patriotic naval forces are on hand to lend assistance to the President in the event of any emergency and ...'

More bollox. They hadn't actually arrived yet but they soon would do. Satellite surveillance and British and American submarines had established beyond any doubt that PLAN vessels, above or below the surface, were no nearer than the Red Sea. How appropriate perhaps. There was only one submarine anywhere near the central Mediterranean in the vicinity of Malta and that was Australian. HMAS Sheean was in transit from Suez to the French naval base of Toulon and she was on a liaison visit following the announcement that Australia's next Attack Class of submarine was to be based on the French Barracuda design. Would she pop into Grand Harbour for a goodwill visit in a week's time after her business in France was complete?

One hundred miles almost due south of Malta, Red Dragon One had just entered the zone controlled by Malta ATC. The earphones crackled to life for the Chinese flight crew. All had gone according to plan years earlier on the evacuation flights and they had been sorry that a diversion to the sunshine island of Malta had not been required. A few days leave in the sunshine would be most welcome on this occasion and the crew on Red Dragon Two were similarly anticipating some hospitality from their compatriots at the Embassy. With good joss the Summit talks would drag on for days. If only they knew.

Denise Grech was once again on duty for another memorable day in her young life. She worked a rota of 'four days on four days off' and this was day four. Tomorrow she would go swimming with friends and family at Delimara which was said to be the clearest water in the Archipelago – after the Blue Lagoon of course. Nothing in the whole world could rival that. She only wished that the whole of her homeland could be turned into a huge marine national park and that future visitors would be attracted to the idyll of preserving nature as well as enjoying the wines and the sunshine. One day maybe, one day.

'Red Dragon One this is Malta ATC. Do you copy?'

'This is Red Dragon One. We copy. I take it we are clear to land on runway 31? Please confirm.'

'Negative Red Dragon One. The wind has changed and strengthened and is now ten knots sustained gusting to fifteen from the south-west. You are therefore cleared to land from the north-east on runway 24. Do you copy?'

'Thank you Malta. Understood 24.'

It was a hot wind blowing in from the Sahara. Feng-shui advocates would say it was dragons' breath and nothing to do with a desert.

Similar instructions were issued to Red Dragon Two within five minutes. It was fortunate that neither pilot had ever seen or even heard of the Game of Thrones – lest they wanted to find their mother, Daenerys Targaryen the Dragon Queen, in the north-east of Gozo. It had been many decades since there was an air strip on Gozo, and biplanes and Spitfires had been the order of the day, not large transports or civilian airliners.

The winds had changed necessitating a change of intended runway but it had the added advantage of being able to tuck the two Chinese Ilyushins away in the military section of the airport and they would never actually be seen from the main passenger terminal. Heard but not seen in this case. It would also assist Victor Tabona's security arrangements in that he could protect three assets at the same time.

The captain of Red Dragon One lined up the plane on the glide path ten miles out and invited President Zhang to join him on the flight deck which spared him the agony of crouching in the 'bomb-bay' which had resulted in so much discomfort. His back still hurt so the fairly comfortable jump-seat behind the First Officer would afford him a superb view of the whole of Grand Harbour.

Throttling back to two hundred kilometres an hour and selecting maximum flaps the Il-76 should land comfortably on the fairly short runway which was only used when the wind was from the south-west quarter. Sitting on the starboard right-hand side of the plane, the President marvelled at the view before him. He saw the breakwaters of Grand Harbour first and then the brilliant white flash of the Christina O at her moorings parallel to the battlements. Ten seconds later and then he spotted what he was looking for – the real reason Malta was hopefully to become the next addition to the String of Pearls. The Red Dock. He knew nothing about the Great Siege, La Valette or the George Cross. All the Communist Party of China wanted was the Dock and then, in time, they would achieve what Suleiman the Magnificent, Napoleon, Hitler and Mussolini had failed to do. And all without firing a shot.

The Ilyushin's multiple undercarriage wheels hit the runway on the centreline and the plane slowed to twenty kilometres per hour within just over a kilometre.

'Red Dragon One, Merhba Ta' Malta, welcome to Malta. Please follow the security vehicle to your designated parking stand.'

As the plane followed the same path to taxi to within a hundred metres of Air Force One the Chinese President resumed his normal seat alongside his First Lady. Had he stayed on the flight deck and been as observant as his Captain he would have noticed a small tri-jet in red, white and blue colours, the red kangaroo in the centre of the Air Force roundels betraying its ownership and nationality. Five minutes later and Red Dragon Two landed and joined its sister on the apron, parking nose to nose with just a few metres separating them. Both Captains couldn't resist speaking to each other via VHF radio.

'It's just like old times, comrade! Remember the time we were both operating out of that base in Western Australia, you know, when we were looking for the wreckage of MH-370. Somewhere near Perth wasn't it?'

'I do indeed comrade. Sad days. I remember the souvenir photograph of several of the planes involved in the search over many days. Australian planes too. Isn't that a similar plane over there on the perimeter? Did you see it? Perhaps the over-fed oafs from the land they call Down Under are here for recreation?'

'Or maybe they are just lost a long way from home.'

'Ha ha! Anyway we'll soon be in the embassy here drinking Tsing-Tao beer from Guangdong Province. I've heard on the grape vine that Tsing-Tao is going to take over a Maltese brewery soon so they can brew our Patriotic Ale under licence.'

Somebody should have told him that rice wine grapevines don't work in Malta.

41

Victor Tabona was relieved that the Chinese delegation had finally arrived in one piece even if two planes had arrived and not one as he had previously expected. The two flight crews were taken by Malta Police transport to the Chinese embassy in St. Julian's. Once there they could do what the hell they liked. They weren't his responsibility. But the President, his First Lady and his interpreter certainly were. He would only ever admit to himself that he cared marginally less for the Chinese President's welfare than his US counterpart. But in the public eye he would be seen to be doing his duty.

He had heard that President Zhang liked boats and enjoyed a swim. This augured well for the trip to the Blue Lagoon he had in mind for tomorrow. For security reasons the area was declared 'off limits' to all pleasure craft for twenty-four hours starting at midnight tonight. If he'd had the time he would have declared the whole of Comino Island a 'No Go Zone' as well but he didn't want to be seen to be unfair to the many locals and visitors alike who had booked into the one available hotel on the island which was less than four square kilometres in total. He had however, under pressure from Al Geister, put certain measures in place in case of accidents. Two helicopters from the Armed Forces of Malta were to be on the ground on Comino carrying supplies of the US President's blood group and presumably the 'nuclear briefcase' much to Victor's amusement. Extra supplies of Cisk lager might have been more appropriate but he would keep that little bit of information to himself – along with the President's alcohol fuelled penchant for singing.

It being the weekend and the patrolling of Maltese territorial waters of paramount concern, Patrol Boat No. 70 was not available. Nor were No's 68 and 69. Roll on the day when the big new boat, No.71 arrived from the Italian builders Vittoria. It would be a quantum leap in capability. The EU had paid for it too as part of their 'southern surveillance budget' and it was seen by many as a 'sorry we haven't been of much help in the past' form of apology.

The problem of the mode of transportation to the Christina O was unexpectedly solved for him when the Chinese interpreter asked if formalities and protocol could be kept to a minimum today. The President needed rest and requested some painkillers for his back which was causing increasing discomfort. Victor was happy to comply and immediately detailed an unmarked police car to transport President and Mrs Zhang and the interpreter to Senglea jetty where the Christina O's tender would meet them and take them to his floating hotel for the next few days. The considerable amount of luggage would follow in the police van that had performed the same function for President Kirk a day earlier.

It was almost exactly 1 pm when the tender conveying the President gently berthed at the foot of the steps lowered to the port side of the Christina O. Captain Leonides and First Officer Skelton stood smartly to attention on the deck. A steward sensed that Zhang was in discomfort and immediately offered an arm for the last two steps. It was much appreciated and the interpreter conveyed his sincere thanks. Leonides snapped a crisp salute with a 'welcome aboard Mr President' as once again the Mandarin and English bi-lingual interpreter performed her job to perfection. At that precise instant the saluting gun at the Upper Barrakka Gardens a half a mile distant thundered out their one thousand decibels. Zhang wheeled round just in time to see the huge volume of smoke from the ancient cannon but, sound travelling much slower than light, the orange flash had long since disappeared into infinity. Thinking that the salute was for him Zhang was very impressed and asked for his personal thanks be conveyed to the battery commander.

Nobody had the heart to tell him that the gun was sounded every day at this time. Nor had anyone the heart, or the courage, to tell him that the Queen of England's late husband had received nine and not one salutations.

Across the harbour in a bar overlooking the whole scene Victor Tabona smiled sweetly to himself as he downed a cool Hop Leaf. He'd got the timing about right. He just hoped that everything else went according to plan. Some hope.

He had detailed his Deputy and others to escort and protect President Kirk for the day's sightseeing that he had requested. Geister & Co. weren't involved as along with the flight crew of Air Force One they were guests of the Armed Forces of Malta who took them up in the Beechcraft Maritime Patrol Aircraft followed by lunch in the Officers' Mess. But tomorrow would be another matter as if anything untoward was going to happen to the President it would be Murphy's Law that it happened away from dry land. Today they would all relax. In the south-eastern part of the Island the US President was on the terrace of the Duncan Hotel in Marsaxlokk enjoying his first ever meal of timpana and

French fries. Walter Bezzina had been tipped off to expect important visitors but this was absolutely mind-blowing. He would have words with 'Admiral McCandless' at a later date. It was perhaps just as well that Geister & Co. were absent as the chance of a trip around the Bay on one of the many colourful dghajsas moored nearby would have been a 'no-no.' Not fancying juggling with two crossed-over oars he declined the offer to 'have a go' despite the wonderful photo-opportunity it afforded. He did however get a 'selfie' of him and the First Lady at sea in the area of the Bush-Gorbachev Summit which he thought would make a great addition to his portfolio – particularly when it came to thinking about his re-election campaign.

By late afternoon they were safely back on board the Christina O for introductory afternoon tea with President and Madam Zhang. The meeting, the first between the two leaders, went very well indeed. Within an hour photographs were released for showing on lunchtime news broadcasts in the US and late night news bulletins on State TV in Beijing.

The New China News Agency reported that President Zhang had received an honorary and ancient gun salute on arrival and pointed out that the American President had received no such accolade. Some things never change. Not yet anyway.

After tea there was time for a short rest and then a change of clothes for the social evening on board the Maltese Falcon. Everybody wanted to look their best and enjoy a convivial evening of chatter and wines. The politics could wait until the Monday, the first real working day of the Summit. Two hours later and the party of six was embarked on the Tender to Christina O for the five-minute journey to the steps beneath Fort Saint Angelo. Travelling at little more than walking pace this little piece of Italian boat building excellence conveyed the two most powerful men in the world across the blue waters which shimmered mirror-blue in the evening sunshine.

Already aboard were Prime Minister Edward Borg Vella and his wife, Alex Pisani, Bruce McCandless, Martin Mifsud, the Australian Consul and his wife, Georgette Fox and representatives from no less than eight Maltese and Gozitan vineyards. All webcams were in place, and diplomatic niceties apart, this was going to be a worldwide exposition for the Maltese wine industry that the major wine houses of the world would give their eye teeth to have taken part in. Not to mention an awful lot of Wonga. If only they knew.

42

This was by far and away the most important speech of the Maltese Prime Minister's life and, boy, did he know it! He had his own elections coming up soon and a good performance tonight would boost his own poll ratings as well as promote Malta on the world stage. For decades Maltese politics had been riven with bitter rivalries, division and rancour. To outsiders it was simply unfathomable that such a small but beautiful country in the very centre of the cradle of civilisation, in the bluest Sea on Earth, could ever suffer from such internecine desecration. This was his chance to look and act like a true statesman. He didn't waste it.

'Good evening, Ladies and Gentlemen.'

He had practised the speech in his study at home and took advice from his wife who had actually spoken on far more similar occasions than her husband in her capacity as a Charity Patron. 'Keep your head up and look the two main dignitaries in the eye from time to time. Speak in short sentences. Keep it simple and above all make sure you allow time in between sentences for the Chinese interpreter to keep pace with you.' So he did.

'On behalf of the Maltese People may I formally welcome you, Mr President, and you, Mr President, to our Island nation.'

He nodded politely to both. They were seated opposite each other either side of a long refectory style table specially set up for tonight's event. Each had their interpreter to their immediate right. There had been a last minute change of seating plan when they were tipped off that President Zhang was slightly deaf in his left ear. It was important that both Presidents felt equally at home.

He deliberately didn't mention either of them by name lest he seemed to favour one of them by announcing his name first. The American probably didn't give a monkey's toss but the Chinaman would have lost face by coming 'second' as it were. Around the world millions were watching live and no less than four webcams were doing their job unseen and unheard. Vella continued.

'Over three decades ago Malta played host to the very successful Summit between Messrs. Bush and Gorbachev.' Pause.

'Unofficially it marked the end of the Cold War and the whole world breathed a collective sigh of relief.' Pause.

'It is with those happy days in mind that I decided to invite you both to our Island to enable you to talk, not as adversaries, but as political equals.' Pause.

'Your serious inter-Government discussions do not commence until Monday. Tonight is an opportunity to relax and enjoy our hospitality on this splendid yacht named after the Humphrey Bogart movie of the same name.' Big pause whilst the Chinese interpreter got her head around it. Suddenly Zhang burst into staccato Mandarin and grinned from ear to ear. She translated, suppressing her own smile.

'The President says he is delighted to be here and it is fortunate that the venue was not in Casablanca, another Bogart movie.'

There was much laughter all round and a polite ripple of applause. Prime Minister Vella beamed. It was a great start to the evening.

'To entertain you this evening we are going to taste a variety of wines from the Maltese Islands but before we do I understand that the American Chargé d'Affaires, Georgette Fox, would like to say a few words. Mrs Fox.'

'Thank you, Prime Minister. As some of you know I am a personal member of the United Nations. The country of my birth, the Lebanon, has been devastated by strife and war for decades. Nobody knows more than I the grief and distress that it brings.' Pause. All eyes were on her.

'So, in my own way, I wish to make a small but I hope meaningful contribution to this evening's proceedings.' She glanced towards two wine waiters each of whom held two bottles of wine, one red one white. They walked down both sides of the long table until every person received a modest measure.

'This wine is from the Château Mussar vineyards in the Bekka Valley, Eastern Lebanon. They have been growing wine there for almost a thousand years – in fact since the Crusades.' Ever the peace-keeper, she had checked in advance that no Muslims would be present to take offence, at the alcohol or the mere mention of Crusades.

'I would like to offer a toast for the success of the Summit. There is a word in my mother-tongue that has no direct translation. That word is *daimee* and roughly speaking it means *may it always be as nice.'*

Everybody clinked glasses with their immediate neighbours and everybody had a go at pronouncing the word *daimee* correctly. Vella was delighted he had invited Georgette along. Already she had solved the problem as to whether to have the welcome toast in English or Mandarin.

He didn't expect it to be in Arabic though. What on earth would La Valette have thought of that? He continued.

'I think I have said enough and with one word Mrs Fox has captured the spirit of the evening.' She interrupted him.

'Thank you, Prime Minister, but I have three more words to say, if I may?' Vella nodded.

'In vino veritas. In wine there is truth.'

Everybody nodded and raised their glasses once again.

'I would now like to hand over proceedings to Mr Martin Mifsud, the Secretary of the Maltese Guild of Sommeliers. Thank you. Grazzi haffna.'

He was determined to get at least two words of Maltese into his short speech. He sat down to polite applause. Had he done enough? Probably. Martin Mifsud adjusted his black bow-tie and walked slowly to the microphone which was fixed to the top of a small lectern set back from the main throng. It was time to hit the 'Buy and Try Maltese Wine' button. He didn't disappoint.

'Firstly we are going to taste the selection of red wines. Then we shall have a break of approximately half an hour when a finger buffet will be provided courtesy of a local caterer called Jimmy's Kitchen.' The buffet was free on condition he mentioned the sponsor's name to the world. Out of sight on the jetty the specialist vehicle conveying chilled food had arrived and staff were busy unloading it and carrying boxes and plates of the finest Mediterranean foods. The phrase 'finger buffet' seemed to cause the Chinese interpreter some consternation. Did he mean fish fingers? She couldn't think of any other edible fingers.

'The first wine for you to taste is a Merlot from the Marsovin winery. This is a vintage from three years ago which was particularly high in the fullness of its fruity bouquet – just swirl it around the glass like this and smell all those summer fruits …'

'The second wine is a Cabernet Sauvignon from the Delicata Winery, the most awarded in the Island.'

There followed much slurping and quaffing around the table as everybody relaxed. With every successive wine there seemed to be a glass raised across the table between the two Presidents and both, via their interpreters, learned to say 'cheers' in each other's language. They finally came to the sixth and final red wine.

'And before we break for the buffet I would like to introduce you to Miss Claudia Camilleri representing the Ambrosia Winery of Gozo.' He stood politely to one side as a stunning thirty-something beauty walked serenely to the lectern, her long jet-black locks cascading almost a metre down the centre of her back accentuated by the cream of her perfectly fitting Armani jacket. Alex noticed McCandless's eyes following her every elegant step. She was the epitome of Vogue. Surely the lady had been hired from a model agency for the occasion. No way would she be getting red wine stains in a bottling plant.

'Don't get any ideas, Bruce. The lady's off limits.' Claudia composed herself before the microphone and began.

'Mr Presidents, ladies and gentlemen. This last red wine of the evening is very special. It is the St. Jean Syrah 2016 from Ambrosia and possibly the finest vintage we have ever produced. Perfection is the word. Before I make a presentation to President Zhang I would like you all to sample it.'

The small measures reflected the scarcity of the vintage. It was simply sensational and everybody beamed. What a finale for the reds. But the gorgeous Claudia hadn't finished.

'Could I now invite President Zhang to join me here for a few moments please?' The interpreter whispered into his right ear.

'She wants you to go up to the lectern. I'll follow you.' So up they went.

'Mr President, I understand that in Chinese folklore the number eight is considered to be a lucky number. On behalf of Ambrosia Winery I would like to present Bottle Number 888 from the total of only 1,680 bottles made that year.'

President Zhang was absolutely bowled over. He wasn't expecting this. He stretched out his right hand expecting her to shake it softly. Instead she quickly kissed him on both cheeks. Madam Zhang was furious. He was openly flirting with her. She quickly sat in his vacant chair so that she could talk with the interpreter instead. She had suspected for some time that he had been spending too much time with Comrade Won-Gah and she knew all about his indiscretions. She made a mental note to have a quiet word with the two female members of the politburo and ask them to keep an eye on him. Zhang responded to the gesture.

'Thank you so much for my gift. I will keep it for a special occasion – perhaps my next birthday or a special celebration.'

The tasting of the St. Jean Syrah brought the red wines to a close and everybody made a beeline for the buffet which looked exquisite. Everybody that is except President Zhang who dashed to the Australian Consul and his wife. His own interpreter had gone to the "Ladies" so her place was taken by Nancy Kwok to make sure the conversation went smoothly. He knew that the Australians were keen to offer assistance to the Chinese wine industry which was still in its infancy. That wasn't all they talked about and when a hand bell was rung to announce that the tastings were about to resume he was irked to see that his wife had pinched his seat. Oh well 'neffer mine' as they say in China. He would just slurp on the whites and keep smiling. Nancy Kwok had just told him quietly and confidentially that Claudia Camilleri had invited him to a private visit of the Ambrosia Estate if time allowed after the Summit talks had finished. He resolved to make sure there would be time. His eyes had wandered too and he couldn't help but notice the size of Claudia's water melons as opposed to his wife's lychees. By all the Gods, this was going to be a much more pleasant Summit than he could ever have imagined.

Martin Mifsud resumed his place at the lectern and announced that the tasting of white wines would now begin.

'The first white wine is a Sauvignon blanc from Mistra Bay in the north of the Island. We hope that one day it will be as famous as its cousin Cloudy Bay from New Zealand. To our guests from overseas I would say be careful if you order a New Zealand white with your dinner because here in Malta a New Zealand White is a variety of rabbit that we breed for the table. There was much laughter from everyone except the hapless Zhang who was now without an interpreter. Whether it was the wine or his libido he simply couldn't take his beady eyes off Claudia's melons. They didn't grow that big in Beijing, that's for sure.

Four more 'whites' followed, and Martin Mifsud thanked everybody for coming. What a fabulous night it had been for Malta's wine industry. Prime Minister Vella had one more small task to perform. He went to the lectern and made sure a webcam was pointing his way.

'President Zhang I understand that in China it is the custom to bring social gatherings to a close with the offering of an orange to all guests.' He nodded to a waiter who bore a crystal bowl of the finest oranges Malta could produce.

'Mr President please accept the first one in your honour.' The waiter moved forward and once again Zhang beamed like a full moon. Vella hadn't quite finished.

'You might be interested to know that the Queen of England believes that Maltese oranges are the finest in the world and a box is sent to her every year from the gardens in Lija. As we speak a bowl is being left in the Presidential Suite on board the Christina O for your enjoyment.'

As the evening came to a close Alex whispered in Bruce's ear.

'Is that true about the Queen or did that Vella guy just make that up?'

'I believe it's true.'

'Wow. If you lived here would you send a box of oranges to me in Maryland every year?'

McCandless just smiled. Maybe he wouldn't have to.

43

The following morning breakfasts were served in the two main suites and conveyed on trolleys by two members of staff. Anqelique took the pre-ordered meals to the Presidential Suite. Madam Zhang had ordered fresh fruits to hopefully include the local figs which were simply unobtainable in China. Prepared by Angelique herself they had been sliced in half and drizzled with prickly pear liqueur, another local delicacy. The immersion course in Mandarin at Fort Meade afforded Angelique just enough to get by with everyday pleasantries and and basic chit-chat concerning food. She was, after all, the designated second chef on board and so far she had got away with it.

'Madam Zhang, the figs are simply delicious. Please try one.'

'She ate one, then another and then a third one.'

'I think I had better get some more packed up for you in the picnic that you're taking to Comino and the Blue Lagoon. Would you like that?'

The smile and the successive nods were exactly the answer she wanted. More figs with extra liqueur. In fact a lot more liqueur. The President's fried eggs in the American 'over easy' style were exactly as he would have wished. If only he could get those at home. The way his wife was treating him these days he would be lucky to get a bowl of congee and a glass of green tea. He had sent an email to comrade Won-Gah late the previous evening after the wine tasting which he will have seen in his in-box as soon as he opened his iPad the following morning, China time. All the necessary financial transactions had been done.

Shortly after ten o'clock a privately owned cabin cruiser tied up at the steps on the port beam of the Christina O. The forty-foot Fairline cabin cruiser named 'Dash' belonged to an expatriate Briton who was a mate of Victor Tabona's. It was normally berthed in Msida Creek opposite the stunningly beautiful St. Joseph's Church. With its sleek lines and blue and white hull it blended in well with a dozen others of similar appearance. It was also one of the fastest boats in Malta, which was useful for activities other than fishing trips and jaunts to Delimara with the family on summer Sundays. When you cranked up the two contra-rotating Volvo Penta engines a sustained speed of fifty knots was not out of the question, assuming good weather conditions. The wind was still from the south-west so they would be in fairly calm waters travelling up the east coast of the Island. That aircraft were still landing on runway 24 gave credence to the fact that those pesky Saharan gusts were still a problem.

Passengers and picnics were loaded aboard as well as the chilled hampers with chicken, Cisk and all the wonders a Swiss chef could cobble together. Christina O's crew could now relax and then start to plan the menus for the dinner that evening.

Himself a qualified helmsman and holder of a 'Day Skippers Licence' Tabona took the helm of the Fairline Squadron himself. They would be safely home to Grand Harbour long before sundown. He steered Dash out between the breakwaters and once again took on the mantle of tour guide as he vectored north-west past Dragut Point, the only place-name in Malta named after a Turk. It was the one sop to the Moslems that had tried and failed to invade them in 1565. Apart from building them a cemetery of course for their war losses. He took the two Presidents up to the 'flying bridge' to get a better view. There was only room for Kirk's interpreter but in any event the Chinese lady had accompanied Madam Zhang to the heads at the for'ard end of the boat. Despite having been at sea for only ten minutes she was already feeling more than a little queasy. Maybe she had overdosed on those delicious figs. Her husband didn't mind. He was enjoying himself no end and despite the early hour was already on his second Cisk. He much preferred it to Tsing-Tao and he hoped to all the Gods that the intended takeover didn't happen. Tabona kept up the spiel as he brought Dash up onto the plane and pushed the speed up to forty knots. The twin contra-rotating Volvo Penta engines purred like tigers over a recent kill.

'And you see all those tall ugly blocks of flats on the left over there? Most of them are empty. They were bought by Russians under a 'cash for passport' scam that my Department is still investigating. Zhang's ears pricked up a tad as he asked Nancy Kwok to clarify that last bit. How interesting. So you could buy your way here? It would surely beat the Spratly Islands. No typhoons here either. Just hot winds from the Sahara. More hot winds, more cold Cisk. Simple.

44

Mario and his taxi had taken them from Fort Saint Angelo back to Valletta and they had missed the last ferry back to to Lascaris Wharf anyway. He dropped them off at the Triton fountain which was bathed in pastel lighting which changed shade every few minutes like an artist's palette caught in the moonlight. It was magical. The short walk back to the hotel was made in total silence. They both knew what they wanted to say but somehow neither had the courage to actually say it. With a head and belly full of wine this probably wasn't the time to say anything of meaning. It would have to wait. Their love-making that night was more spiritual than physical and when Alex fell asleep Bruce just gazed upon her beauty. Before he too fell asleep he finally decided what he was going to do. He would tell her everything. Well, almost everything, anyway.

Their late, lazy breakfast was almost over and by the time they had finished Dash was powering her way past Salina Bay and heading for Comino.

'Bruce, you do realise that our time here is coming to an end, don't you?'

She reached across the table and laid her hand on his, her watery eyes bringing back memories of their first dinner in London when she had reminisced about her Grandfather Pisani, the Illustrious and how she had got her names. She was still no nearer tracing her family connections than the day they had arrived. And when was that anyway? A week ago? A lifetime ago? She was in a Maltese, Mesozoic time machine where 'tempus fugit' meant absolutely nothing. It was now or never.

'Bruce, can we stay here together? You know, make a new life? I need to know how you feel and …'

'You gorgeous girl. Of course we can. I just didn't know how to ask you. And I was scared in case you said no.'

'You scared? I can't imagine you being scared of anyone. Nobody in this whole world would faze you, believe me.'

'Only one person. A part-Maltese American girl.'

They both had watery eyes and just stared, looking as if they wanted to say more, but couldn't find the words. Alex broke the silence.

'Bruce, what the hell do we tell Winchester? He'll think we've gone mad with sunstroke, won't he?'

McCandless thought back to the original memo from Ralph Winchester. 'Have fun' he'd said. Did he mean have a great time or was he playing International Cupid?

'Alex, I can quit now. Officially this mission doesn't exist. In any case we've done what we were asked to do. Haven't we? Or is there something you know that I don't? '

'Bruce, I'm thirty-five and single in a job that I don't think has much future – at least not for me. I'm sure I'm expendable in Winchester's eyes. I'd love to see my staff file. But if we stay here what the heck are we gonna do for money? My pay-checks would dry up in weeks. I can sell my small apartment in Baltimore sure. It would raise maybe two hundred grand, no more. And you?'

'Well I have my Navy pension topped up a tad by the two boring years in Cheltenham. My faux-Georgian house in Cheltenham would raise a half a million …'

'So at the current rate of exchange that would total about three quarters of a million Euros. We could buy a lovely house in St. Paul's Bay, stick what's left in the bank and live off your pension in the sunshine. We can buy a boat, go fishing and maybe buy some small fields in Mistra just over the hill from Xemxjia and plant some vines. Hey yeah, we could too! I was talking to that guy last night from Mistra Bay Winery and he says they're looking for outside investors and me 'n' you could have a ball, Bruce, and just be happy together.'

Her eyes turned into Bombay Sapphire once again as she waited for some reaction. It seemed to her like her whole future was to be decided in the next few seconds.

'Alex, darling, I think I've got a better idea.'

'You have? What?'

'Let's open a new bar cum restaurant right here in Valletta and call it the Ohio Lounge. Like you said it could make a small fortune.'

'Yeah but I didn't mean us, I just meant in general, you know.'

'But why not us? We can recruit young local staff as chefs and waiters. Look how well all those guys did last night. It seems to me that this country's youngsters are amazing and Malta is fast gaining a reputation in the culinary field and they just oozed hospitality, didn't they? Well didn't they?'

'Bruce, there's just one problem. Where do we set one up and how do we pay for it?'

'Well there are suitable premises right opposite the Caffe Cordina in Republic Street. Didn't you see the 'For Sale by public auction' billboard?'

'No, I can't say I did. How big is it?'

'Big enough, that's for sure, on at least two levels. Enough space for a bar downstairs for casual drinkers and a smart restaurant upstairs. And a nice model of the Ohio itself on display in the window. Like you said we can invite dignitaries from the State of Ohio. It's highly unlikely that there are any surviving crew still alive but hey, maybe we can try and trace any descendants of the Master, Captain Mason. Another idea too – one of the very first 'super yachts' ever built ended up here in Malta as the MV Star of Malta. But it was built in Boston, Massachusetts to the order of a rich guy in Cincinnati. His name was Julius Fleischman and he became a millionaire by supplying yeast to the huge brewing industry.'

'No way! You mean Cincinnati, Ohio?'

'Well I sure wasn't aware of another one. It's just another little connection that we can play on. Why don't we take a walk down Republic Street now? It's Sunday and a little quieter than usual. We'll take a few pics of the building. Come on, finish your coffee and let's go.'

McCandless daydreamed about a topless Claudia as the 'front of house' but didn't dare confess his thoughts to Alex. Even less how they were going to pay for the successful bid. There was no question that their bid would be successful. But he still didn't tell her everything. The auction was in two days time on the Tuesday and he would have to move smartly. Neither of them gave the slightest thought to what was happening ten miles away in Comino.

45

Zhang was having a ball and was now on his third Cisk. Victor had let him take a turn on the helm and the throttle but as they passed the Madonna Statue and rounded Marfa Ridge to the west he took back the controls. The sea state changed perceptibly as white water appeared for the first time. The Santa Marija tower came into view on the starboard beam as did a blue and yellow ferry of the Gozo Channel Company which was on the last leg of the crossing from Circewwa to Mgarr. Tabona throttled back the Volvos and gently nudged Dash into the relative calm of the Blue Lagoon. There were no other pleasure boats because of the imposed restrictions but he noticed a crowd of several dozen people on the rising land behind the jetty. The paparazzi had arrived. It was almost inevitable that word had got out that Kirk and Zhang were visiting the Blue Lagoon. A multitude of 'long Tom' zoom lenses perched atop tripods was aimed at Dash, the minute she entered the Lagoon. At least they were only cameras and not rocket propelled grenade launchers. This was Comino not Monte Cassino and nothing was going to happen on his watch. Tabona reached for his Zeiss binoculars and scanned the western half of the island. As requested, two helicopters of the Armed Forces of Malta Air Wing were on the flat ground available just to the north of the Tower and he could see a detachment of uniformed guards who had set up a temporary perimeter with metal stakes and the sort of blue sticky tape that you see following road accidents. At least there wouldn't be any of those today. Satisfied that everything was in place a bow anchor was dropped and Dash was allowed to swing in the breeze. The depth of water was about twenty feet but it was so clear you could see tiny fish swimming on the sandy bottom. Through his interpreter Zhang said that he had never seen sea so beautiful as this and he was dying to take a swim. Secretly he also hoped that at least one of those photographers in the distance was from the Chinese Embassy or Cultural Centre. He wanted plenty of publicity if he wanted to emulate the great Chairman Mao-Zedong's victorious swim in the Yangtze River decades earlier. It had earned Mao almost God-like status and with good joss a couple of laps of the lagoon would afford him similar and deserved accolades. That aspect he would leave to the PR guys back at the CCP in Beijing. He would now go below and change into his swimming attire and when he came back on deck he would make sure he was highly visible from that battery of cameras.

He wasn't sorry that Madam Zhang was by now totally incapacitated with the Maltese version of 'Delhi belly' as she was the sole and almost permanent occupant of the heads. She wouldn't be going swimming today that's for sure and he could hog the limelight. Victor Tabona insisted on accompanying him as he suspected he was a much stronger swimmer than Zhang who, in his sixties, was way past his physical prime. Back pain also seemed to be troubling him. He, on the other hand, although in his late forties, had in his youth been a water polo Junior Champion for Team Ballutta and had a collection of silver trophies on his sideboard at home to prove it. If water polo ever became an Olympic sport then the George Cross Island would take gold, silver and bronze every time. Of that he was absolutely certain. One of his compatriots had just made the swim from Sicily to Malta which made the cross-English Channel swim look like a walk in the park – or even a dip in the Serpentine.

Zhang stood on the upper deck of the Fairline and posed and waved to the cameras at least two hundred metres distant. The clicks and shutters of a dozen Canons, Nikons and Leicas imitating a flight of bats taking off in unison would have been audible from Dash if only the wind had not been in the wrong direction. No matter. Zhang did his best to copy a swallow dive from the height of only two metres and unfortunately misjudged the angle. The gin-clear water had misled him and the resultant splash was not quite the photo opportunity the paparazzi were seeking. Thank goodness for photo-shopping. After surfacing, Zhang did his utmost to copy Mark Spitz and swam out into the lagoon with a creditable freestyle crawl. Victor dived in with a minimal splash and quickly caught up with Zhang who seemed to be moving a lot quicker than his age would normally suggest. In fact a lot quicker. It was a current that was carrying them both along and coupled with that south westerly was taking them at more than three knots in the direction of Cominotto, a tiny rock of an islet that marked the northern end of the lagoon. Beyond Cominotto was the Gozo Channel and beyond that the deep blue sea. Tabona was not the sort to panic and swimming parallel to Zhang shouted to him to swim to the left, not against the current but with it at an angle. Then he realised that Zhang spoke almost no English. His interpreter was a non-swimmer and hadn't even been asked to join them. It might have been his imagination but it seemed that Zhang was almost ignoring him. Didn't he understand the simple sign of pointing to

Cominotto which was by now only two hundred metres distant? And what happened to the bad back?

Tabona analysed the situation very quickly. If the silly Chinaman wanted to swim out into the Channel for propaganda purposes then let him. He struck out for Cominotto and two minutes later pulled himself up onto the rocks. Now he had to attract the attention of those left on Dash and then the boat-boys would haul anchor and come and pick him up. He needn't have worried on that score as the powerful lenses of the paparazzi had quickly picked up on the problem. They shouted urgently to Dash and within seconds they got the message. The anchor was weighed and Dash moved smartly out into the lagoon and headed north towards Tabona who was frantically waving and pointing towards the north of the lagoon. They couldn't hear his shouts of 'forget me go and pick up the Chinese President!' The steady beat of the engines drowned out his pleas and within another two minutes Dash was in 'slow reverse' to maintain a fixed position twenty metres off the rock of Cominotto. Victor dived in and swam the fastest he had swum for years. He pulled himself up the aluminium ladder at the stern and made immediately for the helm on the flying bridge. Grabbing the binoculars he scanned the by now choppy waters ahead to the north. Zhang was nowhere to be seen. Quickly he spoke to President Kirk who by good fortune had not joined them in the lagoon.

'Mr President, I don't like this situation one little bit. I smell a big rat. In this case a water rat. I must insist that you and Mrs Kirk evacuate immediately. I'm calling Geister on his cellphone now. He speed dialled a number and within seconds the rotors started to twirl on one of the AW 139 choppers which lifted off in less than a minute. It swooped low over the lagoon then circumnavigated Cominotto before moving slowly north in a methodical search pattern. Still nothing. The photographers were going crazy. Thank goodness for digital cameras. In the days of rolls of film they would have needed twenty rolls apiece.

An hour later and President Kirk and the First Lady were boarding Air Force One, the second helicopter having flown them straight to the airport. Geister's orders. Dash returned at best speed to Grand Harbour and took Madam Zhang and the Chinese interpreter straight to the Christina O. The flight crews of Dragons One and Two were already on the flight decks of the Ilyushins. They would assist in the search for Chairman Zhang just as they had searched for MH370 all those years ago. If he was still alive then the wind and currents would have taken him well out into the Gozo Channel and quite possibly further east into the open sea. They had several hours of daylight left to find him. After that he would be fish food.

Emergency procedures were initiated for Air Force One in a similar manner to when President Bush had been evacuated after the Twin Towers were hit in 2001. There wasn't even time to top up the tanks but for this short emergency flight it wasn't necessary. In fact the lighter the plane was the better.

'Air Force One, you are cleared for immediate take-off on runway 06. God speed.'

The air traffic controller crossed himself and said a silent prayer. It would be touch and go – hopefully more go than touch. He hoped the pilot knew his stuff and had read the brochure. On the centreline and with the four General Electric turbines pleading to be released he let go the brakes. In his dreams he had always wanted to 'lift this sucker off the deck' in under thirty seconds and if he didn't do it today he never would. He used all but five hundred of the seven thousand five hundred feet of asphalt. Twenty eight seconds – bingo! He wasn't worried about the fuel status. Next stop was Sigonella, Sicily less than a hundred miles to the north-north-east. This was the contingency plan for such an emergency and he followed it to the letter. At least his President was safe. It wasn't his fault that his opposite number from Beijing had gone and done an aquatic walkabout. As Air Force One climbed out over the Three Cities the noise was deafening.

46

Alex and Bruce had looked at the vacant property from the outside and then decided on a snack and a drink in the square almost opposite St. Johns Co-Cathedral.

'Jeez, Bruce, did you hear that plane?'

The ever-present pigeons looked a little restless but didn't take to the air.

'That guy's in a hurry whoever he is.'

Had they been in the Upper Barrakka gardens they would instantly have recognised the most famous Jumbo jet in the world as it screamed to altitude. It wasn't until they were back at the hotel that news of the devastating events reached them. Every member of staff on duty was crowded around a large TV screen in the corner of the main bar. There was normally only this number of people watching when an important football match was taking place. The receptionist sensed that Alex and Bruce were oblivious to developments which were now being beamed around the entire globe.

'Haven't you heard the news? The Chinese President, Zhang, is missing after swimming in the Blue Lagoon. All of Malta's Armed Forces are on alert in case it wasn't an accident. Look, there's another search plane taking off from Luqa. Look!' She pointed to the screen.

'Bruce, I don't like this. Look me in the eye and tell me this is a terrible accident.'

'Alex, I've got a better idea. Let's get a drink in the bar and talk about the Ohio Lounge.'

'Jesus. You mean you knew this was gonna happen? Bruce, answer me! Is this state-sponsored assassination?'

'No, how can it be? Word has it that he wanted to copy Mao-Zedong and it looks like he got into difficulties. I know that over the years several unfortunate people have perished. An English Cambridge University student called Marcus somebody drowned in the Blue Lagoon in an underwater tunnel over a decade ago. Terribly sad.'

'How awful for his family but surely Zhang wasn't scuba diving or snorkelling, just swimming. It looks like our President stayed on the boat. Thank God. Look, there's more news coming in.'

'Prime Minister Vella has announced that he is shocked at developments on Maltese territory. He was recalling the Cabinet from their weekend activities immediately and all MPs were to be summoned to Parliament at ten o'clock the following morning. As we speak President Kirk is being safely looked after and is on his way to a NATO base at an undisclosed destination. Further details will be released as and when they become available.

'You know what, Alex, one thing's for certain.'

'What's that?'

'The Summit is over.'

By evening all major world news agencies were reporting that President Zhang was missing. It was already after midnight in Beijing and the bulk of China's population would be unaware of the potential tragedy until early morning.

In Washington it was around lunchtime and it being Sunday only a skeleton staff were on duty at the White House including leading spokesperson, Sheryl Baguley, who was sailing with friends on the Potomac River. It would be the last one this year as the chill of fall was already in the air. When the news broke she was twenty miles downstream but she knew that tomorrow she would have her work cut out.

The Australian Prime Minister was awoken in Canberra in the early hours with a call from the Consul in Malta. He updated him on the lengthy chat they'd had on the Maltese Falcon. It wasn't all about wine.

It was indeed fortunate that world stock markets were closed but tomorrow might be another story. The Tokyo Exchange would be the first to open followed by Shanghai and Hong Kong. How markets reacted would be anybody's guess. International tensions had been at their worst for years hence the hopeful expectations for the Summit. And it had all turned into sand because a Chinese President had wanted to 'out-swim' one of his predecessors half a century earlier. But twenty-first century China bore little or no resemblance to Mao's China of rickshaws, starvation for millions and dogmatic propaganda. So what was the point? Surely all he had to do was turn up at the Summit and play the considerable hand of cards that decades of progress had dealt him?

In Hong Kong at Chek Lap Kok Airport, a Chinese gentleman in the VIP lounge was awaiting his connecting flight to Melbourne, Australia. His daughter would be waiting for him and he would await developments with interest over the next few days. He checked the electronic screen for his flight and the red and white Qantas logo glowed and indicated 'boarding now at Gate 8.' He walked to the nearest 'lap-sap' bin and having removed the SIM card he then chucked the cheap cellphone into it. Folding his copy of the Far Eastern Economic Review into his expensive Italian leather briefcase, he strolled towards the Gate. Comrade Won-Gah was on the way out.

47

At ten o'clock precisely Edward Borg Vella rose to address the Maltese Parliament. It would be a very short speech and made to award him, indeed the whole Government, some breathing space. He had been up most of the night taking briefs from the Head of the Armed Forces of Malta. The searches had resumed at first light but almost four hours after dawn nothing had been seen of Zhang. Neither survivor nor corpse. Beechcraft maritime patrol aircraft had extended the search patterns to the east and north-east of the Archipelago but to no avail. The PLAAF Ilyushins had done likewise but it was a perfunctory gesture on their part. This was just a hundred square kilometres at the most, not the vast Indian Ocean. They soon peeled off to head for Djibouti and the long haul home. Madam Zhang and the interpreter preferred to return to China via civilian commercial means and were hosted at the Chinese Embassy until arrangements could be made.

'Bongu, good morning everybody. I speak with a heavy heart to inform this House that a guest to our Islands, President Zhang of the People's Republic of China is missing, presumed drowned. I have given instructions that in the absence of positive news at twelve noon today, Malta Time, all search operations will be called off.' He paused for breath. Every Member was in sombre mood.

'When I invited the American and Chinese Presidents to our Islands it was in the hope that international friction would be cooled, divisions mended and mutual trust restored. Those hopes have now been dashed in the cruellest way imaginable. I can tell you that at a social reception held on board the Maltese Falcon less than forty-eight hours ago the foundations were laid for all those aspirations to be fulfilled.' He paused again and took a sip of water.

'It is my fervent hope that a new Summit can be re-arranged in the not-too-distant future and I ...'

But he didn't get any further as a Parliamentary aide tapped him on the shoulder and waved a piece of paper gesturing for him to read it. He donned his reading glasses and what he read hit him like a thunderbolt. Reading the hand-written memo twice for good order and to make sure he wasn't dreaming, he folded the paper twice and put it into his breast pocket. He immediately decided not to say any more just yet.

'I hope to make a further statement to the House this afternoon. Thank you, Mr Speaker.'

Two minutes later and Edward Borg Vella was in his office speaking with his Personal Parliamentary Secretary.

'Dear God. What on earth are we going to do now? Read this. It appears that six members of the Chinese politburo and their wives are seeking political asylum here in Malta.'

'What? Can't we just deny them entry?'

'Too late for that. They're already here.'

48

NSA
Maryland

The Maltese Prime Minister wasn't the only one who had been awake most of the night. So had Ralph Winchester. The difference was that he planned to be. By late the previous evening his member of staff on board the Christina O had emailed him to tell him that Madam Zhang had returned alone, apart from the interpreter. The few drops of phenolphthalein added to the fresh figs via the prickly pear liqueur had done the trick. 'Angelique' could now make her excuses and leave the luxury super-yacht. In any case there were no guests to cater for, only crew. She was free to spend a few days in Malta if she wished, just as a tourist. Her choice.

Winchester mentally reviewed the overall situation. The Summit was as dead as a dodo and there would now be no chance whatsoever that China would ingratiate itself even further into Malta's affairs – and its dockyards. They might try other angles of course but that's what asymmetric warfare had become in the third decade of the twenty-first century. Their cheap offer to build the new tunnel to Gozo might become a bit of a problem. The European Union was running out of money not to mention members. If it crumbled entirely, the NSA would have to offer aid in another guise. It had already been decided that one of the existing Five Eyes had become too unreliable and was already sucking up to the PRC in a manner that was giving the Pentagon more of a bowel problem than even the hapless Madam Zhang had experienced. It was almost time to publicly announce that Malta was to be given full Five Eyes status. It was important though that the announcement, when it came, would be made in the Maltese Parliament. Malta was now a proud and independent Republic and, like America, was a former part of the British Empire. English and Maltese were both official languages and the legal formalities of encompassing Malta into the new version of the original UKUSA Treaty would be a simple matter for the lawyers.

No doubt it would be best left to the Maltese Premier to decide when to make the announcement. He would first have to deal with the adverse fall-out from the disappearing Chinese President. Would China put the blame on Malta? Who would take the rap? Somebody would have to of course, that's politics. Winchester took a sleepy early breakfast in one of the many canteens at Crypto City. The next guy he wanted to hear from was his opposite number in Australia. What time was it in Canberra anyway? Or would he be in Melbourne? Unlike China with only one time zone, Australia had several and even two of those didn't observe 'summer time' so he was always confused.

Back in his office and fortified by scrambled eggs and bacon he sat at his desk and spun the globe. His finger landed smack on Malta. He was getting good at this. He looked at the wall to his right where a photo of his own yacht Hyperion back in San Pedro had once assumed sole occupancy. It had recently been moved up and slightly across to make way for a newcomer – a fine watercolour of the old USS Constellation moored in Grand Harbour. It had arrived by courier. He had to laugh at the receipt for the insurance valuation – one and a quarter million Euros. McCandless must be having a laugh as well as fun.

Winchester thought he knew everything, but he didn't. Not by a long chalk.

49

By three o'clock in the afternoon Prime Minister Vella had sufficient information to make another statement to Parliament.

'Further to my statement this morning I now regret to announce that the search for President Zhang has been abandoned. He is now officially missing, presumed dead. I now ask you all to stand and observe a minute's silence.' All members present rose and bowed their heads in respect.

'I must also tell you that at about the same time I spoke to you all this morning, twelve Chinese Nationals of the People's Republic presented themselves at the Auberge de Castille to claim political asylum and ...'

There was uproar in the House with members from all political parties shouting at the same time and from all quarters.

'Surely you mean Taiwan, not Communist China?'

'Send them back. We don't want them!'

'They'll have to be vetted – we can't trust them!'

'Don't let them build the new Embassy.'

Vella was flustered. What had he done to deserve this? Ten minutes of answering questions which seemed like ten hours and he was back in his office. At his request, Victor Tabona had arrived. If he didn't put up a good show then he was toast job-wise. Early retirement beckoned but he didn't fancy a permanent deckchair on Mellieha Beach just yet.

'I'm telling you, Prime Minister, hand on heart, Zhang deliberately chose to ignore my signals to swim to comparative safety. He refused to notice me. You don't have to be a Weatherman to know which way the wind blows. Do you?'

The Bob Dylan metaphor was lost on the Premier. He was old school and had been around the block a few times. He scratched his chin and shook his head several times in quick succession.

'This is the list of the asylum claimants. You'd better have it. You only have to Google them to see that they are all members of the politburo. Would you believe that they have all been staying at a hotel here in Valletta posing as tourists? It seems that they all have accounts at the BoV with large sums of money already in place. You have the powers already to sequester funds of course but even the bank, which is totally above reproach, might have difficulty in ascertaining the precise origin of the funds. You know how difficult recent investigations have been on other similar but unrelated matters. When millions can be moved around the globe at the click of a mouse what chance have we got?'

'Well at least they're not going to cost us money then! We could maybe charge them a million Euros apiece for a Maltese passport ... only joking of course, Prime Minister.'

'Actually I was thinking maybe two million.' And he wasn't joking.

'This cannot be a coincidence. Would they be seeking asylum if Zhang was still alive? Victor my friend, I suspect there is a lot more to this than meets the eye.'

Even the Fifth Eye.

50

It was Tuesday, the day of the auction, which was scheduled for ten o'clock sharp in the smart function room of the Excelsior Hotel.

'Bruce, this place is smart. Nice! Why didn't you choose this place instead of the ...'

'Women, never happy are you? Because it's a long walk up that hill in the heat that's why. OK? And besides you like all the nice little shops and bistros around South Street don't you?'

'I guess but maybe next time we ...' The microphone clicked on and a sharp suited man in his thirties started to speak.'

'Bongu. Good morning to all of you. We now come to the matter of the sale of the magnificent premises in Republic Street caused by the unexpected and sad passing of the previous owner. It is our pleasure to offer the premises for sale by auction. Technology being what is is today we are also pleased to accept bids online and my colleague here on my left will appraise us of those in real time.'

There were at least twenty people who looked as if they were going to be serious bidders. McCandless would have to be alert if he wasn't to be out-foxed by some smart-arsed realtor who would probably be trying to steer it towards a family friend or business associate for a big back-hander later. He knew the score and the ever-friendly Charles

Caruana back at the hotel had tipped him off that the Group that owned the hotel would almost certainly be bidding themselves as they sought to diversify their assets in the hospitality business. Malta was simply booming following the end of the pandemic. The auctioneer rapped his gavel onto the side of the wooden lectern to attract everybody's attention.

'Will somebody start the bidding at a half a million Euros please?'

A little man in the front row raised his hand. He looked quite elderly. What on earth would he do with it if his bid was successful?

'Thank you, Sir.' Another hand went up.

'Five hundred and fifty thousand.'

'Thank you, Sir.' Another hand went up.

'Six hundred thousand.' McCandless decided it was time to sort out who was serious and who wasn't.' He raised his hand.

'Seven hundred.' Everybody in the room turned round to view this interloper. Who the hell was this? He looked like a Brit on holiday not a local.

'Thank you, Sir. Do I have any more?' The room was humming as the price had now exceeded the realtor's own estimate of six hundred thousand. The little man at the front was on his cellphone and obviously taking orders from afar. He raised his hand again.

'Seven hundred and fifty thousand.'

'Thank you, Sir.'

An online bid came in for eight hundred thousand.

'One million Euros' shouted the little man. His voice faltered. Was this his last bid? He sounded desperate.

The silence was deafening. McCandless would finish this charade once and for all.

'One and a quarter million – and that's my final offer.'

There were no further bids.

'Sold to the gentleman from er, sold to you, Sir. Congratulations.'

Alexandria just gazed at Bruce McCandless in awe.

'How the hell are we gonna pay for it? Are you off your head?'

'Relax. I went to the bank before we came here. I brought an open-ended letter of credit.'

'What?! So who the hell has actually paid for it?'

'Account Number 9988 has paid for it. Everybody has got what they wanted, haven't they?'

But they hadn't. The smart, elderly gentleman whose bid had failed approached them. He was almost in tears.

'I must offer you my congratulations but I am very sad. I was bidding on behalf of a very distant relative in Queensland, Australia. The building in question actually belonged to our family right up until the Second World War. The war changed many people's lives for ever. Some people lost everything, including their lives. I had two uncles who both survived the War but they left Malta – one to New York I believe, the other to Brisbane. Lots of Maltese went to Queensland to make their fortunes in the sugar industry. I'm sorry, let me introduce myself. My name is Silvo Pisani. I take it from your accent that you are from England and your wife also? Or Maltese maybe?'

'Mr Pisani, do you have time for a coffee?'

Thirty minutes later and Mr Silvo Pisani was in a taxi and on his way to Cospicua in the Three Cities. He had a funeral to go to. His sister Carmen was being buried today. Just when she had run out of hope that she would ever find a link to her grandfather Alex learned that he had a brother, also illegitimate. He had moved to Rabat after the War but tiring of the lack of money and austerity had taken one of P & O's great white liners to the land they called Down Under. He worked in Mackay for many years and saved lots of money. He had married and moved south to Brisbane. He said that was most appropriate as the SS Brisbane Star had been one of the survivors of Operation Pedestal and had sailed into Grand Harbour on August 15th 1942. He had been one of thousands who had cheered from the battlements as the ship entered port on the Feast of Santa Maria. Thanks be to God. He died peacefully in the Eighties and left behind several grandsons all living in the suburbs of Brisbane. It was one of them, Richard Pisani, who was wishing to invest in property in Malta. He too, wanted to visit the George Cross Island and meet any relatives. Now he would discover he had a distant cousin called Alexandria. Two more people than expected attended Carmen Maria Assumpta's funeral in Cospicua that afternoon.

Back at the Hotel in the early evening Bruce and Alex had a quiet dinner alone. Words were few and far between. They simply weren't necessary. Alex was deliriously happy, they both were. It was time to tell Ralph Winchester that they weren't coming back. The following morning they visited Alfie Agius's jewellery shop in Merchant Street and bought a ring – a stunning blue topaz gemstone set in twenty-four carat white gold. What else would be fitting for a girl with Roman eyes from Zurrieq?

51

NSA
Fort Meade
Maryland

Ralph Winchester just couldn't stop smiling. He read for the second time the overnight email from Alex and the second shorter one from McCandless. Reaching for the Staff file, he took a red pen to the word 'expendable' alongside Alex's name and replaced it with 'retired' which was at least partly true. Although he didn't play cricket himself, he knew that McCandless 'played with a straight bat' and would look after his fiancée.

He also knew that if required he had two loyal people on the ground ready for when Malta became a bona-fide member of the Five Eyes. It would always be known as that even if the five became six, seven or eight. Soon the formal announcement would be made. Prime Minister Vella would make the formal announcement at a time of his choosing. That was only right.

He also knew, via his Australian colleagues, that the formal announcement of Zhang's death was slightly premature. But what was left of the Politburo didn't ever need to know that. He could now fix a date for his own retirement, perhaps next spring when the warmer weather arrived and he could enjoy sailing Hyperion from San Pedro

Yacht Club. He could watch the massive container ships arriving from China in the hope that the People's Republic, under a new President, had decided that mutually beneficial trade was the way forward and not 'Belts and Roads' and 'Strings of Pearls.' The effective defection of six members of the polituro had been an unexpected development to put it mildly and it had shaken the Middle Kingdom to its core. That their Finance Secretary Won-Gah was also about to apply for Australian citizenship would cause an international sensation when the news broke at a Press conference in Canberra scheduled in a few days time. The Triangle of Trust was as solid and as dependable as ever.

Winchester laughed out loud when he received a scan of a Sydney tabloid newspaper headline:

'ZHANG DOES A HAROLD

In a terrible accident that mirrors events here in Australia over half a century ago when Prime Minister Harold Holt disappeared off the coast of Victoria, China's President Zhang has gone missing in a freak swimming accident. Accusations and speculation at the time that Holt had somehow been spirited away in a Chinese submarine were of course pure fantasy.'

Less well-circulated was this inside-page report in the Italian newspaper La Sicilia:

Eminent plastic surgeon Alberto Arrigoni and his assistant Mario Marchetti were reported killed yesterday in a fatal car accident in the Syracusa region of eastern Sicily. Their car apparently lost control on a mountain bend. The Carabinieri said that no other vehicle was involved, and brake failure was suspected to be the cause.

Winchester reflected over several more cups of coffee in yet more of those dreadful plastic cups. It was time to find his own sea legs again. Hyperion was quite an elderly lady now and a retirement present to himself might be in order. Now where the heck had he put that magazine SuperYacht World? He knew he'd put it somewhere.

EPILOGUE

It was Chinese New Year only three months later, the most auspicious day in the Lunar calendar for all Chinese wherever they are in the world.

Won-Gah's franchise of 'Shau Kei Wan Tram' Chinese restaurants was proving to be a great success and the opening of the first one, in Melbourne, had been well-received. That it was sited beside the main tram lines in Bourke Street had been truly fortuitous. It was packed every night since its formal opening by a Chinese opera singer who had left Hong Hong soon after the clamp-down on democracy in the former British colony. Sister restaurants with the same name, brand and décor had swiftly followed in Sydney, Adelaide and Perth.

A request to open one in Malta from a potential franchisee had caught him by surprise. Sure, why not? The applicant had obviously gone to a great deal of trouble to source suitable premises overlooking St. Paul's Bay. Not that he knew where that was, never having been to Malta himself. Perhaps he should visit during Melbourne's cool winter and Malta's hot summer. Yes he would do that. It would be good to catch up.

He had a special gift to send to the proprietor, and it was something that he had been keeping up his sleeve for a long time. Although not fragile, it was carefully packed with a very personal hand-written message inside on a 'Shau Kei Wan Tram Restaurant' compliment slip.

It arrived by courier an hour before the formal opening at six in the evening. The new proprietor was absolutely thrilled. The protective box contained a stunning Italian leather briefcase, and he couldn't fail to see and grab the note which was tucked into the side pocket.

Best wishes on the opening of your new venture.
Comrade Won-Gah.

It was surely time to open that special bottle of wine – Number 888.

MALTESE GLOSSARY

Bizzilla	Malta lace
Bongu	Good morning, Good day
Cisk	A popular Maltese lager
Dghajsa	A colourful man-powered water taxi
Fenek	Rabbit
Ftira	An open sandwich of hobz, tuna, olives, capers & tomato
Grazzi	Thank you
Grazzi haffna	Thanks very much, a bit more than grazzi
Hobz	Maltese bread
Hop Leaf	A local India Pale Ale
Il-Belt	The nickname for Valletta
Jahasra!	Oh my God! or Oh my goodness!
Karozzin	Horse drawn cab – in M'dina and Valletta
Kem	How much? (money)

Kinnie	A popular Maltese drink made from oranges and aromatic herbs
Lira	The former Maltese currency – pre-Euro
Merhba ta' Malta	Welcome to Malta
New Zealand White	A local rabbit bred for the table
Pastizzia	A puff pastry snack containing peas or ricotta cheese
Sah-ha!	Your good health
Timpana	Malta's favourite baked macaroni dish
Wied	An ancient river valley, usually dry in Malta's summer

ABOUT THE AUTHOR

Mark Harland has lived and worked in the Near, Middle and Far East.

He is a former pupil of St. George's Army School Hong Hong and St. Andrews Army School Malta GC

His other works include:

Novels:
Your Country Needs You
A Very Special Relationship
Her Place in the Sun
The Takeaway

Non-fiction:
MALTA: My Island
One Thousand days in Hong Kong
Sunburnt Pom's Tales of Oz
From UK to Belgium and back

Mark currently lives in North Yorkshire.

www.mvhbooks.com

Printed in Great Britain
by Amazon